MW01174664

The Heart Balm Tort

Thaddeus Lewis Novels

On the Head of a Pin
Sowing Poison
47 Sorrows
The Burying Ground
Wishful Seeing

Other Books by Janet Kellough

The Palace of the Moon
The Pear Shaped Woman
The Legendary Guide to Prince Edward County

Coming Soon

The Bathwater Conspiracy

The Heart Balm Tort

A Thaddeus Lewis Novel

Janet Kellough

All characters in this book are fictitious or used fictitiously. Any resemblance to real persons, living or dead, is purely coincidental.

ISBN 978-0-9937200-6-2 (pbk) - 978-0-9937200-7-9 (epub) - 978-0-9937200-8-6 (pdf)

Cover art:
Portrait of an unidentified woman with a fan c.1858: Library of Congress, Prints and Photographs Division LC-USZC4-13980
Fire at Waupoos cheese factory: Photograph by Janet Kellough

Published 2017 by Janet Kellough
www.janetkellough.com

This one's for me.

CHAPTER 1

A newspaper clipping and a bank draft fluttered to the floor as Thaddeus Lewis tore open the letter that arrived in the afternoon mail. He retrieved the bank draft first. Twenty pounds. More money than he'd had in his pocket for a long time.

He glanced at the signature at the bottom of the letter before he stooped to pick up the clipping. It was, as he expected, from Townsend Ashby, although he would never have been able to tell if he hadn't already been familiar with the young barrister's signature.

The clipping was from *The Canadian Free Press*, and was dated July 14, 1854. It reported the disturbing death of a young woman in the southwestern town of London, Canada West:

> *At first, speculation was that a fire had been started accidentally by marchers in the annual Orange Lodge parade who, it was rumoured, had become inebriated and strayed far from the designated route - an ironic conclusion,* the reporter commented, *as Mr. Albert Warner, the warehouse owner, is a staunch Orangeman. Subsequently, suspicion fell on a group of Irish thugs who had gathered to disrupt the July Twelfth march.*

The Orange Lodge. Thaddeus had yet to see one of their parades that didn't result in some kind of trouble between Protestants and Catholics. Canada should have banned the marches when it had the chance back in the Forties. As he read on, however, the article disclosed a more sinister discovery.

> *A supervisor left to guard the warehouse later informed police that he had seen an unidentified man leaving the premises shortly before the fire broke out and when firemen sifted through the ashes of the destroyed building, they uncovered the charred body of a young woman. From remnants of clothing and the jewellery she was wearing, she has now been identified as twenty-two year old Hazel Warner, daughter of the warehouse owner. She was believed, at the time, to have with her a two-month-old child, although no trace of the infant has been found.*
>
> *Twenty-three year old Nelson Lakefield has been charged with arson and murder. Lakefield is widely believed to be the father of the missing infant.*

There was only a little more information in the accompanying letter. It was a typical Ashby communication – no salutation, no greetings, no catching up with personal news, just straight to the point and an almost indecipherable signature at the bottom.

Ashby's involvement in the case had begun, he wrote, as a tort for seduction brought against Nelson Lakefield by the father of the dead girl.

> *I would scarce have bothered with it except that the accused is the brother of a fellow I knew at school and the father has a ton of money. As far as the other charges go, I'm having a devil of a time getting copies of the witness statements from Earl Jenkins, the local barrister retained by the Lakefields. I need someone with your investigative abilities to pursue the lines of inquiry that seem to have escaped Jenkins' notice. If convenient, I'd like you to meet me in Toronto on October 10th at which time I should have more information in hand. I've enclosed an advance for your traveling expenses, etc. We can sort the rest of it out when we meet.*

It was more than convenient. Thaddeus had completed his disastrous ministerial stint on the Hope Circuit and had not been offered another appointment, nor would he have accepted one. He'd made too big a mess of things. He'd long since overstayed his welcome and the congregation was anxious to have him vacate the manse; after all, they had a new minister coming. But he'd had no idea what he was going to do until Ashby had written to offer employment, and Thaddeus had been waiting anxiously for the details. Now the generous advance and promise of more to come would allow him to finally leave Cobourg.

He tucked the letter into his pocket and wondered if Digger could make it as far as the bank. He whistled for the old dog, who heaved himself up from his place by the stove. Poor old Digger, grey around the muzzle and stiff in the joint.

I know how he feels, Thaddeus thought. *This last year hasn't been kind to either of us.*

He'd inherited Digger from the woman who had been his downfall. She'd sailed away and neither Thaddeus nor the dog had taken kindly to the desertion. At first Digger would escape from the manse and run to the pier every time he heard the steamboat whistle. As soon as he realized that his owner was not on the ship he would wend his way back to the manse again, and after a while, Thaddeus gave up trying to keep him corralled. And then one day, Digger simply gave up. From that day forward he seemed to age at an alarming rate and now he was content to doze the day away while the steamers came and went unnoticed.

As soon as they exited the back door, the dog walked over to the lilac bush that grew by the fence and widdled against it. Then he hobbled over to a patch of sunlight and lowered himself to the ground. It was clear that he had no intention of going any further.

Thaddeus left him where he was, and set off to the bank alone. As he walked along, he tried to recall if he knew anything at all about the town of London.

"What do you mean I should ask Francis if I can go with you?" Martha Renwell was astonished when Thaddeus suggested it that evening. Her father had been absent for most of her childhood and even after he returned he had seldom exercised any fatherly responsibility. It had always been Thaddeus who governed her life. She had always assumed that if her grandfather said something was all right, that was all the permission she needed.

"Technically, it's up to him. He is your father after all."

She supposed Thaddeus was right, it would be polite to ask, but she suspected that Francis would be flattered that she had asked him anything at all.

That didn't stop her from grumbling about it. "You'd think I was five years old or something, not nearly seventeen. I've been keeping house for you for over a year. I don't understand why I have to ask anyone's permission for anything. Besides, you promised I could always tag along with you."

Nevertheless, she'd dashed off a note that very day, then had gone back to thoroughly cleaning the manse in anticipation of their departure.

"I won't have anybody saying I kept a dirty house," she said when Thaddeus asked if it was really necessary to wash all the windows before they left. "There's been far too much talk about us already."

He left her to it. There *had* been a lot of talk, but it had mostly been about Thaddeus and his unseemly preoccupation with a married woman. A woman who, as it turned out, would have had no interest in him even if she had been free.

All he had been left with was Digger, but if he was going to go off to London, he needed to make some sort of arrangement for the dog until he found a more permanent situation. It was a good thing the old boy was so sedate. Mrs. Small, the neighbour who did the heavy laundry for Martha, had taken a shine to him. Thaddeus hoped she would keep him for a few weeks, until he had finished with whatever Ashby wanted him to do in London and had some idea of what he would do after that.

He waited until he saw her hanging sheets on the line, then he sauntered over to the back fence.

"Mr. Lewis!" she said. "Martha tells me you're leaving soon."

"Not before time, I expect."

She looked a little sheepish. "Yes, well, there has been some muttering about how long you've stayed in the manse. With the new man coming and all. It puts them in an awkward position, you see, not having the house ready for him."

"Yes I know," Thaddeus said. "And if I could have avoided it, I would have. And that brings me to another awkward situation. I can't take Digger with me at the moment. I'm going to temporary employment and I'm not sure what my household arrangements will be."

"Oh leave him with me," Mrs. Small said. "Poor old fellow. You don't want to uproot him at this point."

"I'll arrange to retrieve him as soon as I'm settled."

"Don't worry about it. I'm happy to have him. And to tell you the truth, he's so rickety, I'm not sure he has many days left anyway."

Having done Thaddeus a favour, Mrs. Small then felt entitled to enquire about the details of his plans.

"Martha didn't say where you were going. Just that you're leaving."

"It's a bit confidential," Thaddeus said. Mrs. Small looked disappointed. She had a kind heart, but she loved to be the bearer of tidings, good or bad, and Thaddeus was reasonably sure that she was one of the people who had kept the stories circulating about him. "We go on the tenth, by the way, so you can set the congregation's mind to rest over the matter of the manse. I do want to thank you for all the help you and your family have given Martha."

"She's a grand girl, Mr. Lewis. I'll miss her."

And as Thaddeus walked back to the house, he reflected that Digger was possibly the only thing about the Hope Circuit that he was sorry to leave behind.

A week before they were due to leave, Martha heard back from her father. His letter, when it arrived, was much bulkier than anything Francis had ever sent her before. She waited until Thaddeus came in for supper before she opened it.

"Why didn't you open it before? What are you afraid of?" Thaddeus asked.

"What if he said no?"

"Since when has Francis ever denied you anything? It's me who usually says no, not him."

She gingerly opened it, and was surprised to find that there were not one, but two letters for her, as well as a small bundle of banknotes. She quickly scanned her father's letter, and then began to laugh.

"I should have known it was all right. Listen to what he said: *It's fine with me, but have you told Thaddeus yet?*"

And then, in a part of the letter that Martha did not read out loud, Francis wrote:

> *We miss you, but I do understand that Wellington is a small village and you want to see something of the world beyond it. I'm sure you know that, whatever happens, you can always come home. Tuck this money away somewhere in case things go sadly awry and you need to come back in a hurry.*

She teared up a little at this sentiment. She missed Francis and her stepmother Sophie, but she was glad they understood that there wasn't much for her in the tiny lakeside village where they ran a hotel.

"Who is the other letter from?" Thaddeus asked. "Hurry up and open it. I'm dying of curiosity."

She tore it open, then looked up at her grandfather. "Do you remember Horatio? Horatio Joe?"

"Horatio Joe Elliott?" Thaddeus was astonished. It was not a name he had ever expected to hear again. Ten years previously Horatio's mother Clementine had set Wellington on its ear, with her table rappings and séances and contacting of the dead. She and her son had posed as the long-lost family of a local farmer, and had taken advantage of many of Wellington's most gullible citizens. But the real ruse had been an attempt to claim a portion of the farmer's estate.

"Apparently his real name is Joe Corcoran." Martha turned the page over to look at the address. "He sent the letter to Wellington and Francis sent it on."

"And what does Horatio Joe want after all these years?" Thaddeus asked in a wary tone.

Martha looked at him in surprise. "Nothing. Just to say hello, and to let me know that he remembers what good friends we were. He says he thought about writing to me many times, but that he wasn't sure what the reception would be."

"I'm not entirely sure what it is myself," Thaddeus said. "His mother left a lot of angry people behind. Does he say anything about her?"

"He just mentions her in passing. Why?"

"I was sure she'd be in gaol or lynched or something by now, that's all. Be careful. If the boy is anything like his mother, he's probably after something."

"We don't have anything," Martha pointed out.

"No, we don't. But your father does. And as far as I know, it's still sitting in the hotel safe in Wellington. Do you remember when I broke my arm?"

Martha did. "It happened the same night the Elliotts left Wellington, didn't it?"

"Yes. How much do you know about what happened?"

"Most of it, I think. It was all anybody talked about for months. The one son eventually ended up with all of his father's money, didn't he?"

"Yes, but Nathan Elliott took only a little of the money for himself. He gave most of it to Sophie's mother. She used it to buy the hotel. But Nate also reserved a sum to compensate Clementine Elliott for the monies that had been promised to her. He left two hundred pounds behind in case she ever turned up. I don't think anyone really expected to ever hear from her again."

"And now, here she is. Or at least Horatio Joe is. What do you suppose we should do now?"

It was a good question, and one that Thaddeus really didn't have an answer for. "I suppose we're obligated to let her know the money's there," he said, "but bear in mind that it's tainted. It was all a colossal fraud on Mrs. Elliott's part."

"But that's what Nathan Elliott wanted, isn't it?" Martha said. "To give it to her? Even so? After all, it's his money."

"Yes, you're right, but I don't know what the legalities are. I should ask Ashby about it. He's a barrister. He'll know how the whole thing should be handled."

"Should I mention anything to Horatio … or Joe, I guess, since that's how he signed the letter?"

"I don't see why not. Let him know and then the lawyers can take it from there, I guess."

That night Martha got pen and ink and paper from the desk in the parlour and took them through to the kitchen so she could sit by herself while she considered what she should write to Horatio Joe.

She stared at the blank page for quite some time before she began writing.

For starters, she needed to remember that his name was really just

Joe, without the Horatio part of it. Then she had to figure out how she should start the letter. She had been a small girl when she played with Joe along the shores of the giant sand dunes near Wellington, and now she had forgotten a lot of the details, but she did remember that she had been quite taken aback when he and his mother had departed so abruptly, and finally, that was where she decided to start.

Dear Joe,

I was quite surprised to receive your letter. I had long since decided that I would probably never hear from you again, a fact I found distressing, but as I had no notion of where you had gone to, I was at a loss as to how to reach you.

Yes, that was good. The long silence borne with reluctance, but an indication that she was willing to reestablish the friendship. But what should she write next? She was inexperienced in the art of correspondence – almost everyone she knew had been within earshot for most of her life.

I hope you are well, and that your mother is too. I have spent the last year living with my grandfather, whom you probably remember. He went back to being a preacher for a time, and I have been in Cobourg keeping house for him.

Would Joe even know where Cobourg was? Unlikely, since he had probably spent most of his life in the States, but he would at least know that it wasn't Wellington.

We are soon leaving for London, which is in the western part of the province. My grandfather isn't a preacher any more. He's doing some work for a barrister and we expect to be in London for a little while – maybe a couple of weeks or so. I'm quite excited as I haven't ever seen any places besides Wellington and Cobourg.

And then she remembered the horrible news she should tell him.

Sadly, my grandmother passed away a few years ago. She was the lady who limped a little when it was stormy, and was often sick. My father, who made you a jig doll for Christmas, is still at The Temperance Hotel in Wellington, which he runs with my stepmother Sophie.

So far it was an uninspired missive, but Martha wasn't sure what else to include. She felt that the news of the money was best left to Thaddeus to disclose, and she could hardly tell Joe about her adventures in Cobourg – it was such a complicated story that she had no idea how to begin putting it down on paper. In the end, she decided to simply ask him to write again.

I'm sure you have many things to tell me about where you have been and what you have been doing. I would love to hear about them.

Yours sincerely,
Martha

P.S. My grandfather is enclosing a bit of news for your mother.

Thaddeus came in from the parlour just as she finished writing.

"Would you add a note to this letter?" she asked. "I don't really know how to explain about the money." She handed it to him.

"I suppose," he said, although he didn't sound very enthusiastic. He scrawled a few words at the bottom, an addition that Martha thought quite spoiled the look of the page. "I hope Ashby tells us not to give to her."

CHAPTER 2

The lake was choppy as the steamer pulled away from Cobourg Harbour a week later. Several of the other passengers on board looked a little queasy, but Martha was a good sailor and insisted on staying out on the deck.

"The town seemed so large when we were there, but it looks so small from here," she commented.

"Just wait," Thaddeus said. "You won't believe how big Toronto is, although it's hard to get a good view of the harbour itself. It's tucked away behind a spit of land."

Port Hope, Port Darlington, Port Whitby. The north shore of Lake Ontario was dotted with good harbours, and as they passed each one, Martha would peer at them, as if memorizing their locations for future reference.

"Are you afraid of getting lost or something?" Thaddeus teased.

"No, but you always seem to know where everything is. I'm just trying to catch up, that's all."

"We'll be evenly matched when we get to London. I've never been there," he said. "The only thing I know about it is that at one point somebody or other thought it should be the capital of Upper Canada, but it proved to be too far away from everything."

"Is that why they called it London?"

"I believe so. And just to drive the point home, they called its river the Thames. I expect it's nothing like the London in England. Of course, I don't know for sure. I've never been to England either."

Martha was pleased that her grandfather's mood seemed to lighten the further they got away from Cobourg. The last year had been difficult for both of them. Thaddeus had tried hard to maintain their easy relationship, but all too often she would discover him sitting in a chair staring off at nothing, and too many evenings had been spent in brooding silence until she could no longer stand it and had gone off to bed. Now that they were on the move, he seemed quite cheerful. She had insisted that he use some of Ashby's money to buy a new suit of clothes and she had steered him away from unrelieved ministerial black toward a handsome grey waistcoat accessorized with a darker grey cravat. The new clothes seemed to contribute to his improved mood, and she was amused when he drew looks from several of the ladies who had also boarded the steamer.

And as much as Martha found Towns Ashby annoying, she was grateful that he had provided something for Thaddeus to do. Otherwise, she was sure, she would have found herself back at the Temperance Hotel in Wellington, in spite of Thaddeus's promise that she could continue to live with him. And if that had happened, she wasn't at all sure what would have become of her grandfather.

Toronto's presence was signaled long before they reached it by the cloud of smoke enveloping the stacks and steeples that poked up into the sky.

"There's an onshore wind," Thaddeus explained. "It's keeping the smoke inland. The air is better when the wind blows out into the lake."

It seemed to take a long time to round the spit of land that protected the city from the open water, but eventually the steamer chugged up to the quay. Martha could see Ashby waiting for them. She had forgotten how tall he was, and how well-dressed. As soon as they disembarked, he sauntered over to them.

"Thaddeus! Miss Renwell!" He doffed his hat in greeting.

She was apparently 'Miss Renwell' again, she noted. Ashby had begun to call her Martha while he was in Cobourg, but now he had reverted to the more formal salutation. That was fine with Martha.

They flagged a carter and directed him to take their baggage to a nearby inn.

"Are you hungry?" Ashby asked. "I'm famished. We can talk about the case over dinner, if you like. The hotel's just down here."

He indicated one of the main thoroughfares that ran down to the harbour.

"It's only a short way. Easiest to walk it if you've got your land legs back. And close to the quay for when you leave in the morning."

They soon reached what Martha thought was rather a modest building, not really what she expected from a city hotel. Ashby led the way inside, where they registered and then Ashby led them to a small private parlour opposite the barroom.

When the innkeeper appeared, Ashby ordered a brandy. Thaddeus and Martha both opted for tea.

"Now if you don't mind, I'd like to give you the bare bones of my story before dinner arrives," Ashby said. "It's turned out to be a most peculiar series of events. In the beginning it was nothing more than a simple heart balm tort."

"What's that?" Martha asked. She thought it sounded very romantic.

"A heart balm tort is simply what it describes – a civil suit initiated in order to provide compensation for a romantic entanglement that has gone awry in some way. There are various sorts of actions that fall into the category. Reneging on a promise to marry, for example. Another is what they call 'criminal conversation', which is when someone consorts with another's spouse…"

Martha tensed a little, but Ashby appeared not to notice that the conversation was treading perilously close to a sore subject for Thaddeus.

"... but the most common is the charge of seduction. The cases are a nuisance really, but lucrative for barristers. Nine times out of ten the jury finds in favour of the woman, especially if she shows up in court with her infant in tow. They seem to figure that she should get some money from somebody, whether there's any evidence that the accused is responsible or not."

"Tell me about the girl who died," Thaddeus said. "Who was she and what was her relationship with the accused?"

"I don't really know much about her except that she was the twenty-two year old daughter of the warehouse owner. She and this Nelson Lakefield fellow had a longish courtship. The two had been seeing each other for nearly three years. Everyone assumed that they would eventually marry, although no mention of it had been made specifically by either party. And when she turned up in a delicate condition, her parents hoped that the marriage would go ahead and the problem would be solved, as often happens in these cases.

However, Lakefield insists that he wasn't responsible."

"Is there any evidence of extraordinary access?" Thaddeus asked.

"What do you mean by extraordinary access?" Martha asked.

"I think I'll leave that one to you to explain," Ashby said to Thaddeus.

"It's all right. Martha's not been so sheltered that life takes her by surprise." He turned to her. "It used to be that when a couple was already engaged, the girl's parents would allow the young man more latitude. For example, the couple would be allowed to sit up together late at night after everyone else had gone to bed, that sort of thing. Sometimes the marriage was...expedited, so to speak, especially if it was a long courtship and the suitor was a little reluctant to commit. It's not as common a practice as it once was, but in the old days anyway, a betrothal was considered nearly as good as a marriage."

"Did you sit up late at night with grandma?" Martha asked. She said it to tease him, and was surprised when he looked a little disconcerted.

"Well, yes. Not that I was ever reluctant, but there was too much family around during the day. Nobody thought anything of it."

"And did it expedite matters?" Ashby asked. He was joking, too, Martha could see, but Thaddeus's expression was so odd that Ashby quickly turned the conversation back to the matter at hand. "Anyway, Lakefield insists that nothing improper ever occurred between them, and his father objects strongly to the notion of accepting an offspring that isn't blood. When it became apparent that no marriage would take place, the girl's father initiated the seduction suit."

"Why her father?" Martha wanted to know. "Why didn't she do it herself?"

Ashby sighed. "And there you have another of these strange English laws we've inherited. The tort is based on the concept that, due to the existence of a child, the girl's father has been deprived of her services as a servant. I know..." he said in response to Martha's incredulous look, "...it's archaic. It is, however, the framework within which we must work. In any event, the pre-existing suit was enough to convince local law enforcement that Lakefield had a good motive for murder."

Just then the innkeeper arrived with the bottle of claret Ashby had ordered to accompany their dinner. Thaddeus declined the glass that was offered, so Martha decided she should follow his lead. Ashby emptied his glass quickly, and poured out another.

"Are there any other candidates?" Thaddeus asked, returning to the subject at hand. "Was she seeing anyone else, for example?"

"There has been no mention of it," Ashby said. "That's an angle you may want to investigate. The evidence against Lakefield is largely circumstantial. If you can discover who the father is, it may give us a lead on who's really responsible for setting the fire and killing the girl. At the very least, it would provide someone else with a motive and that might be enough to get Lakefield off."

"So what you want me to do is nose around the case to see what I can shake loose," Thaddeus said.

Ashby smiled. "You've got the general idea. First of all though, I'd like you to get the witness statements from Earl Jenkins. I still haven't received them and I can't do much without them. And now here's our dinner and we should talk about more pleasant things."

The waiter set a bowl of unfamiliar-looking soup in front of Martha. She waited until the others had been served before she asked what it was.

"Mock turtle soup," Ashby replied.

"What's a mock turtle?"

"A tortoise with pretensions," Ashby replied.

She frowned at him.

"It's made to taste like turtle soup, that's all."

Since she had no notion of what turtle soup tasted like, she found this answer less than helpful. She resolved to try it, though. After all, she had proclaimed herself open to new experience. She musn't shy away at the first unfamiliar thing she encountered.

But before she sampled her first spoonful, Martha had one more question for Ashby.

"Why do juries in a seduction suit so often find for the woman?" she asked.

"Because it's generally assumed that men are cads, of course." He had a smirk on his face as he replied.

"Oh. Thank you. That makes perfect sense."

To her annoyance, he laughed and reached again for the bottle of wine.

"I have your steamer and rail tickets booked," he said, "and I've arranged rooms at the Western Hotel in London, which is new and, I'm told, rather nice."

Thaddeus looked alarmed. Ashby's payment had been generous, but it wouldn't take too many nights in a nice hotel to use up a large chunk of it. "I had assumed that Martha and I would find a boarding house somewhere," he ventured.

"Far easier if you just stay at the Western through to the end of the assizes," Ashby said. "It will be the most convenient, and the dining room is good. Everything on one bill, you see. Far easier to add it all up at the end."

"Yes, the bill," Thaddeus said. "That's one of the things I need to ask you about. You haven't been very specific about the arrangements."

Ashby looked puzzled. "Did I not write to you about that?" He considered for a moment. "No, I didn't, did I? I'm sorry. A complete oversight on my part. All of your expenses will be met while you're on the case, of course, and then there's a per diem for your services, which I expect will be required to the end of the trial. Minus the advance of course." He pondered this for a moment, then announced, "Why don't I just tell you what I was thinking, and you can tell me whether or not it will be acceptable?"

And then he named a sum that sounded outrageous to Martha's ears. She had managed Thaddeus's household while they had been in Cobourg, and she knew what a preacher's yearly salary amounted to. This was twice the sum.

"I… don't know what to say." Thaddeus seemed as flabbergasted as she was. "That seems rather above the odds to be perfectly honest."

Ashby laughed. "Oh don't worry. It will all get passed along to the client's father, and he's extremely well-heeled. He won't bat an eye. Especially if we keep his son from being hanged."

"And if we don't?"

"Then he pays anyway. Just not as enthusiastically."

Martha thought this was a rather heartless attitude on Ashby's part, but then she supposed that a barrister must win and lose many cases over the course of his professional life, and one probably developed a tough skin. Otherwise, you'd quit as soon as you lost a case.

Their second course proved to be perch in a cream sauce, a dish Martha had herself cooked at the Temperance Hotel. She was very hungry, but knowing from past experience how slowly Ashby ate, she was determined to adopt a leisurely pace, and took only a small serving, which she picked at as though on the lookout for bones.

"I do have a small item, unrelated to the present case, that I would like to discuss with you if you don't mind doing at least a little more business over dinner," Thaddeus said.

"It would be my pleasure."

"It concerns a series of events that occurred a number of years ago, where a man's family had lost track of him for a long time. Then as the patriarch of the family lay dying, the man supposedly turned up again, only to go missing within a few days. His supposed wife and son arrived sometime later, and after a number of rather disturbing developments, tried to claim part of the estate."

"If this is one of the cases you were involved in, then I'm familiar with the broad outline of the story," Ashby said. "There was a murder or two, wasn't there? And a strange wild boy."

"Wherever did you hear about it?"

"Parts of it were reported in the newspapers, of course," Ashby said. "I wormed the rest of it out of your son. It was tough going. He really didn't want to talk about it at all. The real missing heir showed up in the end, didn't he?"

"Yes. And the woman and her son left town in a hurry. No one has seen nor heard from them until recently, when Martha received a letter from the son. They were quite good friends, you see, for the short period of time the boy was in Wellington."

"Surely they're not still attempting to claim any part of the estate?"

"No, although I expect that Clementine would give it a try if she thought she could get away with it. The estate went to the real heir, Nathan Elliott. He left again as soon as everything was settled, but he reserved a sum of money for the woman who posed as his wife. He felt she was owed it. And now I'm asking you if it should be turned over to her, and if so, how we should do it."

Ashby swirled the wine in his glass while he thought, then drained it before he replied.

"There are no outstanding issues regarding the estate? It all went to the one son free and clear?"

"Yes."

"Then he can give money to anybody he wants to. There's no legal reason not to do as he asked."

Thaddeus's look of disappointment was evident at this answer.

"Is there a problem with that?" Ashby asked.

"No, not really," Thaddeus said. "It's just that she's a bit of a charlatan. Table-rapping, calling the dead, that sort of thing. I eventually uncovered how she managed it all, but in the meantime she took the citizens of Wellington for quite a ride."

"I see. Perhaps the best way to proceed is to set up an escrow account for the money. Then she'll have to provide some sort of identification in order to claim it."

"How will she do that?" Martha asked. "Elliott isn't her real name."

"That's her problem. Or her lawyer's I suppose. I'll take down the details after dinner, and if you like, Thaddeus, I can also draw up a document that indemnifies you, so you're absolved of responsibility for anything beyond notifying her that the money exists."

"Yes, I would like that, but it should include Martha's father. He's been holding the funds all these years."

"We can put both your names on it." He turned to Martha. "Why haven't I heard anything about your father before this? I was convinced that you were an orphan, and that your poor long-suffering grandfather got stuck with you."

"He did, for a time," Martha said. "Then my father came back."

"From where?"

"He got caught up in the rebellion in '37 and spent a few years in the States."

"And your mother? Or did you spring out of the ground perfectly formed?"

It was a facetious remark, but Martha met it head-on. "She was murdered."

Ashby had the grace to look embarrassed. "I apologize. I didn't realize."

"It's not me you should be apologizing to. I don't remember her at all. I was an infant when it happened. It was my grandfather who suffered over it."

"Don't." Thaddeus said. "It was a long time ago and of no matter now."

"Yes. Perhaps I should just stop talking," Ashby agreed.

"Excellent idea," Martha replied. "That way you might have time to eat your dinner."

Ashby beamed at her. "You know, Martha, I'm very glad you're here. I really quite missed you."

And with that, their main course, a platter of mutton chops arrived. Martha threw caution aside and dove into them.

CHAPTER 3

Clementine Elliott. It had been a long time since she'd used that name. It had been in Wellington. In Canada. Where everything had gone so badly wrong. Where her husband had been killed. Funny that a ghost from that particular past should pop up just now, when things were sticky again and she knew it was time to run.

How long had it been? She counted it up. Ten years. The little girl who had been Joe's friend would be a young woman by now, just as her son had now grown into a man. Funny that he should take it into his head to write to Martha. Even stranger that the girl had written back with the news that, unaccountably, there was Elliott money to be had after all.

Joe shared the letter with her. The girl and her grandfather were travelling, apparently on their way to another small town in Canada, the preacher no longer tied down by his sickly wife. He had been the devil to deal with all those long years ago. He had been far too observant. Too clever. And completely immune to her charms. She laughed to think of it now. If she hadn't been so desperate at the time, she would have enjoyed the duel of wits. They had matched each other, move for move. And then at the end, when he'd finally bested her, he'd had a choice – and he had chosen to let her go.

The preacher was consulting a barrister, he had written at the bottom of the letter, and she could expect to hear at a later date what she would need to do in order to claim the money. If only she knew where she was going to be.

London, Canada West. She wondered where that was. She could ask at the train station and see if a railroad line extended far enough into Canada to make traveling easy.

London. She'd never heard of it, but it was as good a bolt hole as anywhere, she reckoned, if only she could get this damned wall safe open first.

CHAPTER 4

The next day it seemed to Thaddeus that the steamer took no time at all to reach Burlington Bay, and when they disembarked they were directed to affordable lodgings close to the train station. They were assured that from there it would be easy enough to connect with the train that was leaving Hamilton the following morning.

This was the part of the journey Thaddeus was looking forward to the least. He had never ridden on a train. He had never dreamt that train travel was something that would become available in his lifetime, and had scoffed at the notion that anyone could build a track through the rugged wilderness of Upper Canada. And yet here he was, about to board what amounted to a giant tea kettle that would propel him forward at a frightening speed. He spent a restless night trying to imagine what the experience would be like.

He grew more nervous at the station, and as the conductor called for them to board, he sneaked a glance at Martha's face. She looked excited and eager. Well, he thought, part of the deal we struck was to go off to places we hadn't seen before, and try a few new things. If she can, I can.

They settled themselves on the bench seats that flanked the central passageway. The railway car was long and narrow and reminded Thaddeus uncomfortably of a coffin, and he jumped when the train began to move. They gained speed as they left the city limits, and Thaddeus began to relax, although he twitched a little whenever there was an odd noise. Martha spent the first hour of the journey with her nose pressed against the window, exclaiming now and again at something she saw.

The land seemed much more suited to the laying of rails than the hilly countryside around Cobourg, and he was just beginning to enjoy this new experience when the train slowed, then rolled gently to a stop in front of a small building that looked to be little more than a woodshed. This was, he later discovered, exactly its function. The steam engine that pulled the cars used enormous amounts of fuel, and "wooding up" stations were situated at various points along the route. Soon they were underway again, and in what seemed like a very short period of time, the conductor announced that the next stop was Woodstock. It was a journey that would have taken Thaddeus a day to ride, yet they had arrived in a couple of hours.

The conductor told them that the train would remain stationary for at least fifteen minutes, so they took the opportunity to get out of their seats to stretch their legs. Thaddeus was reluctant to get off the train entirely, but a woman was walking up and down beside the track offering food to passengers. He hopped down, handed over a few coins for some pork pies, then scrambled aboard again, fearful that the train would somehow leave without him. He needn't have worried – he and Martha sat in their seats for a further ten minutes before the whistle finally blew and they got underway again.

They ate their snack and before long, Thaddeus began to nod, lulled by the rocking of the car as it sped along the track. Martha leaned against his shoulder and dozed as well until they reached the next stop, when they both came to with a start.

"It was such a novelty at first, " Martha said. "But now it's beginning to wear thin, isn't it?"

"Never mind, we'll be there before long. It would take ages any other way."

And again, they half-slept their journey away.

The whistle blew them awake again as they pulled into London station, a multi-gabled wooden building with fanciful bargeboard decoration along its eaves. They found a carter as soon as they alit. Just as carters clustered around piers when ships arrived, there was a long line of them waiting at the train station. Thaddeus asked one of them to take their trunks to the Western Hotel, then he and Martha climbed up beside their luggage.

"Is it far?" he asked.

"Not at all," the man replied. "Just on up here on Richmond

Street. It's brand new. They rebuilt the old hotel after half the town burned down a few years ago."

That would explain why London looked so new and prosperous, Thaddeus thought as they rode along. The fire had cleared away the old wooden buildings that posed such a fire hazard and now the town was being rebuilt in brick.

The Western Hotel proved to be an imposing building that occupied fully half of a city block. There were shops on the first floor all along the street – a pharmacy, a barber, a bookseller. It seemed that anything you could possibly want was within a stone's throw.

Thaddeus had expected that he and Martha would share a room, but when they registered, they discovered that Ashby had reserved family lodging for them, two side-by-side rooms with a connecting door. Each of them had a wide bed with a rich woven spread. The floors were covered in soft carpets and the large windows offered a panoramic view of the city. It was far grander than the inn they had stayed at in Toronto.

"This is pretty rich, isn't it?" he said to Martha.

"Yes. More than I expected at any rate. Apparently they don't move the beds around like we do at the Temperance."

The shifting of furniture from room to room was something that happened frequently at the Wellington hotel, the arrangements constantly modified to suit the needs of the guests.

"It looks like everything stays put here," Thaddeus agreed. "Or at least if it doesn't, I'm glad it's not me who has to move it."

Just then two porters arrived with their trunks, deposited them in their respective rooms and informed them of the location of the baths and water closets. As soon as their things had been stowed, Thaddeus and Martha set off in the direction of the dining room. It seemed a long time since their hastily grabbed snack at Woodstock.

The dining room was unlike anything Martha had ever seen. It was huge, with many chandeliers and sconces to light it, a soft carpet on the floor and a sea of tables covered with snow-white cloths. They were handed sheets of paper that detailed the dishes offered.

"What's a la carte?" she asked the waiter who hovered over them.

"It means you choose the dish that appeals to you," the man replied. "And then it's brought to you on a separate plate."

Martha couldn't begin to imagine the trouble this must cause in the kitchen. It was hard enough to cook meals for a crowd when everyone ate the same thing.

"It would make sense to take all our meals here, wouldn't it?" Martha remarked, as she looked over her choices. "Our meal tickets are included with the room."

"That would certainly be the thriftiest thing to do," Thaddeus agreed.

"Good. That way I'll get to try everything on the menu. Tonight I think I'll start with oysters."

The next morning Thaddeus set off to find the local barrister who was partnering with Ashby in the case. Earl Jenkins had a small office not far from the hotel, in what Thaddeus took to be the business district of London.

Jenkins was a small, slow-moving man who looked relieved to hand over whatever evidence he had managed to gather.

"Mr. Ashby seemed to think that I would be able to run around and find out all sorts of things for him." Jenkins held his hands up in despair. "I'm really just a small-town solicitor, Mr. Lewis. I draw up contracts and last testaments. I have little experience with the criminal courts and little time to investigate anything."

He certainly wouldn't, Thaddeus thought, unless he moved a little faster. At least the man seemed amenable to handing over the statements that had been taken, along with a few sparse notes he had made on a separate sheet of paper.

"I wonder if you could answer a few questions for me?" Thaddeus said. "Just some general information, really. I don't know the community at all. What are the details of Mr. Lakefield and Mr. Warner's respective businesses, just for starters?"

"Lawrence Lakefield owns a foundry. He specializes in agricultural implements and steam engines designed for farm use, that sort of thing. Albert Warner is a commission merchant mostly, again, of farm products. Wheat, in particular."

The price of wheat was currently at an all time high, partly because of the anticipated easy access to American markets, and partly because Britain's war in the Crimea had halted their imports of Russian wheat. It was no wonder the two families would have welcomed a union between their offspring, Thaddeus realized. Lakefield sold the implements farmers needed to get their crops in the ground, Warner bought the crops they produced and sold them for a cut of the profits. If they joined forces, they could get the farmers both coming and going.

"Both men are respected in the community?" Thaddeus wanted to know.

"Oh yes. That's why the Warner girl's disgrace was so shocking. It's not the sort of thing that happens in that particular circle. Or at least that we ever hear of. If it does, it's hushed up and the girl sent away."

"Why wasn't that the case this time? Bringing suit makes the whole scandal incredibly public, doesn't it?"

Jenkins looked confused. It was something that hadn't occurred to him. "I'm not sure. Family honour, I suppose. And help with raising the child of course."

Family honour would have been better served if Warner had kept mum, Thaddeus thought. And a wealthy merchant hardly needed help to raise a child.

"And the young man who has been arrested - Nelson Lakefield? What can you tell me about him?"

"Not a great deal. As you say, he's a young man and therefore I have not had occasion to do business with him." Jenkins hesitated, then added, "The Lakefield boys have generally been a trial to their father, or so I understand."

"In what way?"

"In the way of all young men, I suppose. They sow their wild oats a little before they settle down."

"The oats in this case appear to be particularly untamed," Thaddeus pointed out.

"Yes, well, not for me to say. In any event, whatever has been claimed about the suit will be there in the file. You can use my office to look at the statements if you like."

"Thank you, but I think it best that I get out of your way. I'd hate to interfere with your business."

Jenkins looked relieved as just then an old man, a farmer by the look of him, came stomping in the door.

"You see," Thaddeus said. "You have a customer to attend to."

And then he left before Jenkins had a chance to object to him taking the files out of the office.

While Thaddeus was gone, Martha discovered that the Western Hotel provided their patrons with a sitting room that offered solid desks and plenty of pens and paper. It seemed a convenient place to work. They could huddle in a corner of the room away from prying eyes, yet they would be close enough to each other to consult should one of them find something puzzling. As Thaddeus carried Jenkins' files into the room, one of the hotel staff hovered anxiously in the doorway.

"Is this adequate for your purposes, sir?" he asked. "Would you like a desk moved closer to the window?"

"Thank you, but this is fine."

"Is there anything else I could do for you?" The man fussed anxiously.

"I don't suppose you could bring us a pot of tea?" Thaddeus asked. "It would be nice to have a cup of tea while we work."

"Of course, Mr. Lewis. Right away." And he scuttled away.

"That was very odd," Martha remarked as soon as the man was out of earshot. "He's learned your name already."

"Yes, it was, wasn't it? Everyone's curious about a stranger, I suppose."

Thaddeus spread the papers across one of the desks, and when Martha saw how little of it there was, she simply pulled an extra chair up to it. By the time they had sorted the documents into categories, the clerk had returned, not only with a pot of tea, but with a plate of macaroons as well.

"Just set everything down on the table over there," Thaddeus directed. "I don't want to risk spilling it."

The clerk obliged, but not before he craned past Thaddeus in an attempt to get a look at the paperwork on the desk.

"Thank you. I'll ring if we need anything more." The man nodded and left the room, his curiosity unsatisfied.

The papers resolved themselves into two distinct categories: the affidavits, statements and evidence regarding the original seduction suit, and the evidence the police had collected regarding the warehouse fire and the subsequent discovery of Hazel Warner's body. They were both pretty much as Ashby described.

Nelson Lakefield and Hazel Warner had been seeing each other for approximately two and a half years. Everyone expected that an engagement would soon be announced. However, Nelson kept putting Hazel's mother off with regard to any concrete plans. Then, unaccountably, according to the young man, the relationship had cooled, and a few months later, it became evident that Hazel was with child.

Nelson denied any responsibility and Hazel's parents had instituted the lawsuit that would, if not restore respectability to the family, at least provide for the child.

"That part of it seems reasonably straight-forward," Thaddeus remarked. "Her word against his."

"Only if you take her word for it," Martha said. "If you believe Nelson, it's not straight-forward at all – there's someone else involved, isn't there?"

"True enough. But as far as the legalities are concerned, Ashby seemed to think that it would be pretty cut and dried – the jury would find for the complainant. Its only importance is how it impacted the second case."

"I find it a little strange, though. Ashby kept going on about how the Lakefields have lots of money. Why were they defending the suit? Why didn't they just pay up and be done with it without going to all the trouble of a court case?"

"I'm not sure what kind of settlement a jury would award," Thaddeus said. "If it's generally known that the Lakefields are rich, and I don't see why it wouldn't be, given that Mr. Lakefield owns a foundry here in town, then a jury might be tempted to extract as much money as they could. Sometimes the poor like to take it out on the rich, if they get a chance."

"I suppose." Her tone was doubtful. "It may be something to look into, though, don't you think?"

"You have a suspicious mind."

"That's what we're being paid for, isn't it?"

"Well, I am, anyway. I may give you some of it." And then he laughed at her outraged expression.

The notes regarding the charge of arson were even sparser than those regarding the seduction tort. On July 12th, 1854 a warehouse owned by Albert Warner caught fire. At first it was assumed that it was somehow ignited by one of the men taking part in the Orange Parade. There had been a number of fistfights that had broken out between the Orangemen and a group of Irish Catholics. It was only after the warehouse burnt to the ground that Hazel's remains were discovered, at which point one of the men who worked at the warehouse reported having seen Nelson Lakefield leave the building shortly before the fire started. This report, and the fact that it was widely believed that Nelson was the father of Hazel's baby was enough to get Nelson arrested. He denied everything, but was committed for trial mostly, as far as Thaddeus could tell, on the basis of the eyewitness identification.

"I can see why Ashby called us in," Thaddeus said. "This is all pretty circumstantial, but Mr. Jenkins hasn't exactly been stirring himself to discover any other circumstances that would explain it all."

"So where should we start?"

"The obvious place is with Nelson Lakefield. I know it's irregular, but why don't you come with me? I'd like to get your impression of him."

"Won't he wonder why I'm there?"

"I'll tell him you're my clerk." Thaddeus was joking, of course. Women were never employed as clerks or secretaries. "Don't say anything. Just keep track of the conversation and take some notes."

"Yes, Mr. Lewis," Martha replied, and when he looked askance at her, "Well, I can hardly call you 'grandpa' if I'm supposed to be your clerk, can I?"

"I suppose not."

"Or 'boss'. I could call you boss. Yes, 'boss' has a nice ring to it, doesn't it?"

"It does," he agreed. "I like the sound of it. I can boss you around."

"Yes, boss.

The Middlesex County Courthouse was not difficult to find. Its strange crenellated walls and octagonal towers dominated the skyscape from its position on a hill overlooking the Thames River. Its function as a government building was unmistakable – only the government, Thaddeus figured, would build a castle in a small town in rural Canada.

He and Martha were directed to the nether regions of the building where the cell blocks were located, as if the castle concept had been extended to include a dungeon. He almost expected to see prisoners hanging in chains from the walls.

Thaddeus introduced himself to the keeper, offered a brief explanation of his business and asked to see Nelson Lakefield.

"Would the young lady prefer to wait for you out here?" the keeper asked.

"No. She's my secretary," Thaddeus said. The man looked surprised, but led them through a heavy wooden door to a block of narrow cells. They looked reasonably comfortable to Thaddeus's eye, each with a cot and a writing table, and at the end of the hall there was a small stove to combat the dampness that must creep into the cellar, given its proximity to the river.

The keeper stopped in front of a door. "I can leave it open for you. I'll be at the end of the hall, if you can call to me when you've finished."

Thaddeus nodded his thanks. He was used to the rules of gaol, but Martha's eyes were wide.

Nelson Lakefield proved to be an unprepossessing young man. No, unprepossessing wasn't quite the right word, Thaddeus realized. Nondescript maybe? Well-nigh invisible? He was the sort of man who blended into any background he found himself standing against. Ashy brown hair, ashen complexion, neither tall nor short, neither thin nor fat. Thaddeus finally decided that "grey" was the best descriptor. He was surprised that anyone had been able to definitively identify Nelson as the man who had been at the warehouse on the night of the fire. Thaddeus was reasonably sure that he could walk out of the gaol at that moment and not be able to accurately describe Lakefield by the time he reached the street.

He held out his hand. "I'm Thaddeus Lewis. I'm working with your barrister Mr. Ashby. This is Miss Renwell."

Lakefield shook Thaddeus's hand, and nodded at Martha, his eyes sliding over her figure as he did so. Martha appeared to ignore him.

"I would like to go over the events leading up to this unfortunate state of affairs. I know you've told your story many times, but a fresh ear can sometimes hear things others have missed. I report everything I find to Mr. Ashby, who will then use it to help formulate your defence."

"Is he as good as they say?" Nelson wanted to know.

"I have worked with him before, and he is very adept in court, yes."

"So he'll get me out of this?"

"There are no guarantees, Mr. Lakefield. If you are innocent, Mr. Ashby will do his best to prove it. If you are guilty, he will provide an equally spirited defence. But in the end, it all comes down to the jury."

"But I didn't do it."

"Well, then that's a good place to start," Thaddeus said. "We'll work on the assumption that you didn't do it. But I need as much information as you can give me in order to prove it. Why don't you start by telling me about you and Miss Warner?"

"Hazel and I were courting, I guess. We'd known each other since we were children and everybody just seemed to expect that we would end up together."

"And how did you feel about that?"

Nelson shrugged. "All right, I guess. I mean I liked Hazel, and father said it would be good for business, to have the two families connected."

So it had been a lukewarm courtship at best, with parental dreams of dynasty motivating the match.

"Had you proposed to her?"

"No. I wasn't ready to settle down yet. There didn't seem to be any hurry about it."

"Were you often left alone with her?"

"Not often... sometimes... no, not really. I mean, we'd kiss a little when no one was looking, but it was never long enough to...you know." His eyes slid over to Martha. "She isn't writing this down, is she?"

Martha had produced a sheaf of papers and a stub of pencil and was taking notes over by the table.

"Yes, that's what she's here for, to take notes so that Mr. Ashby can refer to them later," Thaddeus explained.

Lakefield looked puzzled, but made no further comment on Martha's presence.

"What did you think when you found out that Hazel was with child?"

"I knew it wasn't mine, that's for sure. Even if we were by ourselves for a few minutes, Hazel wouldn't let me get very far." The young man sounded almost aggrieved, as if he should have been allowed more. "Father was furious when I told him, but then he said it was all her look-out and maybe it was a good thing we found out what she was like before it was too late. I'd say I had a close call – I mean, I could have married her and then found out, couldn't I?"

Martha shifted her position slightly, a movement that distracted Nelson before he could work up too much indignation over his intended's character.

Thaddeus decided to direct the conversation to a different topic. "Where were you on the day of the fire?"

"I lined up with everybody else to watch the parade of course."

"And where did you stand?"

"In front of the town hall. It was the best place to stand. The parade went right by there."

"So there were a lot of people around?"

"Yes."

"And not one of them saw you?"

Nelson shrugged. "None that want to come forward and say so."

Thaddeus thought this odd. Orange Day Parades always drew a great crush of people, and their eyes would have been on the marchers for the most part, but surely one of them would have noticed Nelson Lakefield. Except that he was so unnoticeable. Maybe it wasn't such an odd thing after all.

"There were a couple of fights that broke out," Nelson offered. "Some of the Irish were causing trouble. I expect everybody was watching those."

"Where did you go after the parade?"

"Straight home."

"Did you go anywhere near Mr. Warner's warehouse on the way?"

"No. Why would I?"

"No reason. Just asking. What time did you get home?"

"It was about six o'clock, I guess. I didn't look at the clock or anything. I just went upstairs to start getting ready for dinner."

"And when did you hear that Mr. Warner's warehouse had caught fire?"

"I didn't know anything about it until the next day."

"I see," Thaddeus said, frowning a little. "I think that will do for now, Mr. Lakefield. "But if I have more questions, may I return?"

Nelson looked relieved that his questioning was over. "Of course. Anytime. To tell the truth I'm glad of the company. It's pretty tedious sitting here by myself day after day."

"Surely you have visitors?" Thaddeus said. "Your friends and family are allowed to visit, aren't they?"

"My mother comes," Lakefield said. "My so-called friends came once or twice, but I haven't seen hide nor hair of them in days."

And then, to Thaddeus's surprise, Martha spoke up. "I have a question. What did Hazel look like?"

Nelson seemed surprised by this, as if he hadn't ever thought about it before. "She…ummm… she had sort of yellow hair. She was kind of pretty I guess."

Poor Hazel, Thaddeus thought. *A lukewarm courtship indeed if this is how her suitor describes her.*

"There's a picture," Nelson went on. "She had a daguerreotype done at Strong's Hotel and she gave it to me. It's in the desk in the parlour. Tell my father to give it to you if you want it. I sure don't."

"Let's have a sit down somewhere and you can tell me what you think," Thaddeus said as he and Martha left the gaol.

He headed toward a small cafe near the market that offered beverages and small pastries.

"I thought we were going to stick with the hotel dining room?" Martha said.

"We can afford a cup of chocolate, surely."

They took a seat in the window. Martha drew out the notes she had taken.

"Before you get to those, give me your general impression first," Thaddeus said.

Martha wrinkled her brow in thought. "It sounds like it was a very unexciting romance," she began.

"Agreed. Engineered by the families with some sort of financial advantage in mind."

"And if Nelson Lakefield was my beau, it probably wouldn't take very much to turn my head in another direction." She stopped while she groped for the right word. "He's so… *colourless*."

Thaddeus chuckled. That was exactly what he thought.

"No, I mean, really, he doesn't have much to recommend him. Except for a father with lots of money I suppose. And…"

"Spit it out," Thaddeus said. "We're in the realm of conjecture here, so I'd like to hear what you're thinking."

"It's just that – on one hand Nelson complained that Hazel 'never let him get very far', and then when it became obvious that someone else had, it was suddenly due to her lack of character. He would've thought it was all just fine if she'd given in to him."

"You're right. It's hardly fair, is it?"

"For some reason it never is."

What an odd conversation to have with your granddaughter.

Given the nature of the case, Thaddeus was beginning to wonder if he should have allowed Martha to get involved, but she had, in the past, been remarkably helpful, and she proved her usefulness with her next remark.

"And I think he's hiding something," she said.

"What makes you say that?"

"The whole business of him watching the parade with hundreds of other people and not one of them noticing that he was there. Since when does someone watch a parade all by themselves? And even if he somehow failed to hook up with his friends, there must be dozens and dozens of people who are acquainted with him. He grew up here, after all. His father is a businessman in the town. Someone must have seen him."

"Unless he wasn't there at all."

"Exactly. So if he wasn't watching the parade, where was he? And why won't he say where it was?"

Martha continued to scan her notes. "And what was Hazel Warner doing at the warehouse in the first place?"

"It was her father's place of business. She had every right to be there. I would guess that she was meeting Nelson there."

"But why at the warehouse?" Martha persisted. "She could talk to Nelson anytime, couldn't she? Even if they had fallen out, they were still childhood friends, weren't they?"

"But the Warners had started the seduction suit by then," Thaddeus pointed out. "The families had fallen out as well."

Martha was crestfallen. "Oh. I suppose you're right."

"But you raise an interesting point. Why was she at the warehouse? Nelson claims it wasn't to meet him. Maybe he's telling the truth. He wasn't there. But somebody else was."

"The real father of the child?"

"Exactly." Thaddeus said. "And if we can found out who that is, we'll have a lot better idea of what happened. At the very least it will allow Ashby to raise the possibility of someone with an equally plausible motive."

"But how do we do that?"

Thaddeus thought for a moment. "I'm not sure. Just keep asking questions, I suppose. That's all you can ever do. Now hurry up and finish your drink. And then let's go talk to Lakefield Senior."

The Lakefield residence was a large, imposing house in a prosperous-looking part of the town. When Thaddeus knocked on the door, it was opened by a middle-aged woman, obviously a maid or a housekeeper of some sort, who left them standing in the hall while she went to fetch "Mr. Lakefield".

When Lawrence Lakefield finally appeared he greeted them courteously after he got over his surprise at Martha's presence.

"This is Miss Renwell, my secretary," was the only explanation Thaddeus offered.

They were ushered into a large parlour where Thaddeus was shown to a chair. Martha took a seat at one side of the room, but Lakefield remained standing by the fireplace, one arm resting on the mantle.

"So how does this work?" Lakefield wanted to know. "My oldest son says this Ashby fellow is a whiz in court, but what are you doing here? And how does Jenkins fit in?"

"We will all be preparing your son's defence," Thaddeus explained, without really explaining his own presence. "And yes, Mr. Ashby has been remarkably successful in court. Mr. Jenkins will assist him during the trial."

"Earl Jenkins is a fool," Lakefield grumbled. "He's been well-nigh useless. And with three of you in on it, this is going to end up costing a pretty penny, isn't it?"

Thaddeus thought that it would indeed, but given Lakefield's substantial house and the parlour's stylish furniture, he also expected that Mr. Lakefield could well afford it. He suddenly felt a little less guilty about the amount of money he was getting from Ashby.

"And if this Ashby is such a wonderful barrister," Lakefield went on, "why can't he get Nelson out on bail? It's not right that a young man from a good family should have to sit in gaol until the trial. You'd think he was a common thief or something. It seems to me a few dollars thrown in the right direction would take care of it."

"I believe the gravity of the charges preclude bail," Thaddeus explained. "Even if Ashby petitioned a superior court judge, it would probably not be granted. And in the unlikely case that it was, it would require far more than a few dollars to secure it."

"So what are you doing here? What do you want from me?"

"I've already spoken with your son," Thaddeus began. "But I thought I should speak with you as well. I would like to get as clear a picture as I can of what happened."

"You talked to Nelson? Why? He's already said everything he knows. Is it really necessary to keep grilling him about all this?"

"Yes, it's very necessary. If Mr. Ashby is to mount a defence, he needs to consider every aspect of the case."

"But Nelson's just as apt to say something unintentional and stupid that will only get him into more trouble."

Thaddeus had had enough of Lakefield's obstreperousness. "Might I remind you that I am here in order to help your son? If you find this objectionable, I would be perfectly happy to go away. You can defend him yourself, if you would prefer."

Lakefield glared. Thaddeus glared back. Lakefield blinked first.

"Well, I suppose you're right. Young fool, to get himself into so much trouble in the first place."

"Good," Thaddeus said. "Now that we find ourselves in agreement, perhaps you could tell me when you first became aware that Mr. Warner's premises had burned down."

"I heard that it was on fire the evening it happened – we had a bad fire here a few years ago, so everyone was on the alert in case it spread. I didn't know that Miss Warner died in it until the next morning when Nelson was arrested."

"Hazel and Nelson grew up together, is that correct? They were childhood friends?"

"Yes," Lakefield said. "And if I'd known what sort of girl she was, I would never have allowed her in the house. The things you learn in hindsight, eh?"

"But it would have been advantageous to both yourself and Mr. Warner if the marriage had gone ahead?"

"What are you implying? That I'd let my son marry a trollop just because it would be good for business?"

"I'm not implying anything," Thaddeus replied. "I'm merely trying to find out what happened. When I spoke with Nelson he said that Hazel gave him a daguerreotype of herself last Christmas. He said to tell you that it's in the parlour desk. Could I perhaps look at it?"

Lakefield glared again, then walked over to the drop-front mahogany desk in one corner of the room. He pulled the drawer open and rummaged through the contents until he found a small hinged box, which he handed to Thaddeus.

He opened it, and the likeness of Hazel Warner looked back at him. She was, as Nelson described her, "kind of pretty" in a very conventional way. Her features were nicely proportioned and her nose straight, but her best features were probably her wide, high forehead and remarkably round head.

"Keep it if you want it," Lakefield said. "I had no idea it was there. If I had, I would probably have thrown it out."

"Thank you," Thaddeus said, rising from his chair. "I think that will do for now. I know you're a busy man. If I have any further questions, I know where to find you."

Lakefield nodded a curt goodbye and let Thaddeus and Martha find their own way to the door.

They said nothing to each other until they were half a block down the street.

"What an unpleasant man," Martha remarked.

"Extremely. He seems to be a lot more worried about his money than he does about his son."

"Maybe he's just angry that Nelson got into so much trouble."

"I think it goes deeper than that. Nelson said that his mother was visiting him. He didn't say anything about his father."

"I for one," Martha said, "would find that a relief."

"The other thing that struck me as odd is that Mr. Lakefield said he heard about the fire that evening, which makes perfect sense. Everyone would have been anxious after so much of the town burned down a few years ago."

"But Nelson said he didn't hear about it until the next morning. How could he have been home for supper and not hear about it? His parents would have been worried enough to talk about it at the dinner table, wouldn't they?"

"I would think so. Sounds to me like Nelson wasn't at home after all."

"And yet all he has to do is say where he really was, and the case against him would fall apart," Martha said. "He seems to think Ashby is a magician and can make it all go away with no effort on his part. It's very strange."

"I suppose if I were paying what Ashby charges, I'd think that too," Thaddeus said. "I guess all we can do is keep digging and hope we earn our portion of it."

"And if we don't?"

"Then we're no worse off than before. But I'd hate to let Ashby down."

CHAPTER 5

The next day was a Sunday and, when he asked, Thaddeus was told by the hotel clerk that there was a Methodist Episcopal Church within walking distance. There were in fact two Methodist Episcopal Churches in London, the man said, but one of them was the African Chapel, not affiliated with the Canadian organization that governed Thaddeus's church.

Thaddeus was surprised that there would be an African church in so small a town, but churches grow where their congregations are and there must be enough coloured people in London to support it. Fugitive slaves from the United States could reach London easily once they made it across the lake. Or come through Detroit, he supposed.

The clerk was in a mood to chat. "There's also an African settlement just north of here called Wilberforce," he said, "although I hear it's fallen on hard times. Some of the coloureds in London may have come from there, but I think mainly the local community came up from the States." He shrugged his shoulders. "It doesn't really matter where they came from, I guess. They're peaceable folks and hard workers. A lot of us would rather have them than the Irish."

The poor Irish, despised wherever they go. Thaddeus was curious about the African church, but judged that he should inquire as to whether or not his presence would be welcome, rather than just barge into their service. He would attend the white church first, he decided, and leave the coloured church for another time.

He hoped the change of scenery would help restore the certainty that had been his companion for so many years. He had prayed many times to be struck again by the spirit of the Lord and he felt wholly unqualified to preach until it happened, but so far God had been silent on the subject.

He and Martha found the chapel without difficulty and slipped into a bench near the back. Thaddeus had counted on anonymity so far from home, but as the service started he saw with a sinking heart that the minister was Calvin Merritt, the man who had immediately preceded him on his last circuit. He had no wish to discuss his fall from grace with someone like Merritt, who was an uninspired preacher and sure to offer up nothing but platitudes.

Perhaps he should have gone to the African Church after all.

Any hope he had of becoming suddenly at one with God evaporated with Merritt's entrance. It was not a state that had ever come easily to him, although he had often brought others to it. In times of doubt he consoled himself with following John Wesley's direction to do no harm, to do good of every possible sort, aided of course, by divine support. It would not be enough to gain him an entrance to heaven, where he could be reunited with all those he held dear, for he knew that *without holiness no man shall see the Lord.* But at the moment it was the best he could do.

And nothing astounding seemed likely to occur on this day when his mind fretted over whether or not his personal affairs were public knowledge on this circuit, and Merritt lived up to his reputation by delivering the sermon in a voice so weak that Thaddeus had to strain to hear him.

There was not even any hope of avoiding Merritt by slipping quietly out the door at the end of the service. He and Martha were hemmed in by a very fat woman with two small children. She insisted on waiting until Merritt had stationed himself at the door before she began to marshal her small charges into an exodus.

Merritt's face expressed his surprise when he greeted Thaddeus.

"Mr. Lewis! A pleasure indeed. I had no idea you were in this area."

"A bit of business to attend to," Thaddeus replied. "I don't know if you've met my granddaughter Miss Renwell."

Merritt nodded at Martha, but it was clear that curiosity was consuming him and he turned his attention back to Thaddeus.

"You're not preaching at all now? I know you didn't take a circuit this time around. I wondered where you'd gone."

"No. Not preaching."

"Ah yes, perhaps that's best, for the time being at least." Merritt put a hand on Thaddeus's shoulder and regarded him earnestly. "And you know, Thaddeus, should you wish at any point to pray or at the very least to talk things over, please be assured that I would be happy to meet with you at any time. Please consider me a friend in this."

"Thank you Calvin, I'll consider that."

When hell freezes over. He could not bring himself to share his obsession and subsequent disgrace with the likes of Calvin Merritt, who was thirsty for the details and unlikely to offer any insight.

As he and Martha walked through the churchyard on their way to the street, Thaddeus was aware that here and there a head turned, and there were a couple of whispered conversations. There would be no peace for him here.

He should have known. Unless held in check, the Methodist class meetings were hotbeds of gossip. The Methodists were tasked "to watch over one another in love"; too often they bullied each other with tattle. And yet their offenses were, for the most part, so petty. An unkind thought here, a bit of sharp dealing there. It wasn't surprising that real scandal would be seized upon and repeated many times, especially if it concerned a man who was supposed to be a shepherd to their flock.

He trudged tight-lipped down the road.

"That was a little awkward, wasn't it?" Martha said when they reached the end of the street.

"Yes."

She said no more about it, and again Thaddeus was grateful for her presence and her gift of knowing when to speak and when to keep mum. He didn't quite know where he would be without Martha.

CHAPTER 6

Martha couldn't stop looking at the picture of Hazel Warner. She'd been studying it ever since Mr. Lakefield had given it to Thaddeus, and on Monday morning she brought it with her to look at while she ate her breakfast. It wasn't that there was anything remarkable about Hazel – she could just as easily have been one of the girls that Martha had gone to school with, or someone she encountered on the street in Cobourg or Wellington. It wasn't the young woman herself that was fascinating, Martha decided, but the picture itself. Unlike a painted portrait, it seemed very lifelike. You almost expected Hazel to abandon her stiff pose and rise from her chair.

"I wish they'd had daguerreotypes a long time ago," Thaddeus said. "I'd have liked one of your mother. When people are gone you sometimes start to forget what they looked like." Then he smiled. "Of course, all I really have to do these days is glance across the table and I see her all over again."

"Maybe you should have one done. I'd like a picture of you."

"Why? Are you expecting me to kick off soon?"

"No, I expect you to live forever. At least that's what I'm hoping."

"If I could figure out how to do that, I'd be the most famous man in the world." Thaddeus folded his napkin and pushed his plate away. "I think I'm going to go and have a chat with Hazel's father today. He's not apt to reveal much, given that he's on the other side of the argument, but I'd like to hear what he has to say."

"Would you like me to go with you?"

"Maybe not. I'd prefer it if he doesn't know immediately that I'm working for Ashby."

"Why don't I talk to the daguerreotypist while you're doing that?" Martha suggested. I know it's unlikely, but maybe he remembers something about Hazel. She gave the picture to Nelson just before everything went sour."

"That's not a bad idea at all," Thaddeus said. "I'll meet you back here when we're done."

"Yes, boss."

Albert Warner maintained a set of offices in the centre of the town, a fact that initially surprised Thaddeus. He would have assumed that most of Warner's business was conducted with farmers who were anxious to find a buyer for their crops, and that a warehouse would be a far less intimidating place for them to do it in. Upon reflection though, he realized that Warner's business was probably far more complicated than the simple selling of produce at the local market. He probably had agents who went directly to the farms and signed contracts with the farmers. The offices would host only a bevy of clerks dedicated to tracking the shipments of goods and enforcing the terms of the contracts. There would be no farmers with their muddy boots trudging in to negotiate a price for their wheat.

Thaddeus walked along the town's main business section and soon found a sign indicating that the Warner offices were on the second floor of a newish-looking brick building. There was a further sign at the top of the stairs. Inside the office a clerk was scribbling away at a counter, but he didn't look up when Thaddeus entered.

Thaddeus cleared his throat twice, the second time being loud enough to finally gain the clerk's attention.

"May I help you?" he asked.

"I'm here to see Mr. Warner."

"And may I tell him who's calling?"

"My name is Thaddeus Lewis."

The name would mean nothing to Warner, he knew, but he was reluctant to broadcast his business to anyone who didn't need to know.

The clerk returned a few minutes later.

"Mr. Warner will see you now. Please come this way."

Thaddeus was ushered into a corner room that was mostly taken up by a large oak desk. Otherwise the room was unremarkable, with papers stacked on the table and a cabinet against the wall.

"How do you do, Mr. Warner," Thaddeus said. "I'm here to ask some questions about the recent fire at your warehouse."

"Please sit down." Warner indicated the chair in front of the desk.

Thaddeus sat, and then waited for Warner to respond to his statement.

"I think you'll find that the insurance is all in order. The premiums were all paid on time." He sounded anxious. "There's no difficulty is there?"

Thaddeus realized that Warner thought he was from the insurance company. He also realized that he was far more likely to shake information loose if he let Warner continue to think it. After all, this man was Ashby's opponent, and unlikely to be cooperative if he knew what Thaddeus was really after.

"Not as far as I know," Thaddeus replied. "But there is an open investigation, of course, given the nature of the claim. I have a few questions."

"Of course."

"First of all, the man who reported seeing Nelson Lakefield at the warehouse that day – he was your employee?"

"Jeb Storms. Yes. The foreman in fact."

"How long has he worked for you?"

"A number of years. I don't know how many exactly, just off the top of my head."

Thaddeus smiled. "That's fine, I don't need an exact number. He's a long-term employee then?"

Warner seemed to relax a little. "Yes."

"And where is he now?"

"I'm not sure." Warner shrugged. "I assume he's found employment somewhere else. Until the warehouse is rebuilt, you see, I have no work for him."

It was always the way, Thaddeus thought, the worker gets the short straw. The boss will get his money one way or another, but the employee loses his job with no recourse to anyone.

"He'll need to be in London for the trial, though, won't he? He'll be asked to testify."

"Oh yes, yes, of course. I don't think he's left town or anything. I'm sure he's around somewhere."

"Was he the only person to see Mr. Lakefield?" Thaddeus asked. "Wouldn't there have been other workers there that day?"

"No. They were all either watching the parade or marching in it. I hire only good Protestants, you see, and preferably those who belong to the Orange Order, so I give everyone a holiday on the Glorious Twelfth. Storms would have been marching too, except that I needed someone to keep an eye on the place in case of riot." He shook his head. "There are so many Irish Catholics here now. Everyone was expecting trouble."

"So the fire could, in fact, have been set by someone other than Mr. Lakefield?"

"No. According to Storms no one came near the warehouse except for Lakefield. And my daughter, of course, although Storms didn't see her."

"And why, in your opinion, would Lakefield go to your warehouse?"

Warner's scowled. "I think he went there to meet Hazel. I think he was trying to get her to change her story. And when she wouldn't, he killed her to shut her up forever. Then he set the fire to cover his tracks. He'll be hanged for it, and I hope he rots in hell as a consequence."

"I'm sorry, I know this is difficult for you. I think that's all I need to ask at the moment, but if I have any more questions, I'll be in touch."

Thaddeus rose, but just as he reached the door, Warner spoke again. "Do you know how long it will take for the insurance money to come through?"

"I'm sorry," Thaddeus said. "I don't really know."

Martha wasn't at all sure where, exactly, Strong's Hotel might be found, except that it was somewhere on Dundas Street. She could ask the desk clerk at the hotel, but London wasn't all that big. Larger than Cobourg, but not by many orders of magnitude, and she looked forward to exploring it. She would walk along Dundas Street one way, she decided, and if she didn't find Strong's within a couple of blocks, she would turn around and try the other direction. She began walking toward the court house, reasoning that businesses might have grown up around it and the nearby market.

She had just passed Talbot Street when she saw a knot of young men standing on the sidewalk. They noticed her as well. Every head swiveled to look her over. And then one of them cat-called, soon joined by the others.

She stepped out into the road to bypass them, and as she went by, two of them spat in her direction. And then one of them, bolder than the others, took a half-step toward her. "I know what I'd like to do to you," he said.

She walked as fast as he could without seeming to hurry. Her heart was pounding.

"I do too," another said. "I'd like to…" this was followed by a word so vile that she could hardly believe that anyone would utter it in public. She spun to face the offender.

"Does your father know you have a mouth like that?" she asked. "Someone should tell him how you talk when you're out in public."

"I don't have a father, so there," the boy said in an insolent tone.

"That's exactly what I figured," Martha said and turned to walk away again.

Behind her she heard one of them, a little quicker on the uptake than the others, begin to laugh, then two more realized what she had done.

"Hey she just called you a bastard, you know."

"Ha, ha, ha, Bastard Bill."

"Hey, get back here!" Apparently Bastard Bill didn't like getting the short end of the argument.

Martha kept walking.

"Hey, I'm talking to you, you bitch."

The voice was closer, and Martha knew that he was right behind her. She steeled herself for the hand on the shoulder, the sudden push that would send her sprawling.

And then a short man with a neatly-trimmed beard stepped in front of her. "Are you all right miss?"

"I'm fine, thank you. But as this is the place I was looking for, perhaps you could see me in the door?" She had no idea what sort of store she was entering, but at that moment, anywhere that was away from the mob of boys was a haven.

"Of course," the man said. "You boys go on now," he called. "No loitering in front of my place of business."

The group of boys muttered, then slowly moved off.

Martha's rescuer held open the door and she slipped inside.

When she caught her breath and had a chance to take in her surroundings, she wondered if she hadn't somehow jumped into something far worse than a street altercation. The interior of the shop was small and dingy-looking and seemed to be filled with nothing but heads. The shelves and display cases were full of them. Row after row of skulls, each of them with a placard in front of it. The walls were covered with pictures of heads and diagrams of skulls, many of which had been sub-divided into sections and numbered.

"Don't be alarmed," the man said. "These are merely representations of the science of phrenology."

"Phren..phrenology?"

"The discipline of discerning a man's character from the depressions and protrusions of the skull. Could I get you anything? A glass of water perhaps? Or would you like to sit down for a moment? You must be quite shaken. Those boys were very rude."

"I'm quite fine, thank you. Just a little out of breath because I hurried."

"I'm Dr. Richard Scott by the way."

"I'm pleased to meet you. I'm Martha Renwell."

Intrigued in spite of her initial alarm, she took a step toward one of the charts on the wall. Rather than showing just the bald outline of the skull, this diagram included hair, and was patently female.

"The study of phrenology can tell you many things," Scott said. "For example, this woman has a very refined nature, as signified by the way in which her head is positioned relative to the neck."

"Or maybe it's just her hair style," Martha said.

"Oh no, oh no, we're trained to take that into consideration. Although the manner in which a woman dresses her hair is also indicative of her character."

Martha didn't see how, but she refrained from saying so.

"Benevolence would be a cardinal quality in an individual such as this," Scott went on. "Benevolence and adhesiveness."

Martha wasn't sure what he meant by "adhesiveness" except that she was reasonably certain that he wasn't talking about glue. She moved on to the next diagram, which depicted an individual with a very low forehead and almost no chin.

"This is an example of one of the inferior races," Scott said. "Very underdeveloped reflective faculties, yet at the same time secretive and deceitful. Far easier to comprehend, of course, with a real skull, rather than just a two-dimensional drawing. I'll show you what I mean."

She followed Scott over to one of the shelves, where row upon row of heads were displayed, each inked with lines that divided the surface into numbered sections. *Queen Louisa of Prussia*, she read, *Voltaire, Napoleon Bonaparte.* To her eye, the skulls all looked remarkably similar.

"These are all plaster casts," he said, "but their form has been reproduced faithfully. I have representations of many famous and outstanding individuals – the Duke of Wellington for example – but a particular fascination to me are the casts of those at the opposite end of the spectrum, like this one."

He pointed to a skull that had pride of place in the middle of the shelf. *The Head of Cornelius Burley, Murderer* she read.

"Poor thing was hanged twice," Scott said. "Right here in London."

"Really?" Martha said. "How is that possible?"

"The rope broke the first time, so they hauled him back up and did it again. He was apparently unconscious for the second go-round. Mind you, he may not have been able to fully appreciate the experience anyway. He was little more than an animal. You can tell by the narrowness of the cranial ridge."

The deficiencies in Burley's character were clearly marked, from the face and forehead to various lumps and dents that evidently predicted his fate.

"Concentrativeness, philoprogenitiveness." She stumbled over the pronunciation of the terms. "What's amativeness?" she asked.

"The enjoyment of the opposite sex," the man replied. "You can see that the amative portion of the man's head is over-developed. He was a coarse man, obviously, given to inappropriate appetites."

"Like the boys outside."

He laughed. "That is probably correct, although I haven't had a good look at their heads."

At the back of the room was a glass case. "What's in there?" Martha asked, walking toward it.

"As I said, most of what you see here are plaster casts, but the case holds my collection of genuine skulls. There's nothing to be alarmed about. They're very old."

Martha found them no less alarming because of their age, but she stepped closer to look anyway.

"Most of them have been unearthed from ancient battlefields. Thermopylae, Marathon, the Battle of the Teutoburg Forest. You can see just by the general shape of the heads that these must have been great warriors. And, of course, the collection has been augmented by non-human skulls – there's one there of a tiger, as well as a wolf and a bear."

"Fascinating," Martha murmured, although she found the collection macabre.

"Perhaps you would care to have your head analyzed sometime? Even without examining it in detail, I can tell by its shape that you have a very discerning and sensitive nature."

"Thank you, I'll consider it some day when I have more time," she said, a little bemused by the notion, and not a little disturbed by the skulls.

"Don't dally for too long," Scott cautioned. "I'll be here only until the end of the month, then I move on to the next town."

"I'll think about it," she promised, "but now I must be moving on as well. Thank you for intervening on my behalf." She was about to leave when she realized that she still wasn't sure where she was going. She drew Hazel Warner's picture from her purse and turned to Scott. "Would you, perhaps, know where this daguerreotype studio is? I was told that it was at Strong's Hotel on Dundas, but I'm new to London and I don't know my way around yet." She showed it to him.

He seemed quite startled, and stared at it a moment before he spoke. "This is lovely isn't it? You would think that this young woman must have an extraordinary mind. But then superficial appearance can be so deceiving." And then he seemed to remember what she had asked him.

"Oh yes. Strong's Hotel. It's on Dundas, but up the other way.

Not far. A few blocks."

"Thank you." She peeked out the front window. "I hope those boys are gone."

"I'll stand outside and watch you down the street," Scott said. "I would walk you there, but I'm afraid I can't leave the shop at the moment."

"Thank you, but it's really not necessary. I'll be fine." And then she wondered that he could be so busy that he couldn't' leave for a few minutes. How many people could there be in a town the size of London who would pay to have their heads read?

Martha soon found Strong's Hotel, right down the street as Richard Scott had indicated. A front window had a small shelf with a cardboard sign advertising the services of Mr. Charles Pearsall, who offered to provide daguerreotype portraits "at the best possible prices". His art was illustrated by a collection of wooden frames that held pictures of stern-faced gentlemen and finely-dressed women, although Martha had to turn her head in several directions before she could finally see the images clearly. The sign directed her to "inquire within".

She hesitated before entering. Strong's looked a little seedy, not nearly as grand as the Western. She hoped it wasn't one of the places where local men went to drink. Except that they drank at all the hotels. It was just that some of them had a better clientele than others. She stood squinting at the pictures, trying to make up her mind whether or not she should go in. Finally, she pushed open the door.

The interior arrangement of Strong's bore more than a passing resemblance to the Temperance Hotel in Wellington. No large lobby, just a front hall with a desk at one side. There was no one there, but there was a bell on the desk. She rang it.

A moment later, a young man appeared in the doorway. He was rather good-looking, but a little shabby, the cuffs of his jacket frayed, a small stain on his waistcoat.

"May I help you?" he asked. He didn't sound very interested in the prospect.

"I'm looking for the daguerreotypist," she said.

He immediately brightened. “Are you interested in a portrait? I can do a lovely portrait for you.”

“Are you Mr. Pearsall?”

“At your service, miss.” He nodded slightly.

“Actually, I’m not here on my own behalf,” she said. “I acquired a daguerreotype that I believe was done here some time ago, and I was looking for information about the subject. Do you know who this is?”

She held Hazel Warner’s picture out to him. He looked at it, but didn’t take it from her. Then he took a step back.

“That’s the girl who was killed in the fire,” he said. “Where did you get this?”

“A friend gave it to me,” she said.

“Why would someone give you the picture if you don’t even know the girl? And why are you asking me about it?” He began to look angry.

“I’m sorry,” Martha said. “I meant no harm by it. Thank you for your time.” And she beat a hasty retreat.

“Phrenology? Now there’s a pack of nonsense for you,” Thaddeus said when he and Martha met up and she told him where she’d been.

“I can tell from your tone that you don’t approve, but could you tell me why?”

“It’s utter nonsense. It’s looking at what’s on your head and not what’s in your heart. It’s as though everybody is predestined to be what they are with no prospect of being able to change. It’s an attack on the concept of morals, really, and an excuse for criminal behaviour.”

“I suppose it would be, wouldn’t it?”

“In any event,” Thaddeus went on, “there’s no real scientific justification for it – no two phrenologists can agree on which bumps mean what. And it’s been used most unjustly against certain people, claiming that they’re inferior because of the way their skulls are formed.”

“Like who?”

“Indians. Coloureds. Chinese. If you can prove through phrenology that they’re somehow inferior, then that justifies treating them as though they're not human, you see."

Martha did see how the information could be misused, if one was inclined to take it seriously. "It was interesting to look at the murderer's skull, though," she said somewhat doubtfully.

"Was it a real skull or some faked up nonsense?"

"It was just a plaster cast. But there were real ones too. Old ones that somebody dug up."

"Poor souls. They don't deserve to have their heads paraded around for everyone to gawk at."

Having gawked at them quite avidly herself, Martha was suddenly anxious to change the subject.

"I don't know what to make of the daguerreotypist," she said. "I showed him the picture of Hazel Warner. He knew who it was right away, but he seemed quite upset that I was asking about it."

"Really?" Thaddeus said. "I wonder why? We seemed to have stirred a few things up, haven't we? Mr. Warner was in a lather about when he could get his insurance money. Of course he thought I had been sent by his insurer."

"Lots of threads to follow, whether any of them lead anywhere or not."

"Well, that's how it goes with these things. You just keep pulling until something unravels. Now, what are you going to have for dinner?"

"Whatever is next on the menu. I started at the top and I'm working my way down. I hope we're here long enough to get to the bottom."

Martha was glad that Thaddeus hadn't asked her why she'd gone into the phrenologist's studio. He would have been upset to find out that she had been accosted on the street. He was sometimes a little over-protective and too quick to leap into action. She was afraid that he might go storming off to confront the gang of boys, and there were too many of them. Her grandfather might be hurt.

Besides, it hadn't been anything, really. A little more aggressive with a lot rougher language than she was used to, but the boys on London's main street had been no different than the gaggle in Wellington who used to follow her home from school. Or the students in Cobourg, who had sometimes been quite rude to her as she passed.

She'd keep the incident to herself just in case Thaddeus somehow decided that she shouldn't continue making enquiries on her own.

Then she put it all out of her mind in happy anticipation of sampling the duck comfit.

CHAPTER 7

"I think I'll go have a look at the site of the fire," Thaddeus said to Martha the next morning. "It's apt to be nothing but a pile of ashes, but I'd like to see it anyway, even if it's just to get an idea of where it happened."

"You're not going to wear your new clothes, are you?"

It hadn't occurred to Thaddeus that he shouldn't. "Oh. I suppose not. I'll wear the old ones." Other than a change of shirt, he'd never had "good" clothes before. His old black suit had done for everything.

He set off from the hotel toward the part of town where Warner's warehouse had been. He should head along East North Street, he was told at the hotel, until he came to Adelaide. The area wasn't very heavily built-up, so he should be able to see the site from there.

He wasn't sure what he hoped to gain by seeing it for himself, but he was at a bit of a loss as to where to go next in the investigation, and at the very least a visual inspection of the site would make his inquiries more complete.

The hotel clerk's directions were good. Thaddeus located the mess of ash and charred wood easily. It must have been a large building, judging by the hole the destruction had left. Here and there a partially-burned beam protruded from the rubble and ashes, one of them wound round with a length of chain. The iron rim of a wagon wheel lay in a twisted heap at its foot. It appeared that no attempt had been made to clear the site. No doubt Warner was waiting for the insurance money. And until the court determined that the fire was the result of arson by a third party, and not Warner himself, the company was unlikely to pay anything.

Thaddeus didn't envy whoever had found Hazel Warner's body. It would have been a grim task to pull burnt flesh from this mess. He was surprised that there had been enough left of the body to identify it.

He found a piece of wood that was long enough that he could use it to poke through the ash, looking for anything that might tell him what happened. Here and there he uncovered pieces of metal – carriage bolts, a couple of horseshoes, door hinges, more pieces of chain, another rim from a wagon wheel. But most of the building must have been wooden and had gone up quickly, fed by the fuel of grain and hay.

The coroner's report hadn't specified where, exactly, Hazel Warner's remains had been found. It could have been anywhere in the field of ash. He continued poking. A carriage drove by, slowed while its occupants had a good look at Thaddeus, then drove on. A pedestrian stood by the side of the road and watched him for a few minutes, then he, too, continued on his way.

He soon grew filthy from the sooty grit that billowed up around him as he searched through the ruins. He was under no illusion that the local investigation would have been thorough enough to uncover any evidence that might have remained, but it was clear that if anything of value had survived the fire, it had long since been carted away by scavengers, or lay buried under drifts of ash. Short of sifting through the entire field, he was unlikely to find anything. It was a futile exercise.

It was only as he was walking home that a question occurred to him. If there had been enough of Hazel Warner left to identify her, why was there no trace at all of her infant?

Martha wrinkled her nose at him when he returned to the hotel. "You smell like you've been sitting in a firepit."

"I was," Thaddeus replied. "I've spent most of the day sifting through ashes. I'll wash up, but my jacket may take a while to air out."

"I'll sponge it down," she offered, "and your trousers and waistcoat as well. Your shirt can go to the hotel laundry, but why don't you use the bath? That would help. The baths here are really easy to use – I washed my hair this morning while you were out. The attendant will show you how to use the heater."

He was a little dubious at Martha's characterization of "really easy". In his experience the luxury of a bath had always entailed boiling and lugging huge amounts of water to pour into a tub that was nevertheless so small that only a portion of the body could be washed at any one time. However, the bath attendant obligingly showed him how to fill the copper tub with an adequate amount of water, and fiddled with a gas heater contraption by its side. Then he diplomatically departed with instructions to "call if there are difficulties".

When Thaddeus lowered his body into the tub, he found that the sensation of stretching out and soaking was most pleasant. The tensions of the day seemed to seep away into the warm water. He could get used to easy living, if it meant Windsor soap, hot water on demand and soft towels that had been hung over the heating pipes to warm. He allowed himself to revel in it for a few minutes, then he brought himself up sharply, and began to scrub away the smell of ash and charred, wet wood. By the time he dried off and changed into his good clothes he felt spruce and clean and energized.

"Did you find anything today?" Martha asked as they went in to supper.

"Not a thing. And that in itself is a little puzzling. Everyone assumes that the infant was consumed by the fire, but I can't help but think that there should have been something left of it. A human body isn't that easy to get rid of, even when it's small. A few bones, maybe. A bit of clothing. Something."

"I wonder how they came to the conclusion that it was burned up?" Martha said.

"I wonder that too. There's only one place where I might find out. I think I'll visit the coroner tomorrow. And after that, the newspaper office. I have only the clipping that Ashby sent me. I'd like to see what was reported about the parade that day. I hope it wasn't eclipsed by news of the fire."

"I was looking at our notes again while I was waiting for my hair to dry. I don't know if it means anything, but I found something a little odd. It says in the clipping that the foreman, Jeb Storms, saw 'an unidentified man' leaving the building just before the fire started, but he didn't say anything about it until the firemen found the body. Up until then, everyone assumed it was either the marchers or an Irish gang. But by the time the police got involved, the foreman seemed to be sure that it was Lakefield."

"That is odd, isn't it?" Thaddeus considered this for a moment. "It might just be the way the fire was reported. The clipping is a second-hand version of events, after all. But it might be worth talking to Storms just to clarify when, exactly, he realized it was Nelson Lakefield."

"What would you like me to do while you're seeing the coroner?"

"Why don't you wander around the market and through a few of the stores? Strike up a few conversations and see what local people think about the case. I'll be surprised if you don't hear at least four or five different opinions about what happened. If we're lucky one of them might point us in the right direction."

"Yes, boss."

The coroner, Dr. John Bratton, lived on Picadilly Street, near the corner of Dundas and Wellington Streets. A little bemused by the earnest, almost strained extent to which the town was determined to ape the English London in the choice of its municipal names, Thaddeus set off the next morning to find the doctor's house. It proved to be a pleasant-looking clapboard house with a wide verandah that wrapped around one side of the building. A card tucked into a corner of the front door glazing asked patients to attend at the side door.

Thaddeus walked around the house to the appropriate entrance and knocked.

And waited. After a time, when there was no answer, he wondered if he should knock again, but then he reasoned that there was no point if no one was home, and little point if someone was. They wouldn't be apt to drop what they were doing and hurry to the door any faster, just because they heard a second knock.

Finally, the door was opened by a man with grizzled hair and a heavily-lined face. His jacket was off, he wore a pair of slippers, and he held a pipe in his hand.

"Dr. Bratton?" Thaddeus asked.

"Guilty."

"I hope I'm not disturbing you," Thaddeus said.

"Every time there's a knock at the door, it's a disturbance. That's what happens when you're a doctor. Hardly anyone comes to my door with anything but a problem. I'd even welcome a peddler, if it meant I didn't have to deal with a complaint."

Thaddeus smiled and wondered what it was about doctors that made them so crusty.

"My name is Thaddeus Lewis. I'm investigating the Warner death on behalf of the barrister who is representing Nelson Lakefield." There was no point in pretending to be anything else. The coroner would be impartial in the case, and if he was inclined to vouchsafe any information, he would confide it to either side. "I have a few questions about the death that weren't clear from the documentation I was given."

"Of course, of course, come in."

Thaddeus was ushered into a small book-lined room that obviously served as the doctor's study.

Dr. Bratton settled himself into an easy chair, motioned for Thaddeus to sit in the chair opposite him, banged his pipe a couple of times on the tin pail at his feet and said, "Now, how can I help you?"

"First of all, I guess, I'm wondering if you were able to tell whether Miss Warner died in the fire, or if she was already dead when the fire was set?"

Bratton had been busy filling his pipe, but now he stopped and frowned at Thaddeus.

"No, I wasn't able to tell. The body had been too badly damaged."

"According to your report she was identified by some articles of clothing that managed to survive the fire?"

"Yes, that's right, but there wasn't much. There were a few shreds from the back of her dress, and most of one shoe, if I remember correctly, but the really positive identification came from the earrings she had been wearing. Metal, of course, so they survived. Her father had given them to her for Christmas. The doctor tamped more tobacco into his pipe, then looked up at Thaddeus. "Have you ever seen a body that's been burned, Mr. Lewis?"

"Yes, I have," he replied. He could see that his answer surprised the doctor.

"Well then you must know what it was like. The building was wooden, and full of grain and hay, which is highly combustible at the best of times. It would have ignited in a moment, and then, of course, there was plenty of fuel to feed it."

"But the fire wasn't hot enough to burn the entire body?"

"Oh, no. It takes a lot more than a warehouse fire to completely incinerate the human body. Although the fire may be intense enough to kill a person, usually it sort of sweeps over them. Doesn't burn in one spot long enough, you see."

"But, in your estimation, it was hot enough to destroy all traces of the infant?"

"Well now, that's a good question. All I can say with certainty is that we didn't find any traces of the child. Either it burned in the fire, which I suppose is possible as it was so small, or something else happened to it. It hasn't turned up anywhere else. To be frank, I don't know why anyone else would want it."

"Why not?"

Bratton leaned forward and poked a piece of rolled newspaper into the small parlour stove beside him, and when it ignited, used it to light his pipe. He puffed thoughtfully for a few moments before he replied.

"The child was quite disfigured by a large birthmark – a port wine stain, or firemark, as it's sometimes known. Covered half of its face. Normally, these present no problems in terms of general health, but this one seemed to affect the vision in one eye. There was a suggestion of possible water on the brain as well – a peculiar bulge in its head, although the finding wasn't definitive. No way really, of telling what the ultimate outcome of it might be but in any event, the mark itself was unfortunate enough – not as much of a problem if it had been a boy, of course, but appearance is everything with a girl."

"Would the mark not have gone away over time?" Two of Thaddeus's children had been born with little red marks that looked like strawberries, but these had disappeared within a few months.

"No. Firemarks get darker and more pronounced with time, and this one was quite grotesque to begin with. I'm afraid the child wouldn't have had a very happy life, even if it turned out to be normal otherwise. Other children can be quite cruel, and then, of course, it was probably looking forward to a lifetime spent within the confines of the mother's home. And since the mother wasn't married to begin with, the child would have been quite a burden. In any event, the fate of the infant has no bearing on the trial, really. Lakefield is already on the hook for Miss Warner's death."

"Do you think he did it?"

Bratton shook his head. "Not for me to say. I report what I find. It's up to the law what happens from there."

Poor Hazel Warner.

Thaddeus walked back toward the hotel feeling a profound sense of pity for the girl. Her world had fallen apart in such a hurry. An unwanted pregnancy by a lover who refused her. A child who was disadvantaged from birth. It was no wonder the Lakefields had backed out of the arrangement. They would find it repugnant enough to welcome a bastard child, but one that was disfigured and likely to require a lifetime of support would be an unwelcome prospect indeed. Poor Hazel. Was the lawsuit a desperate attempt to salvage whatever she could from the situation, or was Nelson Lakefield really the father, and in an attempt to extricate himself had sent her to a fiery death? If juries were inclined to award large settlements to pretty women, what would they do for a pretty woman with a blemished baby in tow?

Whatever the answer, Thaddeus was suddenly struck by a second wave of pity for the baby. Marked by fire - first at birth and then by an arson's hand. What a short, sad life.

That afternoon, just as Thaddeus and Martha were finishing their dinners, the waiter came scurrying to their table with the message that someone was looking for them.

"Who is it?" Thaddeus asked.

"I don't know her name," the waiter replied. "But she especially asked for you."

Curious, he walked into the lobby to discover a mountain of luggage, a pale young man and Clementine Elliott. He should have realized that any mention of money would bring her running from wherever she had bolted to.

"Mr. Lewis!" she called as soon as she saw him. "I would have known you anywhere." She hurried over to him while the young man stood glowering by the baggage.

"And I, you," he said. "You look well." Thaddeus was one of the few men in Wellington who had not found Clementine Elliott attractive. Her heart-shaped face had reminded him of a cat, and her subsequent actions had justified his instinctive dislike. But now, as she stood in the lobby in a hat that even he recognized would ignite flames of envy amongst the women of London, he found it difficult to remember what he had found so odious about her. With the onset of what must surely be middle age by now, she had gained weight, but the extra pounds served only to flesh out her thin face and emphasize her pleasing proportions. She no longer resembled a feral cat; she looked more like a pampered tabby who had just lapped up a bowl of cream.

Martha had followed him into the lobby and now she approached the young man. "Horatio?" she asked.

"Actually, it's just Joe."

"Of course. I'm sorry. I forgot. Hello."

Thaddeus remembered Horatio Joe Elliott as a small, pale and somewhat sullen boy. He was still pale, and whether or not he was sullen remained to be seen, but he was no longer small. He was easily a head taller than Martha, with broad shoulders and a solid build.

After the first greeting, Joe and Martha seemed unable to think of anything more to say to each other, and simply stood there while two porters began grappling with trunks and cases. It finally dawned on Thaddeus that the Elliotts were checking in.

"Joe, darling, could you go up to our rooms and deposit the luggage?" Clementine said. "I'm dying for a cup of coffee. I hope the dining room is still open. Would you join me Mr. Lewis?"

And she sailed off leaving Thaddeus and Martha with nothing to do but follow in her wake. She seated herself in the very centre of the room, seemingly oblivious to the heads that turned in her direction. Thaddeus was very aware of the stares he drew when he and Martha joined her.

She scanned the menu, then asked for coffee and a piece of mince pie, handed the menu back to the waiter, and beamed at Thaddeus.

"It really is lovely to see you again," she said. "Martha's letter arrived at a most opportune time for us. Joe and I were in a traveling mood."

"I don't have your money, you know," Thaddeus said. "There are legalities to clear up before you get it. You'll have to talk to the barrister."

His abrupt manner didn't appear to bother her at all. "That's fine. As I said, we're on a bit of a holiday anyway, so there's no harm done if there's a delay."

So she's not desperate for funds, apparently. And then Thaddeus amended the thought – *she might well be, but she's far too cunning to show it.*

"So, what, actually, is your name now, by the way?" he asked.

"Oh, I think you should just go on calling me Clementine, don't you? It will be ever so much easier for you to remember."

"Clementine what?"

"Clementine Elliott will do as well as anything. But I think Joe would prefer to be called just plain Joe. He was never too happy about the Horatio name, were you dear?" She smiled up at her son as he joined them.

"And where have you been all this time?" Thaddeus asked. He was morbidly curious about where she had ended up after she fled from Wellington.

Clementine waved a hand. "Oh, a number of different places. Wherever a poor widow woman could make a living,"

"You never married again?"

She smiled, and once more her face looked distinctly feline. "I didn't say that. I have recently, however, reverted to my previous widowed status."

He hadn't expected that answer. "I'm sorry," he said, falling back on standard niceties.

"Please don't be," she said. "I'm not."

So much for niceties.

"And what about you? What have you been up to? I expected you to still be at the hotel."

"I was never cut out for innkeeping," Thaddeus said. "After my wife died I went back to preaching, but it appears that I'm no longer cut out for that either."

"Really?" Clementine's face showed her puzzlement. And then it softened. "Joe told me that your wife had died. I'm so sorry."

"Thank you," Thaddeus said. But he said it tersely, hoping it was enough to close that particular conversational thread.

But Clementine went on anyway. "She was such a lovely-looking woman."

"Yes."

"I wonder that you haven't married again. But then you never had eyes for anyone but her, did you?"

Martha saved him from answering. "You left Wellington in such a hurry that I never got to say goodbye." Then she blushed. "I mean, I know there were reasons for that, but ..."

Clementine took no offence. "Yes, it was rather a hurried departure, wasn't it? After that, everything we did was a rush. We went here and there, didn't we Joe? First here, then there. Then we landed on our feet. So what is there to do in London, Canada West?" She was obviously as eager as Thaddeus to change the subject. "Are there balls? Concerts? Theatre?"

"There's rather a lot, I believe," Thaddeus replied. "Up until this year there was a large garrison of British soldiers here, and they have established a taste for entertainment in the town."

"Why up until this year? Where have they gone?" To Thaddeus's surprise, it was Joe who asked.

"They've been pulled out to fight in the Crimean War."

Joe frowned. "We haven't heard much about that."

They wouldn't have, Thaddeus realized. It was a British war, and anything concerning the British ultimately had an effect on Canada, but it could easily pass unnoticed by the Americans, who had their own mounting troubles with anti-immigration riots and the slavery question.

"Canada isn't involved really, except for the fact that the soldiers are gone and it's good for business. Wheat is getting top dollar."

"Enough about business and war and all those things men do," Clementine said. "Tell me more about the local entertainment." She looked at Thaddeus and smiled. "Perhaps you could take me dancing."

"No, I couldn't. I may not be a preacher anymore, but I still hold to Methodist principles." At least he was trying to. "Methodists don't dance."

"Ah yes, once a preacher always a preacher. Never mind," she said with a wave of her hand. "I'm sure we can find other things to do."

"I'm not sure that we can. I'm here because I have work to do."

"But you can't work all the time, can you?" she said.

Thaddeus made no answer, but he was quite determined that whatever he did with his free time, he wasn't going to be spending it with Clementine Elliott.

At the other end of the table, Joe and Martha had finally started a conversation.

"I always thought of you in Wellington," Joe said. "It's funny how you freeze someone in time, isn't it?"

"That's exactly what I was thinking," Martha said. "I didn't know what to say when I saw you in the lobby and you weren't Horatio any more."

He made a face. "Honestly. What a fanciful name. I had terrible time trying to remember that I was supposed to be Horatio and not Joe. When did you go to…wherever it was that you ended up? I'm sorry, I can't remember what you said."

"Cobourg. Last year. I went off to keep house for my grandfather." She looked at Thaddeus and smiled. "We decided that we get along, so for the time being I'm his assistant, sort of."

"Assistant at what?" Clementine wanted to know.

"At some business I need to attend to here in London," Thaddeus said. "But you've already informed me that business is a forbidden topic, so I'm afraid I can tell you no more."

"Oh that's right, I did say that, didn't I? Never mind, I'll find out anyway."

"Do you want to go for a walk?" Joe suddenly said to Martha. "I've been sitting for hours on the train. I need to stretch my legs."

"I'd love to," she said.

Now that they had finally started talking, Thaddeus supposed that Joe and Martha had a lot to catch up on, but he hoped he wouldn't be saddled with Clementine while they did it. He couldn't, however, think of any reason to object to Joe's proposal.

"A walk sounds like a wonderful idea," Clementine said as the waiter delivered her coffee and pie. "I'm tired out from sitting too. If you'll wait until I've eaten my dessert, I'll go with you."

Martha's face fell, and Thaddeus realized that she had been hoping to get Joe to herself. He couldn't blame her. So far Clementine had dominated the conversation. Thaddeus hesitated. He had things to do. He wanted to go to the newspaper office that afternoon. But he supposed he could be obliging for once and help Martha out.

"I could use a stroll myself," he said, finally, "but I can't hope to keep up with the young folks." He turned to Clementine. "Perhaps you would accompany me? If you don't mind a slower pace, that is."

Martha beamed at him. He gave her a look that let her know that he was mildly annoyed, and that she now owed him a favour.

She and Joe set off while Clementine dug into her pie. Thaddeus waited in silence while she sipped her coffee, inwardly fuming over the prospect of wasting an afternoon. Eventually she announced herself ready to go and they rose from the table. Thaddeus was aware that a number of heads swiveled to watch them leave the dining room, and several people stared at them as they walked down Richmond Street toward Dundas.

"So tell me about this money," Clementine said before they had gone very far.

"I'm not at liberty to tell you anything. You'll have to wait until Mr. Ashby sends you the proper papers."

"At least tell me how much it is. You didn't say in your note."

Thaddeus should never have written anything at the bottom of Martha's letter. He should have left it all to Ashby to take care of.

"I'm not sure it's for me to say. Wait for Ashby and he can give you all the details.

"Really, Mr. Lewis, I've gone to considerable pains to come here. You can at least tell me whether or not it was a fool's errand."

Reluctantly, he realized that she was probably right. She had travel expenses, and the cost of hotel rooms to cover, and she would find out sooner or later anyway.

"It's two hundred pounds, I believe."

Her eyes widened as she did the calculation. "Eight hundred dollars or so? Is that right?"

"Minus whatever Ashby charges to handle the transaction."

"Well bless Nathan Elliott. He turned out to be not such a bad husband after all, didn't he? Even though I never met him."

"Much nicer than his brother by all accounts."

"That wouldn't be hard. So who is this Mr. Ashby?"

"He's a barrister," Thaddeus said. "I asked him about the legalities of turning over the money. He offered to prepare the necessary documents."

"In other words, you were looking for a way not to give it to me."

"Yes. You can't blame me under the circumstances. As far as I'm concerned the money is there as the result of your scheme to defraud the Elliotts. It goes against my grain that you'll end up with it."

"Well thank you very much Mr. Lewis!" Her raised voice attracted the attention of several people who were walking by. "I worked hard for that money!"

"You worked hard at duping old Mr. Elliott. Don't expect me to feel sorry for you."

They walked along in silence for half a block. Then, unexpectedly, she said, "I missed you after I left Wellington."

"Why? All I did was make your life difficult."

She laughed. "Yes, you did, didn't you? You were the only one who figured me out. I've always wondered, though, why you didn't turn me in as soon as you proved I was a fraud."

"I was more interested in finding out what you were up to than what you had done."

"Still... thank you. I suppose."

"It was nothing to do with you. I wanted to find the truth of the matter. And that's something I wouldn't mind knowing now, as well."

"What do you mean?"

Thaddeus knew his question was on target. Clementine's tone was far too demure.

He stopped walking. She was several steps down the sidewalk before she realized he was no longer beside her and turned to face him.

"You had no idea how much money Elliott left you," Thaddeus said. "It could just as easily have been five pounds. And you're looking singularly prosperous. I don't think it was the money that brought you running as fast as you did."

"You're far too clever Mr. Lewis. Let's just say that it was... an expedient development."

"What are you up to?" A shopkeeper who was sweeping the plank sidewalk in front of his store stopped what he was doing in order to listen to their argument.

"Not to worry," Clementine said. "It's nothing you need be concerned about. Let's just say that it's extremely convenient to have some place to be just now." She started walking again.

In spite of the eavesdropping shopkeeper he called after her. "Are there any detectives following you this time?"

"Of course not," she called over shoulder. "Or at least none that I know of."

Thaddeus hurried to catch up with her, but he was torn between wanting to walk away and not being willing to take his eyes off her for a second.

Joe and Martha walked along in silence for the first few minutes. Martha kept sneaking sideways glances at the young man beside her. She could tell that it was Joe. He had the same fair hair and pale complexion. But he was so grown up and different looking that she felt quite shy with him. Martha had still been a child when the Elliotts had decamped in the middle of the night. She had never been filled in on all the details, but she would have had to be deaf not to catch the general drift of what happened. Clementine had been a trickster, not really Clementine Elliott at all, and had been involved in a scheme to extract money from the Elliott family, although Martha had never been sure just how this was supposed to be accomplished. Joe could in no way have been responsible for any of it – he had been a child like her. But he had been dragged along - first in his mother's schemes, and then quite literally dragged away from Wellington. She wasn't sure what she should say to him.

It was Joe who first spoke.

"Thank you for writing back."

"I was happy to hear from you. I didn't expect you to turn up quite as fast as you did, but I'm glad you're here. Where did you go when you left?"

"My mother wasn't joking. Here and there. Everywhere, while she was trying to find her feet. A hundred different cities, a hundred different plans to make a fortune. We seemed to move every few weeks. And then she married again, and I thought we'd finally be able to settle down."

"What happened?"

"It was just another swindle, really. An old geezer with a lot of money. Then he died, and things got a little strange. That's when I wrote you that letter."

Martha wasn't sure she was following his story, but before she could ask any questions, he went on.

"I was so low when I wrote. I wasn't sure you would even remember me, but I hoped you would." He gave her a shy smile. "Wellington was a happy time for me, in spite of the way things turned out."

"We had fun, didn't we?" But she still wasn't sure she understood.

"It was the best time of my life. We'd been on the run for a long time and everyone in Wellington was so nice. And then there was sledding and snowball fights and messing around at the lake. It was terrific. I was really angry when we left."

"At your mother?"

"Yes. When we found out that my father was dead, I thought maybe we could stay in Wellington. I was even willing to be called Horatio for the rest of my life, if it meant we could stay."

Martha laughed. "It really is a horrible name, isn't it?"

"The absolute worst. I don't know what she was thinking."

"And then I got the wrong end of the stick and thought your name was Horatio Joe. That's how I still think of you, you know."

"That's okay. I don't mind it from you. At least you added Joe to the end of it. For the last little while, I've been Chauncey. Chauncey Hargrave. Now that's a mouthful, isn't it?" He sounded rueful.

"If you keep taking different names, how do you remember who you're supposed to be?"

"Half the time I don't. I got into the habit of not ever saying much at all. That way I wouldn't slip up. Anyway, I didn't really understand what was going on back in Wellington, and I didn't take it well when she said we had to go. I didn't even get to say goodbye."

"I know, that bothered me too. But you're here now, so instead of goodbye, it's hello."

He smiled. "It is, isn't it? How long are you going to be in London? I take it your grandfather has some sort of business here?"

"Yes." Martha didn't elaborate. They were investigating a crime, after all, and she knew better than to be too free with details.

"What happens when the business is finished? Do you go back to Wellington?"

"I'm not sure. My grandfather is having a difficult time at the moment, and I don't think even he knows what his plans are. But for the time being anyway, I go where he goes. I want to see a little of the world while I still can. He's promised me I can tag along with him."

"The world isn't such a great place, you know."

"People keep telling me that. But it's something I need to find out for myself."

"Trust me. I've seen far too much of it. I would like to leave my mother. Go off on my own. But I'm finding it difficult."

"What is it you want to do?"

"I don't know. I'm just tired of the way we live. Maybe I could be a farmer. Stay in one place and stare at the same acre of ground for the rest of my life. Do you think I'd make a good farmer?"

"No."

He laughed. "You're probably right. And I don't suppose Wellington is the same as it was either, is it?"

"Wellington is always the same. Nothing ever changes." It was ironic, she thought, that Joe longed to be in the one place that she herself didn't want to be. "I don't know what the answer is, Horatio Joe, but I'm glad you wrote. And I'm very glad to see you again. Why don't we enjoy the visit and worry about what happens afterwards when it actually happens?"

"Good plan. So what do you think we should do this afternoon?"

CHAPTER 8

Thaddeus was relieved when there was no sign of Clementine at breakfast the next morning, and said as much to Martha.

"Why are you being so rude to her?"

"I'm not rude. Just on my guard. Did you and Joe have a nice walk?"

Martha was thoughtful. "It was kind of odd at first. I didn't expect him to be so grown up. He wants to go off on his own, you know. He says he's tired of following his mother around."

"I can certainly understand that," Thaddeus said. "Did he say anything about how long they intend to stay?"

"No. And I can't just say 'Nice to see you, when are leaving?' Besides it doesn't make any sense for them to leave until Ashby arrives. He has to sort things out so Mrs. Elliott can collect the money."

"That's true enough, but I don't relish the thought of sharing all our meals with them while we're trying to investigate. We may have to rethink our plan to eat only in the hotel dining room."

"Why? What difference does it make? They don't have anything to do with the case." Martha frowned at him. "You just don't like her, do you?"

"It's not that I don't like her," Thaddeus replied. "It's just that I don't trust her."

"I don't see what she could possibly do to harm anything. Ashby will be here in a few days and then she'll probably be on her way. In the meantime, you don't have to wear such a sour face."

"I won't be sour as long as she doesn't interfere. I'm off to the local newspaper office this morning, by the way. Editors and reporters usually have a pretty good handle on who's who and what their business is, and I'd like to find out if they have copies of articles other than the one Ashby sent. I'd also like to see what they wrote about the Orange Parade that day. There may be something there that everyone else has overlooked."

"Do you think they might have any theories as to who set the fire?" Martha asked.

"Maybe. If they're willing to share them. In the meantime, can you continue nosing around town? I'm sure everybody has an opinion about what happened. It would be interesting to hear what they're saying.

"Opinions about what?"

Joe had surfaced in the dining room. He pulled out a chair and sat down beside Martha.

"Um… it's a case my grandfather is working on," she said.

"You should ask my mother. She has an opinion about everything." He sounded grumpy, and Martha wondered if the two had had an argument. "What case? What are you looking for?"

"It's a legal case that I'm looking for information on," Thaddeus said. "I've asked Martha to wander around the stores and the market and see if she can pick up any rumours."

"Now that's definitely something you should ask my mother about. She's an expert at it."

Thaddeus made a face, but Martha was intrigued. "Really?"

"That's how she works the séances," Joe said. "She wanders through a town and picks up information about people, then turns around and feeds it back to them like it's coming from beyond."

"Was that why all those people used to traipse up to your rooms at the hotel?" Martha said. "Oh – that's why you were never around to play with in the afternoons."

"I'm not sure this is something I want to let Mrs. Elliott loose on," Thaddeus said.

"Maybe just once," Martha said. "I'm not getting very far on my own. She could show me how it's done."

"I don't think it's wise to disclose the details of the case," Thaddeus objected.

"It's not like it's a secret. Everybody knows about the fire and what happened. They even know about the lawsuit. They just don't know for sure who's responsible. For either of them."

"I suppose..."

"Whatever you decide, if you want my mother to help, you'll have to wait until she gets out of bed."

"Maybe Joe can go with me this morning," Martha said. "Then if we don't get anywhere we can come back and ask Mrs. Elliott to come along."

Thaddeus shoved his plate away and rose from the table. "Suit yourself," he said shortly. "I'm on my way. I'll meet you back here later."

"Yes, boss." But Thaddeus could tell that she was puzzled by his attitude.

Clementine thought she might get up sometime soon, but just at the moment she was far too comfortable to stir out of bed. The long journey from Philadelphia to London had rattled her bones and frayed her nerves, and there were times when she had wondered if they really needed to go quite so far. But the fact that Joe had been cheerful for once had made the traveling easier, and now that they were here, he had lost the sulkiness that made him so difficult to deal with most of the time.

It was the girl, she guessed. Or maybe not the girl herself, but what she represented. Joe had been happy in Wellington and furious with her when they left. Clementine remembered Martha as a sweet-faced little thing who had been lovely to Joe, including him in her games whenever he wasn't needed at the séances. Now she was all grown up and very pretty. She knew that Joe had been surprised by her appearance, although Clementine suspected that it wouldn't have mattered a bit what she looked like now. It was old times he was after.

And the preacher turned out to be every bit as much fun as Clementine remembered – quick-witted, clever and suspicious. It had been a long time since she had encountered anyone who was such a pleasure to match wits with. She was a little out of practice – she would have to stay alert to keep ahead of him, although this time it would be more for her own amusement than because the stakes were high.

He was also more attractive than she remembered. He had been handsome enough ten years ago, even with the rather harsh lines that carved along the sides of his mouth, a reflection, she supposed, of the black and white certainty of his calling. Now his dark hair was shot through with streaks of grey and the lines had deepened, but that served only to make him look distinguished, and his spare frame had made little concession to the passing of time.

There was something about him, though, that had changed profoundly over the intervening years, and she couldn't quite decide what it was. The old fire was there when he challenged her, but otherwise he seemed to wear an air of melancholy. Sorrow at the loss of his wife, she supposed, but she wondered if there was something deeper as well. She would have to poke at it until she uncovered what it was. And once uncovered, she would decide what she would do with it.

In the meantime she could sharpen her wits on him. Get back on her game. And then, when Nathan Elliott's money came through, she would be ready for her next adventure.

As Thaddeus walked out of the hotel, he began to wonder if he had been hasty in rejecting the notion of enlisting Clementine's help. Joe was right – she had an uncanny ability to worm secrets out of people. She had floated around Wellington gathering tidbits of information from whoever would talk to her. And then a ghostly figure in the séance room would regurgitate it all and convince everyone at the table that they were communicating with dead relatives. Martha was right, too – the details of Hazel Warner's death were common currency. As long as Clementine was apprised of only the general outline of the case, it was perhaps not such a bad idea. He decided he'd say as much when he met Martha later.

He soon reached the corner of Richmond and Carling Streets, where the offices of the *Canadian Free Press* were located. He could tell as soon as he walked into the building that the press was running. Not only was the noise from it audible, but the vibration rattled the windows and shook the floor. He wondered if he should come back at some other time when printing wasn't actually in progress, but before he could reach the door he was hailed by a brown-aproned man with rolled-up sleeves and inkstains on his fingers.

"If you're looking for an advertisement, you've missed the deadline for this week," the man said gruffly.

"No, I don't need an advertisement. Just some information."

"Well if it's information you want, you'll have to wait until the paper comes out. It's got all the information that anybody could want." And then the man cackled at his own joke.

"I was looking for something beyond who was married and who was buried this week," Thaddeus returned, which resulted in renewed laughter. "I'm Thaddeus Lewis." He held out his hand.

"I already know who you are," the man said. "And you don't want to shake my hand – inky fingers." He waggled them to prove his point. "The whole town's been buzzing, trying to figure out what you're doing here."

"And what was the conclusion?"

"Oh now, let me see. Best guess is that you're the fancy lawyer that Lakefield has hired to get his son out of trouble – a sensible move if you know anything at all about Earl Jenkins. I've also heard that you're an investigator for the insurance company here to snoop around as to the cause of the fire; that you're the hangman come to measure young Lakefield for his noose; and that you're a disgraced clergyman who was chased out of his last parish."

Thaddeus found this last pronouncement startling. It was a little too close to the truth.

"I think that's all I've heard about you," the man went on, "but there's also been some wild conjecture about the rather lovely young lady you're traveling with. Of course, that's being rapidly revised now that your wife has turned up for you to argue with."

"She's not my…" and then he stopped. There was no way to explain Clementine's presence without getting into a long, involved story.

"I'm Josiah Blackburn by the way, owner, editor and dogsbody of *The Canadian Free Press.*"

"Pleased to meet you Mr. Blackburn. The grapevine has it partially correct. I'm here to investigate. And the lovely young lady you referred to is my granddaughter."

"Now that's disappointing," Blackburn said. "I was hoping for something a little more salacious. Come in to my so-called office, and tell me who or what you're looking for."

Thaddeus followed him into a tiny closet of a room. Blackburn shoved a stack of newspapers off the only chair and bade him sit.

"Now what is it you're after?"

"I assume you've been covering the Warner case?"

"Oh yes," Blackburn confirmed. "We've reported every last nasty detail."

"And what do you make of it?"

Blackburn had obviously been giving it some thought. "Well, I don't know why Warner brought suit against young Lakefield in the first place. That's one of the things I haven't been able to figure out."

"Just one?"

Blackburn shrugged. "The tantalizing question is who the father is. The big question is who set the fire."

"Any theories?"

"As someone who is well-acquainted with the laws of libel and slander, none that I care to share. But I will tell you one thing - as long as you don't ever claim you heard it from me - if you want to know what's really going on, follow the money. That piece of advice will never take you far wrong. Sometimes sex can gum up the picture, but most of the time money is at the root of everything."

It was good advice. Thaddeus just wasn't sure how it applied in this case. "The Lakefields and the Warners are well-to-do though, aren't they?"

"The Lakefields and the Warners *appear* to be well-to-do. It's often the case, I've found, that people need more money than they have in order to keep up the impression they're anxious to make. I'm not saying for certain that it applies in this case, but it is something to bear in mind. There are a couple of prosperous people I know who are pretty over-extended at the moment."

"Why?"

"The railroad. There was a frenzy over land adjacent to the Great Western route and a lot of people bought. Now, any piece of property that's in the way of the new line to Port Huron is being snapped up. And of course there are all the feeder lines that may or may not ever actually be built, but everyone is hopeful about. They're all jumping in."

"I just came from Cobourg," Thaddeus said. "It was the same there. And some of it was none too ethical."

"Doesn't surprise me in the least. It may not have anything to do with anything, but it seems to me it would be a good place to start looking."

"In the meantime, do you keep back copies of your paper? I'd like to see what you reported about the Orange Parade back in July."

"Of course I do. That's what I just threw on the floor." He pointed to the mess of newsprint at Thaddeus's feet. "Those are from the last six months. We're only a weekly, so it shouldn't take you long to find July. There's a price for looking at them though." He fixed Thaddeus with a glare. "You can tell me what you're really doing here."

"As long as you don't ever claim you heard it from me – I'm working for Lakefield's barrister."

Blackburn nodded. "Fair enough. I figured that might be the case. But it puzzles me that you brought your whole family along to help investigate."

Thaddeus could think of no explanation that would satisfy the newspaperman's curiosity that didn't entail his entire life history. "I don't seem able to leave them behind," he finally said, a little lamely.

"Ah well, family, eh?" Blackburn said. "Sometimes they can be a nuisance, can't they? And now I'll leave you alone to look through the pile. I can't leave the typesetters for more than five minutes before they start mixing up their "p's" and "q's". Eight dollars a week and they still can't spell. I've a mind to replace them all with women. I wouldn't have to pay them as much and they'd do a better job."

"Could I ask just one more question?" Thaddeus said. "I don't mean to offend, but there's a discrepancy between your coverage and the witness statements. Your article says the foreman saw an "unidentified man" leaving the warehouse. But when the foreman talked to the coroner he stated that he saw Nelson Lakefield. How accurate is your report?"

"That was young Burns. Can't string a sentence together properly, but he seldom makes a mistake when it comes to the facts. If he reported "unidentified man", then that's what it was. Now I'll leave you to it. Give me a shout when you're done."

And Blackburn disappeared into the printshop.

Thaddeus spread the papers out over the cluttered desk. It didn't take him long to find the issue he was interested in. As Blackburn had pointed out, *The Free Press* published weekly, so there were not many back copies to go through.

The issue immediately following July twelfth was full of description of the Orange Parade itself, the warehouse fire and the grisly discovery of Hazel Warner's remains. The next issue detailed Nelson Lakefield's arrest and committal to trial. It was the same clipping Ashby had sent him.

He went back to the story about the parade. There had been three other fires that day, all of them small and easily extinguished, set by exuberant, or more likely, drunken marchers. There had also been eight altercations between Orangemen and Irish Catholics, a not uncommon occurrence, and mostly dismissed. No one had been severely injured and there was no property damage, although Blackburn's editorial called for better policing of the parades. It was an almost automatic response, as there was so often trouble at these things.

Albert Warner's claim that he had left Jeb Storms at the warehouse in case of trouble seemed perfectly warranted, even though the parade route had taken the marchers nowhere near that end of town. There were really no questions about why Storms was there; the question was why he had changed his story.

Thaddeus could see nothing else in the coverage that seemed to lead in any particular direction, so he stacked the newspapers neatly and laid them on the chair. Then he peered through the door that led to the printshop and waved at Blackburn to let him know he was finished. Blackburn waved back and then returned to berating a hapless typesetter.

As he left the newspaper office, Thaddeus met Joe and Martha coming along the street.

"Any luck?" Martha asked.

"That remains to be seen. You don't happen to remember if there was an address for the warehouse foreman on those statements we got from Earl Jenkins? I could go back to the hotel and look, but it would save me some time if you can recall what it was."

Martha pursed her lips as she thought. "The foreman's name was Storms," she ventured, then after a moment, "William Street, I think."

"That would make sense," Thaddeus said. "Near the Warner warehouse. How did you make out this morning?"

"People are willing enough to talk about the case, but none of them seem to know anything more than we do. We need a better strategy."

"Why don't you go back to the hotel? It's nearly dinnertime anyway. And I've decided that Joe's suggestion is a good one, if his mother is willing to do a little snooping."

"I'm sure she will," Joe said. "She's probably bored already."

"I'm off to find the foreman. I should be back in a couple of hours. Why don't we meet in the sitting room around four and I'll talk to her then? Bring the clipping and newspaper article Ashby sent me. It's the fastest way to fill her in."

They parted and Thaddeus set off toward the eastern end of town. William Street turned out to be longer than he realized. He finally located the address he was looking for by asking a woman who was throwing a bucket of dirty water over a straggly rose bush in her front yard.

"Jeb Storms?" she said in response to his inquiry. "Just around the corner. There's a big elm tree in the empty lot beside their cottage, and just an empty lot on the other side. I don't think they're home, though."

"Where did they go?"

She wrinkled her brow in thought. "Now then, I'm just not sure. Off to see his sister, maybe? Or was it his aunt? I can't remember now."

"That's all right," Thaddeus said. "I'll just go and knock on the door and see who I find."

He was several paces away before the woman thought to ask why he was looking for Jeb Storms in the first place. He pretended he didn't hear her.

It was as she told him, a small, low workman's house pleasantly situated between two grassy vacant lots, as though it had been plunked down in the middle of a meadow and the rest of the neighbourhood had grown in a circle around it. As he approached, Thaddeus thought he saw movement at the rear of the property, just a flash of something brown, but he couldn't be certain what it was. A dog, maybe, or some small animal that scurried away at his approach.

He walked up to the front door and knocked. There was no answer. He knocked again, with the same lack of response.

Maybe the woman was right – they'd gone away somewhere. Or been sent away, so that Jeb Storms couldn't answer any questions about his statement, but perhaps, Thaddeus thought, he was being too suspicious. Jeb's employment with Albert Warner was in abeyance. Maybe it was just a good opportunity to go visiting.

He walked around the house and had a look at the back yard, but there was nothing to be seen. Annoyed at having wasted an afternoon, Thaddeus began trudging back to the hotel.

When he arrived, he went straight to the sitting room where he found Joe, Martha and Clementine happily sipping tea and nibbling on gingerbread cookies.

"What have you been up to?" Clementine asked. "I couldn't find anybody this morning, and I haven't seen you all day."

"I've been working," Thaddeus replied.

"Oh yes, the mysterious business you need to conduct."

"I'm trying to find some information about a criminal case and I'm not being very successful. The barrister who hired me will arrive in a couple of days and I don't have much to tell him. Joe thought maybe you could help."

Clementine beamed. "I'd love to! Do I get to arrest anybody?"

"Of course not."

"Put them in handcuffs?"

Thaddeus was beginning to regret his decision to involve her.

Then she settled down. "I'm just teasing you. What would like me to do?"

"When you were in Wellington, I seem to recall that you spent a great deal of time floating around the village picking up little tidbits of gossip that you'd later use in your…um…"

"Spirit sessions," she finished for him. "You'd like me to see what I can find out through the London grapevine?"

"Yes."

She took a few moments to reply. "And what do I get out of it?"

Joe groaned.

"The satisfaction of bringing a criminal to justice," Thaddeus said. He knew as he said it that this would be a forlorn appeal. She looked at him dubiously. "And my good will," he went on. "You need someone to identify you as Clementine Elliott in order to claim the money Nate left behind. It would be far easier for you if that someone was in a good mood when the barrister arrives."

"Well, why didn't you say so? When do you want me to start?"

Martha handed the newspaper article and Ashby's letter to Clementine. She scanned them quickly. "And what else have you found out?"

Thaddeus told her where he'd been so far, then Martha handed her the small daguerreotype. "This is the victim, Hazel Warner," she said.

Clementine studied the picture for a few moments, but seemed unimpressed. "A pretty enough girl, I suppose. But nothing special. Amazingly round head. What does the young man look like?"

"You'd walk right past him on the street and never notice him," Thaddeus said. "That's part of the problem. He's so unremarkable I expect he blends into the background wherever he goes."

"So he's not the sort of boy who would have the girls clamouring after him?"

"I shouldn't think so. And the romance with the Warner girl was lukewarm at best. It was one of those matches that the families were hoping for, but I think the participants themselves were ambivalent."

"Nelson seemed very annoyed that Hazel allowed someone else the liberties she wouldn't allow him." Martha blushed as she made this observation. Clementine shot her a glance and then tapped her finger against the arm of her chair for a few moments before she spoke.

"I think Martha and I should definitely make a tour of the stores," she said, and then she grinned. "I'm not sure if we'll pick up any information or not, but it will be fun."

Thaddeus sighed in exasperation.

"Calm down, Mr. Lewis. I'll do what you ask, but I reserve the right to have a good time while I do it." Then she turned to Martha. "Want to go shopping tomorrow?"

CHAPTER 9

Clementine appeared the next morning far earlier than she had the day before, but it was still late by Thaddeus's standards. He had long since finished his breakfast and was on his third cup of tea. He waited impatiently while she consumed a leisurely breakfast of fried oysters and a baked potato. Joe and Martha sat close beside each other across from him, engaged in some private conversation that Thaddeus was reluctant to intrude on. Instead, he sat and watched Clementine with mounting annoyance.

Just as he thought she was finally finished, she signaled the waiter for another cup of coffee.

"I do like staying in hotels," she said. "This is really quite a nice one, isn't it?"

"Are you planning to sit here all day?" Thaddeus asked.

"No, I'm planning to do what you asked me. But I refuse to do it until I've had an adequate amount of coffee."

"How much is adequate?"

"Just this one more," she said. "There's no point in going early anyway, you know. First thing in the morning shopkeepers are busy opening the doors and sweeping the floors. They don't have time to talk then."

"Fair enough, I suppose."

Finally, she drained her cup and set it down. "Now," she said, "you'd better give us some money if you expect us to go shopping."

"What?" Thaddeus hadn't anticipated that he would be financing the expedition. "Why do you need to buy anything? Can't you just look?"

"The wheels turn far faster if a little grease is applied."

Martha looked up. "It's all right," she said. "We can use the money my father gave me."

"No," Thaddeus said. "He gave you that money to use for yourself, not for my benefit."

"Actually, he gave it to me in case something happens to you and I need to find a way home."

"You didn't tell me that." Thaddeus felt a little nettled that Francis thought he might leave Martha stranded somewhere. "Well that was a vote of confidence, wasn't it?"

"Oh I don't know," Martha said. "I haven't had to use it so far."

"And we're not going to use it today either." Clementine glared at Thaddeus. "I know perfectly well that the lawyer is covering your expenses. Just think of this as another expense. The client will get the bill for it and none of us will be out of pocket."

That made a certain amount of sense, Thaddeus supposed, but he was still leery of handing over any great sum.

"Come on, we just need a little. I promise we won't go overboard. A couple of dollars. The client can afford that, surely."

Thaddeus stood up, dug in his pocket and extracted a handful of coins. "Bring back what you don't spend," he said.

His movement attracted the attention of the diners near them. One man looked up and chuckled. "Wives and daughters," he said shaking his head. "They're always looking for money, aren't they?"

There was no point in trying to explain. If everyone wanted to believe that Clementine was his wife, Thaddeus decided that there wasn't much he could do about it.

They waited in the hotel lobby while Clementine ran up to her room to fetch an umbrella, though the day was warm and sunny and Martha wasn't at all sure why she needed it.

"What are you going to do today?" she asked Joe.

"I heard there are some horse races at the fairgrounds or the parade grounds or somewhere on the edge of town," he said. "I thought I'd go along and have a look. Maybe I can win a dollar or two."

"Do you gamble?"

Joe looked surprised. "Yes, of course. I nearly always come out ahead, too." He shrugged. "It's a nice day. It'll be good to be outside."

Martha didn't know what to say. She knew that not everyone took a dim view of gambling, but she had been raised with the Methodist view of it. She must endeavour to be more open-minded, she decided, and not judge others by her grandfather's strict standards.

And then Thaddeus astonished her. "Want some company?" he asked.

Joe looked pleased. "Yes. That would be great."

"It's a good place to eavesdrop on conversations," he said to Martha. "It's possible to watch a race without wagering on the outcome."

Just then Clementine reappeared, and once they were out on the street, she took Martha by the arm.

"This is going to be so much fun," she said. "I can't remember the last time I had another woman to go shopping with."

"Don't forget, we have other things to do as well," Martha replied, although she, too, was looking forward to browsing through the stores.

"Oh, don't worry, we can do both."

They went to a dry goods store first, where Clementine spent an enormous amount of time examining the fabrics and notions.

"Was there something in particular you were looking for?" the shopkeeper finally asked.

"I'm just visiting for a few days," Clementine said. "I didn't realize that fashion in London was so progressive, or that there would be so many social functions to attend. I'm beginning to feel that my wardrobe is quite dowdy."

Martha stifled a laugh. "Dowdy" was hardly a word that could be applied to anything Clementine Elliott put on her back.

"I'm wondering if I can find a few little flourishes to add," she went on, "to update things a little, if you know what I mean."

"We do have a nice selection of lace," the shopkeeper pointed out. "Lace can add a nice touch. What sort of functions will you be attending?"

"Some dances, I believe, and a concert or two. And everyone seems to be atwitter over some murder trial that's happening next week. I've been asked if I would like to see it, but I'm not sure what I should wear. I've never been to a trial before."

"Ah yes, that would be young Lakefield's trial."

"Yes, I believe that's the one. I'm not at all sure about going. Do you think it's likely to be a spectacle?"

The shopkeeper leaned forward, pleased, Martha could see, to pass on what he knew. "Oh, I'm sure of it. It's quite a thrilling case. A young woman and her baby burned up in a fire. Lakefield is accused of setting it."

Clementine gasped. "My goodness," she said. "How dreadful! Whyever would someone do such a dreadful thing?"

"The girl claimed that Lakefield was the baby's father, that's why. It makes sense he'd want to get rid of her."

"Do you think he did it?"

The man shrugged. "Not for me to say. But the Lakefields have hired a famous barrister. I expect you'll see a lot of fireworks in court. They say this man is a pistol and there will be some sharp questions asked."

"That sounds entertaining, all right," Clementine allowed.

"Now if the boy hangs for it, that really would be a spectacle. Maybe you should wait for that."

"What does one wear to a hanging, I wonder?" Clementine said. "I've never been to one of those either." She must have judged that there was little more information to be gained, because she now cut the conversation short. "I'll think we'll just take these," she said, holding up a handful of Chinese frogs. They'll look lovely if we add them to my young friend's dress."

She was right, Martha realized. The dress she was wearing was a soft loden green; the frogs, made of covered piping, were a green of the same tone, but lighter and brighter in colour.

Clementine held them up against the dress. "Down the front of the bodice, I think. And then two more across the top of the pockets." She counted out the number they would need, then paid for the purchase and they left the shop.

"Not much news there," she said. "Or at least not anything we don't already know. We'll have to see if we can do better in the next place."

They walked along the main street, turning heads as they went, the women noting Clementine's quite frivolous hat and her elegant velvet jacket, the men's eyes fixed on other things. Ahead of them, Martha could see a knot of boys at the corner.

"Be careful of that bunch," she said. "I had trouble with them the other day. Apparently they have nothing to do but stand in the street and make rude comments."

"Don't worry," Clementine said, but Martha noticed that she took a firmer grip on her umbrella.

The group started whooping as soon as they spotted the two women. One of them elbowed the other as Martha and Clementine went by, and again repeated the same odious remark as before. Then one of the young men, the one called Bill, started following quite closely behind them, while the others continued their rude commentary. Clementine quickened her pace and Martha followed suit. Bill stayed close - so close that he occasionally bumped against their heels, hampering their stride.

Suddenly Clementine came to a dead stop, turned slightly and drove the heavy wooden handle of her umbrella into the boy's stomach. He emitted a soft, "whoompf", then clutched his stomach and fell to his knees.

"Oh, I'm so sorry," Clementine said sweetly. "I didn't realize you were right behind me. I do hope you're all right."

Bill was unable to answer. The others were unsure of what had just happened. They rushed forward to cluster around their friend while Clementine set off briskly down the street. Martha scrambled to keep up with her.

"That was neatly done," she ventured when they were out of earshot.

"He's lucky he only got the butt end of the handle," Clementine said.

"What do you mean?"

"Oh, I have other weapons when the going gets sticky," she said. "But I expect the handle did the job. I think he got the message. You should always carry an umbrella, you know. They're extraordinarily useful."

Martha was mightily impressed and profoundly intimidated. She resolved on the spot to never, ever cross this woman and to purchase an umbrella at the earliest opportunity.

"Ah, here we go," Clementine said, "Just what we're looking for."

It was a jeweller's and silversmith's. Martha had no idea why in particular they would be looking for it, but she trailed through the door after the older woman.

Again, Clementine took a long time to look everything over. She lingered over the necklaces and rings, then sighed and turned to the silverware. Martha thought some of it looked quite fine, but as silver serving pieces were things that seldom made their way into Methodist manses, she decided that she had no way to judge. Clementine seemed quite dismissive of them, but then she picked up a silver water jug that was initialled with an ornate "W".

"This is quite nice," she said to the clerk. "It's a shame it's engraved. My name, unfortunately, does not begin with a "W".

"I told Mrs. Warner that would be a problem," the clerk said, and Martha was instantly alert. "I think you'll find, however, that the price reflects the difficulty in the resale."

"My friend Mrs. Williams might be interested in this," Clementine said thoughtfully. "Is there just the one piece?"

"No, there's a tea service as well. Five pieces, all told. All engraved, of course."

"I will let her know. She'll have to come in and look at it herself, of course. Do you handle a lot of resale items?"

"Only occasionally. And only if they are of the highest quality."

Clementine reached into her pocket and removed a small box. "Perhaps you would like to take a look at this. It was left to me by my grandfather." She opened it to reveal a heavy gold watch. "It's far too large for a lady's use, and as I barely knew my grandfather I can't claim any great sentimental feeling for it. Perhaps you could advise me."

The clerk lifted it out of the box and examined it carefully, opening up the back of it to check the action.

"This is a first-quality piece," he said. "Your grandfather must have been a well-to-do man."

"Yes, he was," Clementine said. "That's why I was so disappointed to be left only a watch."

The clerk chuckled. "I could take it off your hands if you're interested in selling." He named a price.

Clementine countered with a higher figure and they haggled back and forth for a few minutes until they settled the deal. The clerk counted out the bills, Clementine pocketed them, and then motioned for Martha to follow her out the door.

"Let's go look at hats," she said brightly. "That's the most fun of all."

The horse races took place on what had once been the parade ground of the British Regiments stationed in London. It had become a convenient place for community activity, from races of all sorts, to wrestling matches to rowing on the nearby, artificially-constructed Lake Horn. Thaddeus was surprised at the number of people in attendance, given that it was a workday.

Joe led the way to the pens where the waiting horses were corralled.

"There's some good horseflesh here," he said, looking them over carefully. "The trick is to discover which one wants to run today."

In spite of himself, Thaddeus became caught up in Joe's appraisals.

"That's a nice bay over there," he ventured.

Joe squinted toward where he was pointing.

"Hmmm.... I don't know. I think she's got a bit of a spavin on the near side," he said.

He finally settled on a handsome chestnut who was fighting his handler. "He's agitated," Joe said. "Let's see if that makes him run." He found a man who was taking wagers and placed his bet, then he and Thaddeus walked to the edge of the makeshift racetrack.

The horses were lined up at one end. The chestnut was led out, still shying and bucking. Eventually they were judged to be more or less in an even line and a flag was dropped. The chestnut bucked once, then went flying down the track. The noise was deafening as everyone shouted, urging on their favourites. It was neck and neck between Joe's horse and a dun-coloured mare, but in the end the chestnut put on a burst of speed and crossed the line first.

Joe's face was split in a grin as he pounded Thaddeus on the back. "There's a day's work. Let's go get our money. Then we'll check out the next bunch."

"I'm going to wander around for a bit," Thaddeus said. "I'll catch up with you later." As exciting as the race was, Thaddeus saw no point in wasting the day standing at the side of the track. He walked over to the pens and pretended to be inspecting the herd of horses that would compete later that day. Most of those in attendance were laying their bets on the next race, but here and there knots of men were clustered in conversation.

Thaddeus walked by each of these groups slowly, but all he overheard were comments about the horses. He wondered that so many had so much time and money on their hands. Out of work farm hands, he judged, at loose ends until the next spring, eager to spend their hard-earned cash; a few prosperous-looking gentlemen, most likely the horses' owners; several packs of well-dressed young men with nothing more to do on a fine October day than drink and gamble.

One group of these young men drew his attention because of the noise they were making. Thaddeus pretended to be interested in a big roan at the far end of the paddock, and walked along the fence until he was close enough to hear what they were saying.

"I can't pay up right now," one of them said. "You know I can't. Lakefield owes me a packet, and I can't collect. I'll get it to you when I get it from him."

"And when will that be?" another sneered. "Right after they dangle him?"

"That's what got Nelson into trouble in the first place," another quipped. "His dangle."

They all laughed.

"It's a wonder Gert hasn't gone out of business with Nelson locked up," he went on. "Maybe that's what was wrong with Hazel's kid – old Gert had a go at her and it didn't work…"

"Nah, that's not it – the kid just took after Nelson, that's all. Ugly as sin. We'll have to wait and see what the next one is like…"

"There won't be a next one if they hang him…"

"Sure there will. He's probably got two or three in the oven that he didn't have time to do anything about…"

Another race was about to get underway and the group was moving slowly in the direction of the track. Thaddeus didn't bother following them. Their attention would be riveted by the horses thundering across the field. He was unlikely to learn anything more just by standing with them.

Nor did he hear anything else about Nelson Lakefield over the course of the day. Everyone was far too busy counting money – either the amount they had won or the amount they had frittered away, but Thaddeus counted the time well spent – Nelson Lakefield, it seemed, was notorious among the young blades of London.

"You know," Clementine said, peering over the supper menu at Thaddeus, "it would be easier to find what you want if you could focus the inquiry a little. It's not very productive to just wander around town asking if anybody knows anything."

Thaddeus just grunted in reply. He was deep in thought and wasn't paying any attention to Clementine's prattle.

"And you might consider responding in a complete sentence," she said. "Otherwise you might just as well be a husband."

"Apparently everyone thinks I am anyway."

"Nevertheless, that's no excuse to be inarticulate."

"Stop." Martha was beginning to be annoyed by the low-level squabble that broke out between Clementine and her grandfather every time they were in the same room together. It was clear that Clementine was amused by it, but Thaddeus just seemed grumpy and rude.

"Would you like to hear what we found out today or not?" Clementine said.

"I thought you said it was no good just wandering around town," Thaddeus pointed out.

"All right, have it your way." Clementine studied her menu while the silence stretched out. Joe shrugged and rolled his eyes.

Thaddeus sighed. "All right. What did you find out?"

"Are you actually listening?"

"It would be hard not to hear you."

Clementine ignored this last slight. "The Warners are in financial straits. Rather dire ones, if I'm any judge. Mrs. Warner has sold off her silver. Including her tea set."

She had Thaddeus's full attention now. A sliver tea service was one of the first symbols of prosperity a Canadian wife acquired. It would be one of the things most reluctantly parted with.

"Follow the money," Thaddeus said softly. "That was good advice."

"It usually is," Clementine replied. "At least in my case, it is."

"Do you think it's possible Mr. Warner set fire to his own warehouse in order to collect the insurance?" Martha asked.

"I think it's something we need to consider. He was awfully anxious about when the insurance money would be paid. And one of the things that has everyone puzzled is why he brought the seduction suit in the first place. If he didn't need the money, he would have hushed up his daughter's predicament in order to save face."

"We still don't know who's responsible for that. Or if it has any bearing on what happened afterward," Martha pointed out.

"That's true. But at least it gives us a little more idea where to look."

"I told you," Clementine said. "You really need to focus, Mr. Lewis."

Thaddeus ignored her. "I think I'll have another chat with Earl Jenkins tomorrow. See if he can shed any light."

"I'm wondering if I should have my head read," Martha said. "Dr. Scott reacted very oddly when I showed him Hazel's picture."

"I'm not sure he has anything to do with it. After all, it was pure accident that you talked to him at all."

"Who?" Clementine wanted to know. "Really, if you want me to help, you need to fill me in."

Martha turned to Clementine. "I told you that I had trouble with that gang of boys before. I was more or less rescued by a gentleman who had a nearby shop. He turned out to be a …phrenologist?" Martha looked to Thaddeus to confirm that she had the proper term. He nodded.

"I showed him Hazel Warner's picture. He seemed a little startled at first, and then…I don't know…sad? In any event, he wanted me to come back so he could examine the bumps on my head. I know he was just hoping to drum up business, but maybe I should. At the very least I can ask some questions."

"I think the daguerreotypist is a more promising lead," Thaddeus said. "Maybe you should have your picture taken."

"But I'm sure he'd recognize me and know why I was there. He became quite angry when I asked about the picture."

"I could do it," Clementine said. "He doesn't know me."

"If you're going to do it, do it soon. He may not know you yet, but news seems to spread like wildfire in this town. He's sure to hear that you're somehow connected to me."

She smiled at him. "Yes, I am, aren't I? Now there's a state of affairs that could never have been predicted."

"Fortunately it's only temporary."

"I'll enjoy it while I can."

"Oh for heaven's sake," said Martha. "Will you two stop it?"

CHAPTER 10

"Follow the money," Josiah Blackburn had advised. "Sometimes sex can gum up the picture, but most of the time money is at the root of everything."

With this advice in mind, Thaddeus headed off in the direction of Earl Jenkins' law offices the next morning. He stood in the outer room for a full five minutes before Jenkins finally emerged to see who had come in, and when he did, he seemed disconcerted to find that it was Thaddeus.

"I have a few questions."

Jenkins sighed. "I'm very busy right now."

"It will take only a few minutes."

"Very well."

They stood in silence for a few moments until Thaddeus finally said, "I suggest we not hold our discussion in your public waiting room. My business has become far too public as it is."

Jenkins blinked, then nodded, and ushered Thaddeus into his small office, where he took a seat on the far side of the desk.

Thaddeus sat in the chair reserved for clients. He leaned back and crossed his legs, his hands resting comfortably on the arms of the chair.

"Tell me about Mr. Warner's money problems."

Jenkins looked aghast. "I can tell you nothing. You should know that. Client confidentiality is paramount."

He had not denied that the problems were there. Clementine had it right. No wonder Warner was so anxious about his insurance.

"Mr. Warner is not your client in this case," Thaddeus said. "And you deal mostly, as you pointed out to me, in deeds and mortgages and last testaments, so you must have an idea of the financial status of every man in London. I see no breach of confidence."

Jenkins opened and closed his mouth several times, as if groping for a response to this.

"If you prefer, I can ask questions and if I'm wrong you can answer with a simple shake of the head."

Jenkins glared, but Thaddeus went on anyway. "Is Warner heavily invested in lands that he hopes a railway will be built on?"

There was no reply.

Thaddeus heard the outer door open and the sound of heavy footsteps.

Jenkins jumped up. "I must attend to this." He went rushing out. In his haste, he left the door partially ajar.

"Have you got anywhere yet?" a voice demanded. "I need my money if I'm to get through the winter."

"Now, now, Mr. Forbes," Thaddeus heard Jenkins say. "I'm working on it."

"You tell Warner credit doesn't cut it. I need cash. I've got a family to support."

"I told you, I'm working on it."

"Well work harder," Forbes said. "I want to hear something by next week, or I'm taking my business to another solicitor, do you hear?"

Jenkins murmured something that Thaddeus didn't quite catch. Then the outer door slammed and Jenkins came back into the room. He was red-faced and obviously flustered.

Thaddeus waited until he was seated, then he said, "Warner's been offering credit instead of paying the farmers cash, hasn't he? And he's over extended."

Jenkins glared.

"That's why he brought the suit in the first place instead of covering up his daughter's mistake. He needed the money."

Jenkins still made no reply.

"So the question is," Thaddeus went on, "why didn't Lakefield just pay him off? Why go to all the bother of defending a lawsuit that he had little hope of winning? After all, there would sit pretty Hazel Warner with a babe in her arms. The jury would be anxious to compensate her, especially if the money was coming from someone as prosperous as Mr. Lakefield."

Then Thaddeus took a shot in the dark and hoped it would hit something.

"Lakefield is in as bad a shape as Warner, isn't he? He's been speculating too."

"Just because a gentleman is temporarily embarrassed, it doesn't mean he would stoop to criminal activity," Jenkins sputtered. "Yes, Warner and Lakefield both owe some money, but that has nothing to do with the fire."

"I didn't mean to imply that it did. But if you expect Mr. Ashby to successfully defend Nelson Lakefield, you're going to have to be more forthcoming. We're all on the same side after all."

"I suppose you're right," Jenkins mumbled, but Thaddeus had no hope that he meant it.

"I think that will do for now." Thaddeus didn't bother waiting for Jenkins to see him out the door.

As he walked back toward the hotel, he went over what he had just learned, trying to decide who stood the most to gain. It was still Warner, he decided. In fact, Lakefield would have gained nothing, unless he'd known that Hazel Warner was in the building. Unless... he stopped in mid-stride as another notion hit him. He almost went back to Jenkins' office, but then he decided that he had shaken loose as much information as he could that day. Besides, there were other ways to find out.

Richard Scott smiled as soon as Martha walked in the shop door. "Hello again."

"I wasn't sure you'd remember me," she said.

"How could I forget such a pretty damsel in distress? I hope you experienced no ill-effects from your unfortunate encounter."

"None whatsoever, thank you. It was all just foolishness, really."

"I'm pleased to hear it. And now what may I do for you?"

"I thought I might take you up on your suggestion to have my head examined," she said, "but I wasn't sure about the proper procedure. Do I need to make an appointment and come back later?"

Scott made a great show of going to his desk and consulting what appeared to be an appointment book.

"As it happens, I have some free time this morning. I could take you right away if that would be convenient."

This answer didn't surprise Martha at all since there was no one else in the shop at the moment. Nor had there been anyone the first time she'd been there.

"That would be most convenient," she said. "Thank you."

"Please, follow me. I do the examination away from the public eye. There's always a danger of gawkers, you see, and most people prefer a little privacy."

She hesitated. She didn't really know anything about this man, and she wasn't at all sure she wanted to anything privately with him. Truth be told, she would have preferred a few gawkers.

Scott smiled. "It's all right, don't be shy." He swept aside the curtain that covered the doorway and motioned her to walk through.

The back room was tiny, with only a cabinet, a small table, a stool and a bookshelf. She scanned the titles that were lined up in a row on the shelf. *Self Instructor in Phrenology and Physiology*; *Love, Percentage and Amadivaness; Self Culture and Perfection of Character.*

"That looks like heavy reading," she said.

"Oh yes. Phrenology is a complex science that requires a great deal of study. The human skull is constructed of myriad parts, not only depressions and protuberances, but various conjunctions where the different plates form a union. Every minute detail can reveal the character and propensities of the individual."

Unless you believe it's all poppycock, but Martha didn't voice this opinion.

"Would you remove your cloak and hat, please, and take a seat."

She did as she was asked, hung her things on a hook on the back of the door, then perched on the stool. Scott opened a large book that sat on the table.

"Name?"

"Martha Renwell."

"Address?"

She had to think for a moment. "My address here in London is The Western Hotel, but my home address is Wellington, Canada West."

"You're just visiting?"

She considered whether or not she should say anything about why she was in London, then decided that a direct approach was in order if she ever hoped to get any information. Besides, everyone already seemed to know that Thaddeus was investigating the arson. "I'm here with my grandfather. He had some business to attend to and asked me to come along with him. He's looking into the unfortunate warehouse fire that occurred a few weeks ago."

Was it her imagination, or was there a slight hesitation on Scott's part. If so, he covered it quickly.

"Oh yes," he said. "A young woman was killed, wasn't she?"

"And her infant, as well," Martha added.

"Yes, yes, most unfortunate." And then he retrieved a pair of calipers from the cabinet. "I'm going to measure your skull now. Don't be alarmed by the instrument."

He anchored one point of the calipers near her left ear, then swung the other arm around to her right. He stopped, and entered the information in the book. Then he did the same across her forehead. Martha tried to stay very still. She was a little alarmed that the points of the calipers came so close to her eyes.

Scott took measurement after measurement until, finally, he appeared to be satisfied with what he had found.

"Now comes the actual examination," he said with a smile. "I'll be touching your head in various places. That's the only way I can feel what's there. Is that all right?"

She nodded her assent.

He began with her forehead, running his hand along it, stopping in places when he apparently found something, then stepping to the desk to write down what he had found. Then he moved across her head, poking, prodding, documenting. Martha found it quite unpleasant.

"Did you know the girl who was killed in the fire?" she asked at one point.

"No," was the only response she got.

"I just wondered. The Warners seem to be a very prominent family."

"So I understand."

"The Lakefields as well."

"Yes."

So much for getting information. She couldn't get him to talk at all.

He hesitated when he reached the back of her head where her hair was looped up into a bun.

"I'm afraid I may need to disarrange your hair somewhat," he said. "It's so thick."

"That's all right. I can just jam it under my bonnet until I get back to the hotel to fix it," she said.

She could feel his fingers working through her hair to the scalp underneath. She hoped he would finish soon.

"Women should wear their hair down, anyway" he said suddenly. "Pulling it this way and that constricts the blood flow to the brain."

"I must admit it's a nuisance. It was much easier when I was little and could just put it in braids."

"Even that is too much," he said. "The same is true of corsets. They constrict blood flow and breathing. Women should just stop wearing them."

Martha found this an extraordinarily odd thing for him to say.

"I have no intention of dispensing with mine," she said.

"I wasn't implying that you should do anything at this moment," he replied. "I meant just generally."

"Yes, of course. Are we nearly finished?"

"Almost." He felt around the nape of her neck and behind her ears, jotted a few more things down in his book and then he said, "There. That wasn't too unpleasant, was it?"

It was. "No," she said.

"It will take me a few days to do the analysis. Could you come back on Wednesday, perhaps. I should have it ready by then."

The assizes would have started by Tuesday. Martha hoped Ashby wouldn't need her to be at the trial. And then she realized that, unless she and Thaddeus managed to find something more substantial about this case, neither of them would be needed for anything.

"Wednesday would be fine."

To Clementine's surprise, her picture was to be taken upstairs on the roof of Strong's Hotel.

"The process needs a very strong light to work," Charles Pearsall explained. "Fortunately, it's sunny today. Otherwise you would have to come back at a more propitious time."

He collected a wooden box and then she followed him up the stairs and out onto the roof. He pulled aside a tarpaulin to reveal an armchair placed in front of a painted backdrop of a large potted plant.

"Have you ever done this before?" he asked.

"No."

"It takes quite a long time. I'll need you to stay motionless for at least four minutes, which doesn't sound like a lot until you try to do it. There is a brace on the chair which I'll put at the back of your neck so that your head remains steady. I suggest you put your hands in your lap and get as comfortable as you can."

She shifted in the seat until she felt that she was in a posture that she could maintain. Pearsall had his back to her while he fiddled with something, some chemical preparation required for taking the picture, she assumed.

"I just need to prepare the slide," he said, as if he had read her thoughts.

"Have you been in London long?" she asked.

"Since December," he called over his shoulder. "I stay in one town until business starts to drop off, then I move on. I'll be packing up soon, so you've come just in time."

"And where do you go from here?"

"Brantford, I think, or maybe Hamilton. I haven't been to either place before. I'm sure there must be all sorts of people who would like a picture of themselves to admire."

"Or for others to see," Clementine said. "I suspect most of your work is given away."

"And I don't mind at all when it's a beautiful woman and she gives her picture to an admirer. But you'd be surprised at how many fat, bald old men want to have a stern representation of themselves sitting on the mantelpiece. I suspect they do it to scare small children."

Clementine laughed.

"So which admirer will you be giving this picture to?"

"You're a dreadful flatterer, Mr. Pearsall."

"Not at all. I think it's a reasonable assumption that you'd have many."

He appeared to expect no answer and to have readied the apparatus. He walked over to where Clementine was sitting, reached behind her and pulled forward a wooden brace that clamped around her head and cradled her neck. Then he spent a few moments fussing with her hair.

"I want to make sure the brace is completely hidden," he said, smiling down at her. She caught the smell of some fragrance as he bent over her. Cloves, perhaps. Pomade. Or the wax he used on his moustache. It was a peculiarly intimate moment, although he seemed to take no notice of it.

The brace was digging into her neck. She tilted her head slightly to remove the pressure.

"Is that all right?" she asked.

"However you are most content is fine," he said.

She rested one elbow on the arm of the chair, and shifted around until she was, if not comfortable, at least not in actual pain.

Pearsall seemed happy with her pose and went instead to fuss with the box-like camera. It was not unlike the camera obscura she had once used to project apparitions on a wall, and must work in much the same way, she decided, although she had no notion of how the image was permanently fixed onto a metal sheet.

"I came to you because I saw a sample of your work," she ventured when the silence had stretched out for what seemed a very long time.

"Is that right?" he said, absorbed in what he was doing.

"Yes. It was a picture of the Warner girl. The one who died."

He stopped, and turned to face her, an annoyed look on his face. "Mr. Warner has already asked me about that portrait. I don't know anything about the girl. She asked for a picture, I took it and sent her on her way. Is that why you're here? To ask about the fire?"

"No," Clementine said. "A friend showed it to me and I thought it was lovely work. I wanted one of myself, that's all."

He glared for a moment more, then returned to the box-like camera.

"Now remember, once I start the exposure, don't move, don't talk, don't do anything," he said. "It blurs the image."

More than most, Clementine was used to arranging expressions on her face. She set her lips in a half smile and stared directly at the camera.

"All right, it starts now," he said. "Be very, very still and try not to blink."

As soon as he said it, she felt an overwhelming urge to close her eyes. She fought the feeling, and remained motionless, her gaze fixed on a point where she thought the lens must be. At first each second seemed like torture. She needed to think about something other than the fact that she was trying to maintain a pose, so that she could forget that she was trying to stay motionless.

Her current predicament was as good a topic as any. She knew she needed to consider what her next move would be. She was safe, here in this small town, for the moment. She had booked her train ticket under one of her many pseudonyms. She had signed in at the hotel under the name Clementine Elliott – an alias she had not used for ten years. It was unlikely anyone could trace her here. She wondered if anyone was trying to. By now, someone would have noticed the bits and pieces she had walked away with. They were hardly worth chasing. But she was unsure if anyone else had known about the safe. The bits and pieces would keep her going for now and Nathan Elliott's money would see her through until she could find a reliable fence. After that, she would be able to do whatever she wanted.

She would need to give some of the money to Joe. He had earned it, after all. He had been her accomplice ever since his father died. He was tired of it, she knew and would soon strike off on his own to do who knew what. She'd be alone, then, for the first time in a long, long time.

"I'm finished now."

She came back to the present, blinking and slightly disoriented. It had never been four minutes, had it? And yet, there was Pearsall bustling over to remove the brace.

"If you can come back on Wednesday, the picture will be ready for you. You'll need to pick out a case to keep it in, so it won't get scratched."

And then he escorted her down the stairs and out into the street.

Thaddeus saw Clementine coming out of Strong's Hotel. He almost turned around and went back the other way, but then he realized that she must have seen him too, for she waved an arm in greeting, and stood and waited until he caught up with her. He supposed it would be uncivil to do anything but walk back to the Western with her, and he prepared himself for another round of challenging statements and impertinent comments. To his surprise, though, she seemed in a pensive mood.

"Do you have sons, Mr. Lewis? I don't think I ever heard whether you do or not."

He debated whether he should answer. Then he decided that it was unlikely that information about the number of his sons could ever be used to wrong him. "Yes, three. One is in Toronto. Two are farming not too far from here."

"But no girls?"

"We had more girls than boys. But only one of them lived for long. And even then, it wasn't long enough."

"Oh of course. Martha's mother."

"Yes." He didn't add anything more. There was nothing to add, really, except that sometimes, especially late at night, he still felt the sorrow of it all.

"Martha looks like her grandmother, doesn't she?"

"Like her mother as well," Thaddeus said. "Sometimes I get mixed up between the three."

"Your wife was a lovely looking woman. I know she was quite sick by the time I met her, but you could still see how beautiful she must have been."

"She was indeed."

"How did you meet?"

"She was a friend of my sister's." Thaddeus remembered it as if it had been yesterday. She had been standing in a field of wildflowers.

"And was it love at first sight?"

"It was for me. She, quite rightly, took a little more persuading."

"And why was that Mr. Lewis?"

"I wasn't much of a catch." He found it very strange that Clementine was asking questions about his long-ago love affair with his wife. Her interest made him a little suspicious. "Why do you want to know this?"

"In polite circles, it's called making conversation," she said in an exasperated tone. "You know – taking an interest in another person, that sort of thing? So you weren't a dashing young minister back then?"

"I'm not sure such a thing exists as a dashing minister," Thaddeus said. "And if it does, it surely wasn't me. I'd gone charging off to fight in the war, full of myself like all the young men were. I was shot in the leg, and it didn't heal well. I was sick. I drank too much. They were going to send me to Britain, to a pensioners' hospital. I knew that if I went I'd never see Betsy again."

"What happened to intervene?"

"I prayed for God to do something."

"And did He?"

"Yes, He ended the war and that was the last I heard about the hospital."

Clementine abruptly stopped walking. "Oh. So that's why you became a preacher. You made a deal."

"Not exactly."

"Oh yes, exactly! You bartered with God so you could get what you wanted. You old fraud, you!"

"What do you mean?" Thaddeus felt quite nettled by her reaction.

"All this time I thought you were somehow moved by the holy spirit or whatever it is that's supposed to happen, and it turns out you just made a deal."

"I did not!" The vehemence of his reply drew the attention of the other people on the street.

"And now you're angry because He took her away too soon. That's why you're not preaching anymore."

"That's not true!"

Clementine laughed. "And here I thought you were struck with the glory of the Lord when all you really struck was a bargain. I had no idea that the Methodist God works that way. Maybe I should start paying more attention."

"That is not how the Methodist God "works" as you put it."

"So does He give you every little thing you ask for as long as you promise to be a good, go-to-meeting Methodist? Or does it always have strings attached?"

Thaddeus refused to let his temper rise. This was Clementine Elliott, after all. "I'd gladly debate theology with you if I thought you were sincere," he said in a deliberately mild tone. "But I know perfectly well that you're just trying to bait me."

"Bravo, Mr. Lewis!" She giggled. "You're the only one who ever sees through me."

"I don't know why I told you anything."

"Because I'm a good listener," she replied with a sweet smile. "I always was."

They had all agreed to meet again in the sitting room before they went in to dinner. When they arrived, each of them was thoughtful and had more questions than answers after a morning of inquiry.

Thaddeus's news was the most straight-forward.

"You were right," he said to Clementine. "Mr. Warner is hard against it."

Martha thought Clementine showed great restraint by not crowing over this small victory.

"Jenkins wouldn't confirm much, but his silence told me a lot. I wouldn't be at all surprised if Lakefield is in the same boat."

"So Mr. Warner brought the seduction suit because he needed the money. And Mr. Lakefield refused to pay because he didn't have it, is that right?" Martha said.

"I would think so," Thaddeus said. "I'm not sure how much farther down the road it gets us in terms of proving Nelson Lakefield's innocence, but at least it tells us what the original motives for the suit were."

"Nelson Lakefield," Joe suddenly remarked. "I heard his name down at the market today."

"What were they saying about him?" Thaddeus asked.

"It was name-calling mostly. Something about ugly babies and Nelson's talent for fathering them, which resulted in a great deal of hilarity amongst a group of well-dressed young men."

"What was meant by ugly?" Clementine asked.

"The Warner child had a large birthmark," Thaddeus answered. "On her face. Apparently it was quite disfiguring."

"You might have told me that before," Clementine said. "Again, Mr. Lewis I don't know how you expect me to be of any assistance if you don't give me the whole picture."

"May I continue?" Joe said, "or have you heard everything you need to know, in which case I'll just stop talking."

"I'm sorry, my darling," Clementine said. "Do please go on."

"After that, someone made a remark about Nelson's preference for low women. That's when it got really interesting. A fistfight broke out. From what I could gather from all the shouting, there's another young woman who was involved with Lakefield, and a young man – not very well-dressed at all, by the way, and who is known as "Bastard Bill" - took objection to her being called a hussy. He went at it hammer and tongs with the gentleman who made the remark."

"Interesting," Thaddeus said. "That certainly squares up with what I heard about Nelson at the races."

"Who won the fight?" Martha wanted to know.

"It was pretty much a draw," Joe said. "They both looked pretty battered by the end of it."

"I'd like to have a talk with this Bill fellow," Thaddeus said. "Do you know where I might find him?"

"I do," Martha said. "Or at least I know where you can find him most days. He'll be down along Dundas Street making nasty remarks to ladies."

"Is he one of the boys who catcalled us?" Clementine asked.

"He's the one who followed us."

"How do you know his name?"

Martha turned bright red. "I think part of his name may be my fault. He said something nasty and I asked him if his father knew that he had such a foul mouth. He said he didn't have a father. I told him I figured as much."

Clementine threw her head back and laughed so loudly that it drew the attention of the waiter, who peered anxiously in the doorway. Thaddeus, however, looked worried.

"You didn't tell me you had trouble in the town."

"It wasn't trouble, really. Or at least it's the sort of trouble that most young women come to expect whenever they're out walking. I took care of it that day. And then Mrs. Elliott took care of it when it happened again."

Thaddeus turned his outraged gaze to Clementine. "What did you do?"

"I whacked one of them with my umbrella. Don't worry, he's not entirely sure what happened. I made it look like an accident."

"I wish you'd told me," he said to Martha.

"I took care of it. And that sort of thing happens all the time. You soon learn how to deal with it."

"What is wrong with these young men," he fumed. "They should be horsewhipped."

"Oh, don't worry about it," Clementine said. "Your delightful granddaughter has shown that she's perfectly capable of taking care of herself."

"Still… honestly," Thaddeus grumbled. "Well, that's certainly helpful, Joe. Thank you. It sounds like I should have another conversation with young Lakefield as well."

Joe gave him a mock salute. "Happy to be of service," he said. And then he grinned at Martha. "And how did your day go?"

"Not nearly as well. I really didn't find out anything useful at all, except that it takes forever to measure the lumps and bumps on my skull."

"Did you have a lot?" Joe asked.

"Apparently. I'm supposed to go back Wednesday and he'll have a written report for me. I'm on tenterhooks in case he discovers that I have criminal tendencies or something."

"It's all nonsense," Thaddeus said.

"I know. But I found the whole process kind of strange. I've never had anyone feel my head like that before. It seemed kind of forward on his part. And then he went on about how women should wear their hair down and throw away their corsets." She looked puzzled. "He didn't do anything improper or anything. It just alarmed me a little. And, as I said, I didn't find anything out for my pains."

"Nor did I," Clementine said, "although having my picture taken was a fascinating process. I had to sit still for a very long time while he took the picture. Did you know that he takes them up on the roof?"

"Yes," Thaddeus said. "The light has to be very strong to register the image, or so I'm told. The process uses a metal plate that's specially treated."

"It looked just like a camera obscura to me."

"Yes, I believe the principle is the same. The breakthrough was in being able to fix the image."

"Anyway, Mr. Pearsall was quite charming, but distinctly unhelpful when it came to providing any useful information. I kept trying to talk and he kept telling me to be quiet."

"Fancy that," Thaddeus said. Martha frowned at him.

"I mentioned the trial, and he grew quite agitated. He said Mr. Warner asked him about the daguerreotype, but Pearsall says all he did was take a picture and he knows nothing beyond that."

"I wonder how Warner knew about it?" Thaddeus said.

"Hazel gave it to Nelson at Christmastime," Martha pointed out. "Maybe she showed it to her parents first. And her father probably paid for it."

"But why would Warner connect that with the father of the child? And wouldn't he have to have it in his possession in order to show it to the daguerreotypist? It was Nelson who gave it to us."

"That's true," Martha allowed. "Did Mr. Pearsall say when Mr. Warner asked about it?"

"No," Clementine said. She glared at Thaddeus. "I didn't realize it was important. Oh well, I'm supposed to go back next week and retrieve my portrait. I can ask him about it then, I suppose, although he made it pretty clear that he wasn't happy with the topic."

"Maybe I should talk to him," Thaddeus said.

Martha smiled at him. "Maybe you should go and have your portrait done. I would like a picture of you."

"I'd probably break the camera," Thaddeus joked. "I'd rather have one of you. Let's see where we are when the dust settles, and then we'll see about pictures."

"Was it hard to stay still?" Martha asked Clementine.

"At first it was, yes. He has a brace that holds your neck so you can't move much, but it's hard not to fidget. After that it was very odd. I was sitting in the sun and I grew quite… sleepy isn't the right term exactly. It was very mesmerizing."

"Maybe he put you into a trance," Joe said. "He could have done all sorts of things with you if you were in a mesmerized state. Maybe he hypnotized the Warner girl and had his way with her."

"That isn't really possible, is it?" Thaddeus said.

"Only to a degree," Clementine replied. "My husband practiced animal magnetism. He was quite successful at getting people to do all sorts of things they ordinarily wouldn't dream of doing. Of course they were minor things – barking like a dog, for example, or standing on one leg. I'm not sure you could get someone to do something that was fundamentally against their principles."

"But that was just part and parcel of your bag of tricks, wasn't it? Like the séances and the mechanical writing?"

"No." Clementine was quite thoughtful. "There was more to it than that. There really wasn't any trickery involved. He was just very good at getting people into a suggestible state. I've done it occasionally, myself, but I'm not nearly as good as he was."

"Just as well," Thaddeus said. "You'd get into even more trouble."

Clementine smirked at him. "I could probably mesmerize you, if I wanted to."

"I doubt it."

"Is that a challenge?"

"What? You don't seriously think you could induce me into a trance and make me do something, do you?"

"Would you like to make a wager on that?"

"No, I wouldn't. I don't make wagers of any description. That said, I still don't think you can do it."

"I'll tell you what," Clementine said, a challenge in her eyes. "We won't bet anything, since you find that so offensive. But let's try it, just to see what happens. After supper, when you'll be full and sleepy."

"So you stand a better chance of making it work?"

"Yes," she allowed. "But you seem to think I can't do it at all. My room. After supper, if you dare."

Thaddeus laughed. "Fine. But it won't work."

When they had finished their meals, Clementine asked Thaddeus and Martha to wait for fifteen minutes before they came to her room. When they arrived, they discovered that the curtains had been drawn and there was only one lamp burning, and that Clementine had lit some sort of incense. It was extraordinarily like the scene she had set for her séances, Thaddeus thought, and he was all the more determined to be on guard because of it.

"Please, take off your jacket and sit down," she said in a low voice, and Thaddeus took the only chair in the room. Joe and Martha stood by the door to watch.

Clementine began by asking Thaddeus to make sure he was comfortable. He wasn't sure he could be, but he shifted in his seat until he felt, at least physically, at ease. She stood behind him and began massaging his shoulders. She was very good at it, and in spite of himself, he felt the tension of the day begin to float away. After a few minutes she moved in front of him, her knees touching his. She then held aloft a silver pendant and asked him to concentrate on it. It was in a position just above his head, and he had to look up slightly to get it into his line of vision.

"Think of nothing but the necklace," she said. "Concentrate all of your thought on nothing but it." And then it began, very gently, to sway back and forth.

At first he was intensely aware of her physical proximity, the rustle of her skirts, the scent she wore. But after a few minutes he forgot these things and became attentive to nothing but the slight swinging back and forth of the pendant.

The next thing he knew, he became suddenly aware of his surroundings again. His eyes felt heavy and he was slightly disoriented.

"What a shame you wouldn't wager," Clementine said. "I'd have won."

"What are you talking about? Nothing happened."

"Oh didn't it?"

Thaddeus looked to Martha for confirmation. "You went under all right," she said, a rueful expression on her face.

"Oh that's ridiculous, I did not."

"Yes, you did," Joe confirmed. Thaddeus felt foolish, and a little angry that he could so easily be persuaded into an altered state of mind.

Then Martha said, "Try me next, so he can see what happened."

"Good idea," Thaddeus said. "I'd like to see this." He went to stand by Joe while Martha took his place on the chair.

"She's not nearly as tense as you were," Clementine said to him as she massaged Martha's shoulders.

Again, the silver pendant was held in the air, while Clementine stood against Martha's knees.

"Concentrate."

Martha looked up at the necklace.

"Concentrate. You are very sleepy."

Martha shifted slightly in the chair.

"Keep looking at the pendant. You are very sleepy. You will do whatever I ask until I release you."

"Nothing's happening," Martha replied.

"Oh. All right. Concentrate fully on the pendant."

Back and forth it swung, while Martha followed it with her eyes. Back and forth and back and forth, but every time Clementine spoke, Martha reported that she didn't feel in the least sleepy. Finally Clementine lowered her hand and backed away from the chair.

"Didn't you feel anything at all?" she asked.

"No," Martha replied. "Nothing, except that my neck hurts from looking up for so long."

Clementine threw her hands up in surrender. "As I said, I'm not as good as my husband was. And there are some people who just aren't susceptible. Martha may well be one of those."

Martha looked disappointed. Thaddeus was skeptical.

"Then how do I know it worked on me?" he said.

It was Martha who replied. "Oh, don't worry. It worked."

He saw the confirmation in all their faces. "This is just a load of nonsense," he sputtered. And then he left the room.

Later, when he heard Martha come in, he knocked on the connecting door between their rooms. She opened it and bade him enter. He stood in the doorway.

"Was I really mesmerized?" he asked.

"Yes."

"What did she make me do? I didn't bark like a dog, did I?"

Martha blushed a little. "No. She made you kiss her on the cheek."

He was silent while he absorbed this startling piece of information. "Well," he said finally, "that's certainly something I would never do if I were awake."

CHAPTER 11

The next morning Thaddeus apologized handsomely. "I would never have believed that it was possible to be induced into a hypnotic state, but Martha assures me that I was. My apologies for doubting you."

Clementine accepted this with a gracious wave of the hand. "The amazing thing to me is not that you succumbed, but that Martha didn't."

"Does that happen often?"

"Occasionally. There are some people who really can't be fooled into anything. Apparently Martha is one of them." She grinned at Thaddeus. "She must get her strength of character from the other side of the family."

From her grandmother. Betsy could see through everybody. Especially me.

But he was a little taken aback that he had proved to be so weak-minded.

It suddenly occurred to him that Clementine had appeared at the breakfast table at an uncharacteristically early hour.

"We don't usually see you at this time in the morning," he commented. "Is this some sort of special occasion?"

"Yes," she said. "It's Sunday, isn't it?"

"I like your dress," Martha said. Clementine was wearing a beautifully-cut dove grey dress with darker lace across the bodice and at the sleeves. It was far more understated than anything Thaddeus had seen her in before.

"Thank you," Clementine said. "It's my Sunday best." She had a wicked look in her eye. "It's my Sunday-go-to-meeting dress."

"You're going to church?" Thaddeus asked. It was so unlike her.

"Isn't that what respectable people do on a Sunday? They go to church."

"I'm not going," Joe said.

Clementine ignored him. "I thought perhaps I could accompany you, Mr. Lewis. What you've told me about Methodism is quite fascinating. I'd like to see for myself."

Thaddeus stifled a groan. There was already far too much gossip about him within the Methodist community. What sort of nonsense would the tongues wag forth if he showed up at a meeting with a strange woman in tow? And even if she was sincere about learning more, Calvin Merritt's services were the worst possible examples of Methodist preachings. Even Thaddeus had been bored at the last one. And then there was Clementine herself. Would she behave, or was she likely to do something outrageous that would scandalize the congregation for years to come? And then, after a long moment's reflection, he decided that he just didn't care.

"I would be pleased to have you accompany me," he said, and was rewarded when she looked a little startled. So her intention had been to annoy him and he had called her bluff. So be it.

The streets were full of people on their way to church, both on foot and in passing carts. Thaddeus thought their little trio must be making quite an impression as they walked along the street toward the chapel, judging by the stares they drew. Clementine's hat matched her dress perfectly, and although it had its share of ruches and rosettes, it was not nearly as excessive in design as the ones she usually wore. All in all, she looked extraordinarily elegant. Martha, as always, was very pretty in her Sunday dress, but the appreciative glances that came her way were due to her youthful good looks and not her wardrobe. They each took one of his arms, and he allowed himself a small moment of smugness to be walking with two such fine-looking women.

They arrived only just in time for the service. The back rows were already filled. The only seats left that would accommodate all three of them were in the front row. Thaddeus stood very straight as they made their way down the centre aisle. Every head turned to look at them as they walked by. He heard a couple of gasps and a great deal of whispering. They were like rows of crows, he thought, all lined up in unrelieved black, cawing and commenting on the alien birds that had wandered into their flock.

Calvin Merritt, no great speaker at the best of times, nearly dried up completely when he saw Thaddeus and the two women sitting right under his nose.

Clementine seemed to be on her best behaviour. She politely attempted to join in the responses and stood for the hymns, Thaddeus feeding her the lines on the assumption that she would know none of them. She had quite a lovely contralto voice. If she were really a Methodist she would immediately be asked to join the choir. She then fixed her attention on Merritt as he sputtered his way through the sermon, giving every appearance that she found his discourse fascinating.

At the end of the service, when they finally made their way to the exit, Thaddeus realized that none of the congregation had gone scuttling home for their Sunday dinners as they usually did. They were huddled in twos and threes in the yard, glancing now and then at the door, waiting for him - or more to the point, he supposed - Clementine to come out.

Merritt was standing by the door to greet them. His mouth hung open as he drank in the details of Clementine's appearance until he finally recollected himself. "Good day Mr. Lewis." Then, in a low voice, "I must apologize for my remarks at our last meeting. At the time, I had not yet heard that you married again." He bowed slightly to Clementine. "Good day, ma'am."

Thaddeus was annoyed that all the conjecture about him that currently preoccupied London had so quickly reached the ears of the Methodist congregation. But, he realized, there was no way to set the record straight without initiating a fresh round of gossip and everyone knew far too much about his business as it was.

"How do you do," Clementine said, and bestowed a radiant smile on Merritt. He blinked and nodded in the glare of it. "I enjoyed your talk…"

"Sermon," Thaddeus prompted.

"I enjoyed your sermon very much. Thank you for allowing me to participate."

Thaddeus could see that Merritt was about to explode with the questions he wanted to ask. His eyes kept darting from Clementine to Thaddeus and back again, with several detours in the direction of Clementine's elegant hat. A hat that in all probability cost more than a Methodist minister earned in a month.

"You're most welcome," Merritt finally stuttered. "And congratulations on your marriage. May we hope to see you at the women's meeting, ma'am?"

"Oh dear, I'm so sorry," Clementine said with a little pout. "That would present some difficulties. I was, of course, very curious about your church, but I'm Jewish you see, so I'm afraid coming to any more meetings would be out of the question."

That was taking things much too far. Thaddeus gave her arm a surreptitious jab.

"But who knows?" she went on. "Perhaps Mr. Lewis will someday manage to convert me."

"Unlikely," Thaddeus said. "But I'll give it my best effort. Good day, Mr. Merritt, I hope you have a pleasant afternoon."

The crowd parted to let them through. Thaddeus took Clementine by the arm while Martha walked ahead, her shoulders shaking. Thaddeus waited until they were at the end of the block before he began to chuckle. Martha let loose the laugh she had been trying to control.

"Well that was fun, wasn't it?" Clementine said.

"You are reprehensible."

"You could have stopped me. But you didn't."

She was right, he could have. He should have. Thaddeus knew that he would have to pray earnestly for forgiveness for what he had just allowed to happen. But at the moment, he found it difficult to feel contrite.

Ashby arrived late that afternoon.

After dinner Thaddeus returned to his room planning to spend a quiet afternoon in prayer and contemplation as befitted a Sunday. He wasn't very successful. Every time he thought of the look on Calvin Merritt's face, he began to laugh again. He gave up and went over the notes of the case instead, reading through the information he had jotted down and the information he still needed to find. There was far too little of the former and far too much of the latter. He could hear Clementine and Martha in the next room, but wasn't foolish enough to think that they were reading the Bible as was appropriate for a Sunday afternoon. No doubt they were engaged in some female pursuit. He wouldn't admonish Martha for it. He had no moral high ground left to stand on. He was just cleaning himself up in preparation for going down for supper when there was a gentle knock on the door. It was one of the porters with a message.

"Mr. Ashby asked me to tell you that he has arrived and that he will meet you in the dining room in about half an hour, if that's convenient."

"Yes, of course, thank you." Thaddeus rapped on the connecting door to Martha's room and relayed the message when she opened it. Her hair was hanging in a tangle down her back.

"We'll meet you down there," she said. "Mrs. Elliott just finished sewing the frogs on my dress and now she's going to help me with my hair." Then she firmly closed the door.

Thaddeus was no expert on women and their hair, but from the state of Martha's he judged that she would be far longer than half-an-hour, and that Ashby would no doubt be late as well, given his history. Thaddeus had no wish to sit in the dining room by himself, so as soon as he was tidied up, he sat at the desk again and summarized the evidence so far. Ashby would want a report. And after all, he was paying for everything, so he was within his rights to demand one, but Thaddeus was disappointed that he didn't have more to say.

When he judged that enough time had elapsed, he went down to the dining room to discover that the young barrister was waiting at a table. When Thaddeus drew closer and saw the bottle of wine that was already half empty, he realized that Ashby must have been sitting there for some time.

"Towns! Good to see you! How was your journey?"

"Tedious as usual. The train, however, is a welcome improvement."

"Yes, it's quite astounding, isn't it, the number of hours it cuts off the journey. Not so long ago it would have taken days."

"So how have you been getting on? Or should we wait until your charming granddaughter arrives? I seem to recall that she gets quite annoyed if she's left out of the conversation."

"She may be some time yet. And Mrs. Elliott and her son will be joining us as well."

When Ashby looked puzzled, Thaddeus suddenly realized that he needed to explain the presence of the two extra people. "Mrs. Elliott, or at least that's the name she's using at the present, is the lady I consulted you about when we met previously. She had money left to her and has come to claim it."

"Ah yes, of course. And you need me to produce some paperwork with regard to that, don't you?"

Thaddeus was mildly annoyed. He had been hoping that Ashby would arrive with everything drawn up, so that Clementine would soon be on her way. It appeared, however, that Ashby had forgotten all about it.

"Well, yes, but in the meantime I'll fill you in on where we stand. The others may have something to add when they get here, but you'll have the broad picture anyway."

Again there was a questioning look from Ashby.

"It was impossible to keep Joe – that's the son – and Mrs. Elliott in the dark about what I was doing here," Thaddeus explained. "They have, in fact, been extremely helpful in furthering the investigation. And don't worry, they understand the need for discretion."

Briefly he outlined what he had discovered so far. "Nelson has not been particularly forthcoming with information," he pointed out. "He seems to have no alibi at all, but I'll talk to both Lakefields again tomorrow, and see if I can track down this Bill fellow and find out what the fight was all about."

"It sounds like our Nelson has been a busy boy," Ashby said. "I wonder if there have been other settlements? It would explain why his father was so determined to defend the suit."

"It may have been a contributing factor, but I think the fact that Lakefield is so over-extended has more bearing on his decision. And by all accounts the child would have needed life-long support as well. The Lakefields and the Warners were building an empire. An unmarriageable daughter is a useless pawn in the alliance game."

"And the eyewitness? Have you talked to him?"

"I haven't tracked him down yet. He was let go when Warner

didn't have any work for him. Finding him is one of the things I need to do in the next couple of days."

"You've got that, but not much more," Ashby said. "The assizes open tomorrow, although the Warner case will be reserved to last on the docket. I've picked up two other cases, by the way, one as prosecutor, the other as defence. It won't take more than a day to get through them, I expect. And then we'll have another day while the prosecution presents its case. After that I'll need something to argue."

So the trip to London would be lucrative for Ashby. Thaddeus supposed it made sense for anyone else who found themselves on trial to retain his services if they could afford them. No wonder Ashby hadn't batted an eye about footing the hotel bill.

"There's a discrepancy in the eyewitness account, for starters," Thaddeus said. "According to the newspaper reports, the foreman at first claimed to have seen an "unidentified man". It was only later that he changed his story and said it was Lakefield. The local editor says the reporter is reliable."

"So it may be possible to shake his story?"

"It would certainly be worth a try."

"I need to introduce myself to Nelson tomorrow morning. Since you want to talk to him as well, perhaps we should double up. Maybe we'll get more satisfactory answers if there are two of us, and then we'll see where we go from there."

Just then there was a stir as Martha and Clementine entered the room. Martha's good dress was newly festooned with the frog piping she had purchased and even though Thaddeus had no idea why, the addition made the dress look wonderful. Clementine had sewn the fasteners in a row down the centre of the bodice, and had looped two more over the pockets at the sides of Martha's skirt. They gave the dress a vaguely military air. Martha's hair was dressed in a becoming style that swooped softly over her ears and was held in place by a netted snood that she must have borrowed from Clementine, for Thaddeus had never seen it before. She looked considerably older than her sixteen years.

Thaddeus happened to glance at Ashby as the women walked toward them. He looked surprised, his mouth slightly open, his gaze fixed on Martha. Then he seemed to recover his wits and leapt to his feet to pull out a chair for her. Thaddeus similarly rose and seated Clementine.

"Mrs. Elliott, this is Townsend Ashby. Mr. Ashby, Mrs. Elliott," he said by way of introduction.

"Oh, the man with my money!" Clementine said. "I'm so pleased to meet you."

Ashby's mouth twitched a little. He was evidently amused by Clementine's shameless focus on monetary matters. "And I you," he said. "And of course it's lovely to see you again Miss Renwell."

Martha merely nodded in acknowledgment.

Just then Joe came loping into the dining room. All of the chairs at the table were now occupied, but he grabbed one from an adjacent table and pulled it up beside Martha. She looked at him and beamed, but left it to Thaddeus to make the introductions.

"This is Mrs. Elliott's son, Joe…" he hesitated. He'd completely forgotten Joe's last name. Or at least, the name he was using at the moment.

"Corcoran," Joe finished for him, nodding rather curtly at Ashby. Then he turned again to Martha. "There's a concert tomorrow night at the Music Hall," he announced. "Would you like to go?"

"I was about to ask what there was to do of an evening in this town," Ashby said. "And now my question has been answered."

"There are a surprising number of things to do," Clementine said. "Alas, Mr. Lewis has proved to be a disappointing escort as he refuses to attend anything that involves dancing or cards."

"Perhaps I could take up the slack," Ashby said smoothly. "Would you care to attend this concert with me?"

"I'd be delighted." She was smug in her acceptance.

Thaddeus knew that they were all expecting him to go along with their plans and offer to go as well, but he felt a stubborn reluctance to join in. He'd stay in his room and read, he decided. Read, and think about the looming court case, which seemed to be more than Ashby was doing.

"So, Mr. Ashby, tell me about yourself," Clementine said.

"Oh, I'm nothing special," he replied. "Just a poor barrister struggling to establish a practice. Fortunately at this stage of my life I have few responsibilities to meet, other than to keep myself in food and drink."

"Oh dear. I'm afraid Martha and I spent a little bit of your money in pursuit of evidence. I hope you don't mind too much."

"Not at all. Just report it to Mr. Lewis and he can itemize it on the bill. I trust your inquiries were productive."

"That remains to be seen, but I hope I've been able to assist if only to prove to Mr. Lewis that I'm not such a flibbertigibbet after all."

"I've often thought many things about you," Thaddeus said. "Flibbertigibbet wasn't one of them."

"No, I don't expect it was, was it?" she replied airily.

"What are your plans for tomorrow?" Martha asked Thaddeus.

"I'll talk to Nelson Lakefield in the morning. What I do in the afternoon depends on whether or not I get anywhere with him."

"What would you like me to do, boss?"

"I think you and I should talk to this Bill," Clementine said before Thaddeus could answer.

"I'm not sure I'm happy with that idea," Thaddeus said. "I don't want Martha anywhere near that gang of boys."

"You see, Mr. Ashby, in what little regard Mr. Lewis holds me? He's expressed no concern whatsoever for my safety, only for his granddaughter's."

Ashby laughed.

"But you can't do it," Martha said to Thaddeus. "You don't know what he looks like. Don't worry. Mrs. Elliott can take care of us both."

"I'll take my umbrella," Clementine said, and then they both giggled.

"I'll go with you if you like," Joe offered. Clementine looked surprised. Martha looked pleased.

"Thank you Joe, that would make my mind easier," Thaddeus said. "Do you think this Bill will talk to you?"

"I think Mrs. Elliott can probably make Bill do whatever she wants once she gets hold of him," Martha said. "The difficulty will be if he's in a crowd."

Joe turned to his mother. "I'll take care of the crowd. You can cut Bill out."

She nodded. Thaddeus wondered how many times they'd "cut" somebody out in the past, and to what purpose.

Ashby looked on in amusement. "I'm beginning to understand why you got these people involved, Thaddeus."

"Mr. Lewis really couldn't manage anything without us," Clementine said.

"The problem with Mr. Lewis is that he has principles," Ashby pointed out.

"Always a handicap, in my experience," she agreed.

Clementine and Ashby continued to banter with each other throughout the meal, while Martha and Joe carried on a quiet private conversation, ignoring everyone else at the table. Thaddeus began to feel very left out.

When he had finished his meal, he stood up abruptly.

"Well, I've got a long day ahead of me tomorrow," he said, "so I'll wish you all a good night."

And then he left the dining room, unsure as to why he felt so out of sorts.

CHAPTER 12

The next morning Ashby and Thaddeus left the hotel before the others had even come downstairs for breakfast.

"I don't know how far we'll get with Nelson," Thaddeus remarked to Ashby as they reached the gaol. "Both Lakefields have been uncooperative. I'm beginning to think everybody is hiding something, and I'd include Earl Jenkins in that assessment as well."

"Jenkins? No, I think he's on the up and up. You have to remember that he's really nothing more than a small town solicitor. He knows everybody's business, I expect, and he survives by being extremely circumspect about it. Let's see what we get from the Lakefields and then, if necessary, I'll deal with Jenkins."

The keeper was swabbing the anteroom in front of the heavy wooden door that led to the cellblock, and was reluctant to leave off his activity in order to let them through.

"It's too early for visiting," he grumbled. "We've only just got through breakfast."

Ashby turned on his charm. "I know it's a terrible inconvenience," he said. "I'm Mr. Lakefield's barrister, newly arrived in town. I have another case to try this morning, and I hoped to introduce myself before I have to be in court. If you'll bend the rules a little this time, I promise to be more considerate the next."

The keeper jangled his keys and after a moment's consideration, unlocked the door.

"The cells are open already, so's you won't need me from here. Holler when you want back out."

Thaddeus led the way down the long hall. Nelson Lakefield was lying on the narrow cot in his cell. He lifted his head when they stopped at the open door. "Oh, it's you," he said. He slowly sat up.

"This is your barrister," Thaddeus said. "We need to talk."

Lakefield showed no inclination to rise any further. He merely slumped back against the wall. "So you're the famous Mr. Ashby," he said.

Ashby entered the narrow space and stood, arms folded, while he regarded his client. "I am. And if you expect me to defend you, you'd better start telling me what you know."

"I already said everything I know."

"Might I remind you that your case goes to trial this week? And might I also point out that we have precious little evidence with which to argue your innocence?"

Nelson only shrugged in reply.

"Has anyone explained to you what will happen if a jury decides that you deliberately set the fire that killed Hazel Warner?" Ashby went on. "They'll put a rope around your neck, Nelson, and they'll hang you until you're dead."

His speech didn't have the effect Ashby was hoping for. Nelson's face remained stubborn. "But that's what you're for, isn't it? To get me off. Not that I did it," he added hurriedly.

"Did you know that some of your friends were in a street fight yesterday?" Thaddeus said.

"So?"

"Apparently the fight started with remarks some of your friends made about Hazel Warner's child."

"You can't blame them for that. There was something really wrong with it. That great purple blotch all over its face. Ugly as all get out."

"Some of your so-called friends said it looked just like you."

"That's a tired old joke. They've said it before. Name-calling, that's all."

"They also speculated that there might be more around that you didn't have time to do anything about before you were arrested."

The shot hit home. Nelson looked astonished, then his face set into a stony stubbornness.

"I don't know what you're talking about."

"The word 'hussy' was used. Another young man took exception and the fists came out. Who are the other girls Nelson? How many others have there been?"

At this point, Ashby jumped in. "Did any of them file suit? Or did your father just pay them to go away?"

Nelson was angry, and it made him incautious. "There's better ways to deal with them."

"Do you try to deal with Hazel that way too?" Ashby asked. "Is that how her baby got damaged? You tried to get rid of it and it didn't work?"

"Hazel's brat wasn't mine."

"So who were the others?"

"They were just common sluts," Nelson said. "Nobody important."

"Who's the girl your friends were fighting about?"

"Just some servant girl," Nelson said. "She doesn't matter."

"She doesn't matter as long as your father doesn't find out, isn't that right?" Ashby said softly. "You know, Nelson, it's quite immaterial to me whether I win this case or not. Your father will pay regardless. And you've already cost him a pretty penny, haven't you?

"Look, he doesn't have to know about it, all right? Just get me off, and then nobody has to worry about it."

"I'm not a magician," Ashby said. "Come clean and I'll do what I can, but unless you start telling the truth, I might just as well send them in to start measuring your neck."

With Ashby's words, the enormity of his predicament finally seemed to register with Nelson. He looked angry, frightened and confused. He took a few moments to think it through and then he said in a low voice, "I was with Nora Tobey."

"On the day of the fire?" Ashby asked.

"Yes."

"All day?"

"Yes."

"Will she vouch for you?"

"I don't know."

"What were you doing that day?" Thaddeus asked. But he was sure he already knew.

"We were over in East London. There's a woman there you can go to when pills don't work." Then he looked anxious again. "My father doesn't have to know about this, does he?"

"That depends," Ashby replied. "If she testifies in court, he's going to hear about it. If she doesn't, it's not likely to matter anyway, because you'll be dead."

"Where can we find this Nora Tobey?" Thaddeus asked.

"I don't know. She used to work for the Warners, that's all I know. They hired her to help with the kid."

"For the Warners?" Thaddeus was stunned at Nelson's audacity. Accused of one indiscretion, he'd had no compunction about perpetrating another – and with the woman who had been hired to deal with the results of the first.

"You might look over in Tipperary Flats," Nelson offered. "She has no family, so she may have ended up there."

"She no longer works for the Warners?"

Nelson looked astonished. "Of course not. Hazel's dead and so's the baby. Why would they need her anymore?"

"You've done very well," Ashby said. "Now we have something to work with. And if you think of anything else that might be helpful, you'll pass it on, correct?"

Nelson nodded, and a little of his bravado returned. "You'll get me off, right?"

"I'll see what I can do," Ashby said, but Thaddeus thought his response lacked enthusiasm.

As for Thaddeus, he was beginning to wish that they would just go ahead and hang Nelson Lakefield and be done with it.

It took Joe a long time to find the gang of boys they were looking for. They weren't on their customary street corners, but it was a Monday morning, and Martha supposed that the streets were not as busy as they might be at other times. People were only just stirring from the slow, reflective Sunday respite, not yet back into the full bustle of the work week. The boys would find few girls to heckle on a Monday morning.

Joe finally located them in one of the lots left vacant by London's fire, where the rubble had been cleared away but nothing had yet been rebuilt. Someone had leveled a piece of ground near the adjacent building, which had largely survived, and now the boys were throwing dice against its wooden wall. Joe had a wolfish grin on his face when he ran back to where Martha and Clementine were waiting and reported that Bill was amongst the group. "Give me some money," he said to his mother. "I can have some fun with this."

Clementine handed over some coins, then she and Martha followed him to the vacant lot.

"Now, remember," Clementine said as they approached the group. "We'll watch for a while, then when I move over to Bill, come up on the other side. We'll each take an arm and gently lead him away. With any luck, the others will be so engrossed in their game they won't even notice."

"Really?" was the only remark Martha could think to say in light of this rather extraordinary instruction.

"Just follow my lead. You'll be fine."

A number of young men were crowded around the players, watching the game. One or two of them looked up at their arrival, but the rest had their eyes fixed on the dice. Martha would never have dared come close to this group on her own, but the fact that she and Clementine were accompanied by a male seemed to grant them immunity to the kinds of remarks that she had come to expect from gangs of boys.

There was a pile of coins in front of one of the onlookers. He appeared to be taking wagers on the outcome of the next throw.

"Eight", the shooter called, and then threw the two wooden cubes along the ground. They bounced against the wall and ricocheted. There was a groan when they finally settled in the dust. The dice showed a five and a four.

"Chance seven," he called and threw again. There were several cheers when he threw a one and a two, and another shooter took his place.

"They're playing Hazard," Clementine whispered in Martha's ear after they had watched for a time. This information meant nothing to Martha. She had no experience with games of chance.

Two more shooters dropped out after a series of unsuccessful throws and Joe judged it was time to step forward. He called out his prediction, rattled the wooden cubes around in his hand and tossed. His throw didn't seem to settle anything, although Martha wasn't sure why. There was no decision with his next two throws either, then he appeared to fumble the dice, and one of them went shooting off sideways into the crowd.

"Sorry, misthrow," he said, and retrieved it.

After that, his luck seemed to change. He won on the next toss, and then the game started all over again.

Only Martha seemed to notice that Joe's fortunes had changed with his mishandling of the dice. He had added a tiny flick of the finger just as he let go. It was obvious to Martha that he was no stranger to the game, and that whatever he had done had affected how the dice fell.

Just as he was winning again, Clementine nodded over at Martha and shifted her position as if she were trying to get a better view. Martha did the same, moving slowly until she was right beside Bill.

As soon as Clementine was on the other side of him, she took his arm. He looked up, startled. Martha grabbed the other arm.

"Let's go for a walk, Billy," she said in a low voice. She jabbed the handle of her umbrella into his stomach.

"Wha..?" But she was already tugging him away. "Don't make a fuss, Bill. I just want to talk. And I brought my umbrella, just in case you're not in a chatty mood. But you'd be smarter if you just came along. Otherwise I'll stick you like a pig."

None of the players and only one or two of the other spectators noticed that Bill was being marched away from the crowd. None of them made any move to stop it. Clementine increased their pace until they were out of earshot and sheltered from sight by a nearby building.

"That should do," she said, although Martha noticed she didn't let go of Bill's arm, so Martha hung on as well.

"Let me go! What do you want?" Bill's eyes were wild with alarm, but Martha noticed that he made no real attempt to pull away. Apparently he was taking Clementine's warning seriously. He also looked quite the worse for wear from his fistfight of the day before. His face was bruised, and Martha thought his nose looked a little crooked. Poor Bill. He'd been out-classed three times now.

Clementine gave his hand a reassuring pat. "Poor Bill. It looks like you got beat up pretty bad yesterday."

"Nah, I did not! I gave as good as I got." A little of Bill's swagger returned, although he still slid wary glances sideways at Clementine.

"That's what I said to … whoever it was who told me about it. You must have been pretty angry though, to start a fight like that. Your nose took the brunt of it I can see."

"Aw, it's all right. Yeah, I was pretty mad. Is that what you want? To know about the fight?"

"I want to know why it happened," Clementine said.

Bill's mouth was set in a stubborn line. "He had no call to say what he did."

"Who?"

"Tom Rankin. One of the fancy Dans. He said she was loose."

"Who? Hazel Warner?"

"No," Bill said. "I don't care what they say about Hazel Warner. They was talkin' about Nora."

Clementine sighed. "You're not making a lot of sense, Bill. Why don't you start at the beginning and just tell me what happened."

Bill's face was screwed up in thought as he tired to marshal a coherent narrative. Along with his bruises and crooked nose, Martha thought the effort made him look rather like a gnome.

"They was talkin' about Nelson Lakefield and the Warner girl's ugly kid. Rankin said Nora Tobey's bastard would turn out just as ugly, and that's why she didn't want it. Then he called her a whore, and that's when I lit into him."

"Who is this Nora Tobey? Is she Nelson's young lady now?"

Bill snorted. "Not likely. She worked for the Warners and that's how Nelson got at her. He'd wait at the corner until she was done work, then he'd follow her."

"Did he force her?"

"No, not really. She was all happy about it at first – said she had a fancy boyfriend and would be set for life pretty soon. Then after he got at her, he made her get rid of the baby he made and she wasn't so happy no more. That's what Nelson does – if the pills don't do the trick, he trots 'em over to Gert Mossman."

Martha wanted to ask who Gert Mossman was, but Clementine shook her head slightly to warn her off.

"Them?" Clementine said. "How many have there been?"

"Nora, of course, and Minnie Storms - Gert damn near killed Minnie - Lettie Quinn. I heard she wouldn't go along with what Nelson wanted her to do, so old man Lakefield gave her some money to go away. I don't know where she went. I haven't seen Lettie in a long time. And Ethel Kelly, too. That's all I can think of right now."

One of the names tickled Martha's memory. Storms. The foreman who placed Nelson at the scene of the fire was named Storms. She was sure of it.

But Clementine had seized on an entirely different tack. "So why, in particular were you upset about what they called Nora?" she asked. Then she reached up and patted his cheek. "Aw, are you sweet on her Billy Boy?"

Bill turned bright red. The flush made a strange contrast with the purple bruises on his face.

"Yeah, I guess." And then the confession seemed to give him courage. "I was hopin' I'd get taken on at the cooperage and then I was gonna ask her if she wanted to court. But Nelson got to her first, before I could ask. And now he doesn't want her after all."

Clementine fixed him with a perplexed stare. "So tell me, Bill, why do you say such rude things to women in the street?"

He looked puzzled. "I dunno. We all do it, I guess."

"But you didn't like it when Tom said a bad thing about Nora. Didn't it ever occur to you that the women you pester have husbands and beaus as well. Don't you think they'd be upset too, if they heard the things you say?"

"But Tom meant it," Bill protested. "We don't mean anything when we do it. It's just a joke, that's all."

"Women don't find it funny, Bill. It scares them. And when they get scared, they start carrying umbrellas." Clementine poked him a bit, just to make the point. "Now, be a good boy and tell me where I can find Nora."

In spite of the umbrella threat, Bill was still prepared to be wary. "What do you want Nora for?"

"I just want to talk to her. I don't like Nelson Lakefield any more than you do. Maybe I can help her out a little."

"I guess that's all right then," he said after a moment, "if it means trouble for Nelson. Over in Tipperary Flats. She moved in with an old woman. Old Annie."

"Good boy!" Clementine said. "You've done just fine." She let go his arm and reached into her pocket. She pulled out a banknote and pressed it into his hand.

Bill looked astonished. "That's all you want? Just to know about Nora?"

"That's all I want. See how well things can go when you're not unpleasant to ladies?"

"Gee, thanks."

"Just before you go can you answer one more question?" Martha said.

Bill's face fell, as though he should have known better than to believe it had all been so painless. "What?"

"This Minnie Storms, who almost died – what's her father's name?"

Bill's face cleared. "Jeb. Jeb Storms. He's the one that saw Nelson at the warehouse."

And with that he bounded away, clutching his money.

Clementine beamed at Martha. "That went well, don't you think?"

"Yes, it did. What should we do now? Go get Joe?"

"Good heavens, no. We'll stay well away from the game in case he needs to make a hasty exit. He'll meet up with us later. And I have an errand to run, so that suits my purposes."

She led Martha back along the main street until she found a jeweller's, a different one than they had visited before. Again, she spent some time looking at the rings and brooches, then inquired if the store dealt in resale items. When the clerk answered in the affirmative, she drew a pearl necklace from her pocket and held it out for his inspection.

"This is quite lovely," the clerk said. "He held the necklace up to the light, then, to Martha's surprise, rubbed it against his teeth before he took a small eyepiece and inspected it closely.

"First quality," he said. "You don't often see such fine pearls here. What are you asking?"

Clementine named a figure, then haggled over the price until she seemed satisfied. She pocketed the money and motioned for Martha to follow her out of the shop.

"And now, she said. "Let's look at shoes. I think I'd like a new pair of dancing slippers."

Ashby would be tied up in court for most of the day, but he

suggested that everyone meet in the hotel sitting room before dinner.

"I'm anxious to hear how Mrs. Elliott made out with Bastard Bill," he said with a grin. "If nothing else, it's sure to be entertaining."

Thaddeus agreed, and set off for the Lakefield house, where he hoped to find Nelson's father. Lakefield hired a manager to run his foundry, according to Earl Jenkins, and only occasionally attended at his place of business, so he was apt to be at home even though it was a Monday morning. He might be in better financial condition, Thaddeus thought, if he did a little more of the work himself.

The door was opened by the same squat housekeeper who had answered before. Thaddeus was informed that Mr. Lakefield was "not receiving" at the moment.

"Get him anyway," Thaddeus said. "Tell him his barrister has some questions."

The maid looked frightened and started to close the door.

Thaddeus put out a hand to stop her. "I'm not waiting on the step. Let me in and let him know I'm here. Either that or get out of the way and I'll get him myself."

She relented, but left him standing in the hall. The parlour was to his right, Thaddeus knew. That was where he and Martha had been shown to on his previous visit. He took a few steps further down the passageway. There was a door to his left. He opened it. It was Lakefield's library, spacious, with book-lined walls, thick carpets and a massive oak desk. It was the sort of library Thaddeus could only dream about having.

He walked over to the bookshelf, scanned the titles, then pulled down one of the books. To his disgust, he found that the pages had never been cut. The book had never been read. He replaced it and pulled out another. It was the same. The books were for show. Thaddeus had always read whatever he could get his hands on, but it was never enough to satisfy him. He couldn't afford many books. Certainly not books like these. And yet here they sat, where no one ever looked at anything but their leather-bound exteriors.

He put the book back on the shelf, then walked over to the desk and sat down, not in one of the chairs that were obviously meant for visitors, but in the chair behind the desk. Mr. Lakefield's chair. He idly opened the top drawer. It was full of the usual accessories – pens, rulers, wax, seals. He opened the next one. It was full of papers.

He pulled them out. They seemed to be invoices and receipts from Lakefield's foundry. He put them back and opened the bottom drawer. More papers, bound together, and a ledger.

He folded out the topmost bundle. "Well isn't that interesting," he said aloud. It was a mortgage taken out on Albert Warner's warehouse and issued by Lawrence Lakefield. The document had been witnessed by Earl Jenkins.

Thaddeus quickly flipped open the other bundles. They were all deeds to properties that were identified only by lot, concession and township. He didn't know where any of them were, but if he were a betting man, he'd put his last dollar on them being along the routes of proposed railway lines. He'd also wager that Albert Warner's drawers were full of similar deeds.

He set them aside and opened the ledger. It did not hold, as he expected, details of the ebb and flow of business at Lakefield's foundry. It was a personal record, amounts on the credit side apparently flowing in from the foundry, but on the debit side, other than the minimum needed to run his household, there were only recurring amounts for repayment of mortgages. Lakefield must have taken every penny he could spare and plowed it into the purchase of lands. Even with a cursory inspection, Thaddeus could see that the payments were bleeding him dry.

It had all been a gigantic roundelay. Warner owed money to Lakefield, but didn't have enough to pay up. When his daughter turned up pregnant, he hoped to recoup some of his losses by filing the seduction suit. Lakefield wanted no part of Hazel and her child, but he didn't have enough money to simply settle out of court.

Had one of them hatched the notion of burning down the warehouse? It would solve at least some of their problems quite neatly. Monies from the insurance on the warehouse would go first to clearing the mortgage, which would give Lakefield cash in hand. And with the mortgage paid off, Warner's troubles would ease, at least temporarily. Neither of them could have anticipated that Hazel would be present when the fire was set, or at least Thaddeus hoped they hadn't.

Follow the money. If what he suspected was true, who had gained the most? Hard to say, but he didn't need to decide anyway. All Ashby needed was reasonable doubt. A little seed planted in the jury's mind.

The rationale for Nelson's arrest had been shaky at best. Both Warner and Lakefield, Sr. had far better motives for setting the fire, although Thaddeus suspected that the prosecution might argue that Lakefield had sent his son to strike the match.

And then there was the eyewitness, Jeb Storms, the watchman who claimed to have seen Nelson leaving the warehouse that night. Unless Storms' testimony could be shaken, there might still be a noose around Nelson's neck. And, he suddenly realized, around his father's as well, if his financial situation was disclosed in open court. No wonder Lakefield had hired Ashby, in spite of the cost. He was desperate.

There was no point, Thaddeus decided, in confronting Lakefield with the information he had discovered. Lakefield would simply deny it all. He shoved the ledger and papers back into the drawer he had found them in and walked back out to the hall just as the housekeeper was coming down the stairs.

"Mr. Lakefield insists that he is not receiving today. You'll have to come back some other time," she said.

"All right," Thaddeus said. "Goodbye."

"Warner or Lakefield?" Thaddeus asked when everyone had gathered in the sitting room just before supper. "Either of them would have benefitted from a convenient fire, if Lakefield's accounts are anything to go by."

"I thought you had principles," Clementine said.

"The Lakefields obviously don't," Thaddeus replied.

"That makes it all right to rifle someone's desk? It's something I might have done, but I thought you were all upright and everything."

"Now, now, that's enough," Ashby said. "Honestly, you two can scarcely be in the same room for five minutes before one of you starts an argument. London is all atwitter with breathless accounts of your public squabbles, you know. I heard all about it at the courthouse today."

"We don't squabble in public," Thaddeus said.

"Yes you do," Martha said. "That's all you've done since she got here."

Thaddeus wanted to reply that it was Clementine who had started this one, but he realized that it would make him sound like a six-year-old. Ashby saved him from having to reply at all.

"If need be, I can subpoena both Lakefield's and Warner's financial records, but I'd much rather surprise the prosecution with this. The simplest thing to do is to put one of them on the stand and ask about it."

"Won't they lie?" Clementine asked.

"They'd be under oath," Thaddeus pointed out.

Clementine shrugged. "So?"

"They won't dare," Ashby said. "If I ask a specific question about the mortgage, they'll know that I know it exists. Neither of them will run the risk of having the other contradict him."

"But if Lakefield is first in line for the insurance money doesn't that give Nelson an even better motive?" Martha asked. "Wouldn't a jury think that Nelson was just doing his fathers dirty work for him?"

Ashby grinned. "Logical as always, Miss Martha. Yes, it would supply a motive, but not the one the prosecution has built its case on. There's an advantage to going second. And it would be a toss-up whether the jury figured it was Nelson or his father. That's reasonable doubt – and that's all I need."

"And if they decide it was Mr. Lakefield who set the fire, he'll probably keep you on for his trial, in which case you'll get to bill him twice," Clementine pointed out. Ashby roared with laughter.

"That's hilarious," he said, "and also perfectly accurate. I love it. You and Martha should open your own law firm. Martha can supply the argument and you can do the accounting."

"What about the foreman, Jeb Storms?" Thaddeus asked. "I haven't been very successful in finding him. Do I still need to?"

"If you can. I'd like to cast some doubt on his testimony as well," Ashby said. "The prosecution argument hinges almost entirely on Storms' identification of Nelson at the scene. And as Mrs. Elliott and Martha so deftly discovered today, Storms has a reason for wishing harm to Nelson Lakefield. I'm assuming he must know about Nelson and his daughter. After all, she almost died." He mulled this over for a few moments. "Let's see what the Tobey girl has to say first. If she's willing to vouch for Nelson's whereabouts, that's all we need. Try to find Storms as well, if you have time, but I don't really expect him to change his story."

"What about this Gert person?" Martha said. "Couldn't she confirm that Nelson was with the Tobey girl?"

Ashby shot a glance at Thaddeus before he answered. "You could ask her questions from now until the end of time," he said. "She's unlikely to say anything at all, given the nature of her business."

"I suppose you're right."

"Even if Gert would talk, Nelson could then be faced with the charge of procuring a miscarriage. It's a far less serious charge than arson, of course, but given the current climate, the court would definitely take a dim view of it. And then, of course, his father would find out about it as well, which is the prospect that really seems to have him terrified."

"I wonder how many other girls he's got into trouble?" Clementine said. "I expect they all tried Beecham's Pills first and ended up with Gert as a last resort. You can get those here, can't you? In the States you can buy the stuff at any pharmacy."

Thaddeus wondered at her familiarity with the subject. But then it would have been difficult to have a brood of children when she was so often on the run, he supposed. He and Betsy had never made any attempt to limit the number of their children, but had welcomed each one as it came. And then he realized with a start that he really didn't know if that was true. If Betsy had taken steps, she had never told him about it. And it had never occurred to him to ask. It had been women's business, and in his time, men had been expected to stay out of it.

"Attitudes are changing," Ashby said. "It used to be that it was perfectly acceptable, as long as it was accomplished in the early stages, but the courts are starting to crack down on the whole business. It's my understanding that the powers-that-be are alarmed by the falling birth rate in the better classes and the rather astounding fertility demonstrated by immigrant women. Especially the Catholic ones. They're starting to make size of family a concern of the state, and that's reflected in changing laws."

"Typical," Clementine said. "Men decide and women pay."

Martha was following the conversation closely, and Thaddeus suddenly realized that in most circles, this topic of discussion would be considered highly unsuitable for a young woman's ears.

Fortunately, Joe arrived at that moment and everyone's attention turned to him.

"Did you have a successful day, my dear?" Clementine asked.

Joe grinned. "Cleaned them out. What a shame we weren't playing for bigger money."

"By the way, somebody owes me for the stake."

Joe was reaching into his pocket when Ashby rose to his feet and said, "Oh, just get Thaddeus to put it on the bill. Now I suggest that we go to the dining room for the early sitting. After all, we have a concert to attend this evening."

It was just a few minutes after ten when Martha returned to her room. She must have seen that Thaddeus had a lamp burning, because she knocked on the connecting door and poked her head in to say good night.

"How was the concert?" he asked, looking up from the book he was reading.

"It was all right, I suppose," she said. "It was all a little wasted on me, since I have no idea if it was any good or not. The others decided to go to one of the taverns afterwards. I didn't want to go, so Joe walked me back."

Thaddeus knew that "didn't want to go" really meant "didn't think she should" and he was grateful that Martha was so mindful of his convictions. It was hard for a young girl to resist the temptation to go along with friends.

"May I talk to you for a minute?" he said. The conversation of that afternoon had been bothering him all evening.

"Of course." She came and sat at the end of the bed.

"Ummm…" he wasn't sure how to start. For the millionth time, he wished his wife was still alive. He could have left this conversation to her. "Did you understand what we were talking about in the sitting room earlier? The business about the woman named Gert? You looked like you had some questions."

To Thaddeus's enormous relief, Martha said, "Yes, I understood. If I looked puzzled it was just because I was trying to figure out whether or not any of it could prove useful to Ashby, that's all."

His relief must have shown in his face, because she went on, blushing a little. "You wouldn't believe how women talk when they think there's no one else in the room. I know what Beecham's Pills are. I didn't know for certain about the other thing, but I suspected it."

"I wasn't sure how much your stepmother might have told you, that's all."

Martha hesitated for a moment before she spoke. "I don't know if it's really up to me to tell you this, but Sophie lost another baby a couple of months before I left Wellington. She was taken quite suddenly, and I was the only one around to help her." Martha shook her head. "It was a bit ridiculous. As soon as Francis came home, I sent him for the midwife just to be on the safe side and as soon as she got there, I was hustled out of the room as though I hadn't already taken care of everything."

"I'm sorry," Thaddeus said. "You shouldn't have had to do that."

"It's all right. It was a good thing I was there. There was an awful lot of blood. Anyway, in Sophie's case it wasn't on purpose, but the end result was the same, so don't worry, I wasn't shocked by anything anybody said this afternoon." She sighed. "It was just...sad. The poor little thing was already dead and Sophie wanted her so much. It doesn't seem fair, does it? Why does God let these things happen?"

"I don't know," Thaddeus said. It was a question he had asked himself many times, but beyond the standard response that "It's God's will" he had yet to come up with a completely satisfactory answer.

"Oh well," she said, getting up. "There really isn't anything we can do about it, is there?" She leaned over and kissed him on the head, one hand on his cheek. "Good night, boss."

Just as she reached the door to her room she stopped for a moment and looked back at him, a bemused expression on her face. "Isn't this is a really odd conversation for a girl to be having with her grandfather?" Before he could reply, she went off to bed, closing the door behind her.

CHAPTER 13

Ashby and Thaddeus were the first ones downstairs for breakfast again the next morning.

"Did you enjoy the concert last evening?" Thaddeus asked.

"Oh, the concert was acceptable enough," Ashby said, "but the company was extraordinary. Your Mrs. Elliott is quite something, isn't she?"

"She's not my Mrs. Elliott."

"No, that's right – she's Mrs. Lewis, isn't she?" Ashby teased. "Or at least that's what people seem to think. Is she really Jewish?"

"I have no idea. I doubt it. I don't think she's anything but a charlatan," Thaddeus said. In spite of the fact that it had been amusing at the time, he was beginning to regret having let Clementine go with him to the Sunday meeting. Especially since it appeared that reports of her performance had spread so fast.

"I like her. She's fun."

And Thaddeus was left to wonder what kind of fun Clementine had got up to the previous evening, especially if she got up to it with Ashby. Oh well, none of his business, really, was it? She'd be leaving soon anyway. Just as soon as Ashby got the papers together.

"Who's fun?" Martha joined them at the table.

"Mrs. Elliott," Ashby said. "And here she is herself."

Clementine floated into the dining room and beamed at Ashby.

"Good morning."

Joe was behind her. As usual he took a chair beside Martha, but rather than beginning a huddled conversation with her as he usually he did, he spoke to Thaddeus. "Martha says she's going with you to find the Tobey girl today."

"Yes. She's more apt to talk if there's another girl there."

To Thaddeus's surprise, Joe objected to the plan. "That's kind of a rough end of town. I don't think Martha should go."

"Is it?" He was surprised that Joe knew so much about London after only a few days.

"It's a shantytown," Joe said. "There are a lot of migrants. If anything happened to you…"

"Fair enough," Thaddeus said. "I'll go by myself. Although I'm not sure how successful I'll be."

"I have a suggestion," Clementine said. "First of all, I agree that you'll have far better results if a woman talks to her, but I don't think it should be Martha. I think it should be me. A woman and a preacher won't be threatening, but if something should happen, I can take care of myself."

Thaddeus was surprised that Martha was making no objection to being left behind. And then he realized that Clementine was, for her, dressed quite plainly. There had obviously been a discussion that he had not been privy to, and everything had been arranged to everyone's satisfaction but his own. He had no wish to spend the day with Clementine. But he couldn't think of any convincing reason not to go along with the plan.

"It's too far to walk, and if it's a shantytown we can't take a cart," he said. "Do you ride?" It was the only thing he could think of that might get her to stay home.

"Not well enough to take a horse on my own," she said, "but I can certainly ride pillion."

And with this objection dealt with, she turned her attention to bantering flirtatiously with Ashby, until the young barrister finally rose and announced his departure.

"I'm devastated that I have to leave you with the most unsatisfactory Mr. Lewis as a companion, but duty calls," he said to Clementine. "My apologies."

"You'll have to make it up to me later," she replied. "In the meantime I'll endeavour to cope."

"We'd best be on our way as well," Thaddeus said. "I'm not sure how long this is going to take."

"I'll just get my things."

She returned wearing a plain cloak and a subdued bonnet that was unlikely to draw much attention. She also carried her umbrella.

"Why do you need that?" he asked. "It will only get in the way."

"I can tuck it into my belt once I'm on the horse," she said. "Are you going to be this disagreeable the whole way?"

"Possibly," he replied. "I'm a very unsatisfactory companion."

"Oh don't be so sour," she said as they went down the hotel steps. "Towns is only teasing you."

"You and he seem to be getting on awfully well," Thaddeus grumbled.

She looked at him with mock astonishment. "Oh my goodness, is that jealousy I hear?"

"Of course not."

"I'm astounded. And here I thought you had a heart of stone."

"I'm not jealous."

"Towns is a charming boy, but I'm fairly certain that any attention he pays to me is intended purely to catch Martha's eye."

"But Martha doesn't like him," Thaddeus objected. "I think she liked him a bit when she first met him, but now she's scarcely civil to him."

"That's what he finds so appealing. And now all of a sudden Joe is in the picture, too. That's really made him sit up and take notice."

This wasn't news that Thaddeus wanted to hear. He had been relieved when Ashby had fallen out of Martha's favour. Ashby wasn't the sort of man he wanted for his granddaughter. And he suddenly realized that he hadn't considered Joe at all, although he should have. He wasn't sure how he felt about Joe. Martha had been pleased to see her old friend, of course, but was it really a budding romance? He knew so little about the boy. Not for the first time, he wondered if he hadn't been hasty when he decided to take responsibility for an adolescent girl.

"You may be right," he said finally. "I'm not very good at reading these things. My wife was far subtler than I, and she sorted things out with the children. Any advice for a poor old obtuse preacher?"

"Don't do anything. Martha's quite capable of dealing with it all by herself. You, on the other hand - you're a different story."

"What do you mean by that? What have I done?"

"Nothing. And that's the problem. You nurse your wounds far

too long Thaddeus."

It was one thing for her to comment on Martha, he felt, but quite another for her to stick her nose in his affairs.

"You have no right to say that. You don't know anything about me."

"Yes, actually, I do. I know you grieved a long time over your wife, and fair enough – you loved her very much. It's a shame that you got hurt again just as you were getting past it, but that was nothing more than bad luck. And it doesn't even compare in magnitude. You need to chalk that one up to experience and get on with things."

She could only be talking about what happened in Cobourg.

"How do you know about that?" Thaddeus demanded. "Did Martha tell you?"

"Of course not," Clementine said. "I tried to worm it out of her, but she wouldn't tell me a thing. I think you can rest assured that Martha will take your secrets to the grave with her. Towns Ashby, on the other hand, is a perfectly wonderful gossip."

Thaddeus was speechless. The monumental gall of the man, to confide the details of another's personal life. He had half a mind to pack his bags and leave on the next train.

"Don't be angry with Towns," Clementine said. "He's very fond of you, and sorry about the way things turned out. He's only trying to help."

"How dare you? How dare either of you interfere in my business?"

Their altercation was once more drawing curious looks from people on the street. Clementine stared back at them until they turned away. Then she took Thaddeus's arm.

"You can't keep it bottled up forever, you know." Her tone was glib. "You're going to have to talk to someone about it sooner or later. It might just as well be me, since I'm such a good listener."

He pulled his arm away. He was seething. What had happened in Cobourg was a matter between God and himself, not a thing that could be trotted out and exclaimed upon by a casual acquaintance. Particularly not someone like Clementine Elliott. Or Towns Ashby, for that matter. A proven huckster and a callow youth who was well on the road to becoming a drunkard. What right had they to judge?

What right had anyone?

And then that small annoying voice at the back of his mind piped up – it was the voice that spoke when he least wanted to hear. Was that not, after all, the purpose of a Methodist meeting? To own up to one's failures and seek help in addressing them? To ask God to judge – and to forgive?

And yet, he had never been able to confide his shame and embarrassment to anyone. Was it possible that Clementine was right? Did he bottle things up, mumble over them, treasure them, almost? He had held his grief over Betsy's death close, until his son Luke had cracked it open and spilled it into the light. Was he doing the same with the humiliation he had suffered in Cobourg?

He had no time to think it through. They had reached the stable.

After a brief discussion with one of the grooms, Thaddeus chose a grey mare that he was assured was mild-mannered. The horse was a little small to carry two people, but Thaddeus would trade speed for temperament any day. They would take it slow, and it was not so long a ride that the mare would be too taxed.

The stableman helped Clementine up into the saddle behind Thaddeus. She wrapped her arms around him, which she quite rightly needed to do to stay on the horse, but he was acutely aware of her physical proximity. They rode without talking, Clementine seemingly unconcerned with his sulky silence.

Their destination was at the northwest end of the town, far past the old barracks and Lake Horn. It was not hard to find. Tipperary Flats was, as Joe had described it, a shantytown, a huddle of small wooden houses and shacks. It would fill up with people as the harvest ended and labourers were no longer needed on the farms. Here they would stay to nurse their earnings over the winter, until spring came again and it was time to fan out over the district in search of work.

The laneways were too narrow and twisting to make riding easy. Thaddeus slid out of the saddle and reached up to help Clementine to the ground, holding her steady until he was sure she had found her balance.

It was Clementine who asked directions, inquiring not for Nora Tobey, but for "Old Annie".

"Anybody with a name like that is apt to be known by

everybody," she explained.

It was a good strategy. They were soon directed to a shack at the end of a muddy path.

Thaddeus rapped on the door, hoping the force of the knock wasn't enough to cause the flimsy structure to fall over. An old woman with straggly grey hair answered.

"Sorry to bother you," Thaddeus said. "We're looking for Nora Tobey."

"Who wants her?"

"Someone who's willing to pay for information," Clementine said quickly.

The old woman slammed the door.

"I never said anything about paying her," Thaddeus protested.

"Trust me, it's the only way you'll get anything out of her."

The door opened a crack.

"Can we talk to you? Just for a minute?" Thaddeus asked.

"Old woman says you'll pay money for talk." Judging by her thick Scottish accent, she could not have not been in this country long.

Clementine was right, Thaddeus thought. It would be the easiest way. "Yes, we'll pay," he said. He hoped Ashby's pockets were as deep as they seemed.

The door opened further and Nora stepped out into the laneway. She could have been a pretty girl if she were cleaned up, but her hair was lank and dirty, the skirt of her cheap dress muddy, her shoulders slumped as a hedge against the next blow the world chose to send her.

"What do you want to know?"

"Do you know Nelson Lakefield?" Thaddeus asked.

The girl's suspicious face hardened still further. "I hope he hangs."

Clementine poked him to be quiet, then tried a different approach. "We're trying to find out what happened to Hazel Warner." Thaddeus noticed that she had adopted a Scottish-sounding brogue. Not as thick as the girl's, but unmistakable.

The girl shrugged. "Hazel got herself into a mess all right. She should've married Nelson when she had the chance. Then maybe he'd have left me alone."

"Did Nelson get at you?" Clementine asked softly, her face set in a concerned sympathy. "Did he force you?"

Nora shrugged again. "Not exactly. More like pestered me to death. Every time I turned around, there he was."

"And after a while you gave in?"

"At first it was all right. He gave me things. Nice things. Then he said if I didn't keep doing what he wanted, he'd tell the Warners and I'd lose ma job. I lost it anyway, didn't I? As soon as Hazel was gone, they didn't need me nae more." She glared at Thaddeus. "Nice clean work it was, too. Not like workin' in the fields."

"You looked after Hazel's baby?"

For the first time, the girl's face softened. "Aye, I did. Poor wee mite."

"Did Hazel ever tell you who the father was?"

"No, but I think it must have been somebody down along the high street. After the baby was born the Warners wouldn't let her go enna'where by herself. Even goin' to the market, I had to go with her." Nora eyed Thaddeus suspiciously. "Is this just between us?"

"Yes," Thaddeus said. He hoped it was true.

"Sometimes she'd tell me to make ma'self scarce while she ran an errand or two. I don't know who she went to see, but she'd come back cryin'. Seems like the father didn't want the baby enna'more than the Warners did. Only one wanted her was Hazel. Hazel loved her in spite of everythin'."

"Did you make yourself scarce on the day of the Orange Parade?" Thaddeus asked.

"Hazel told her father that we was goin' to watch the parade. Like I said, they'd let her out if I went with her. We weren't out of the house five minutes before she told me to go away. Suited ma purposes, all right. But the next thing I knew, she was dead in the fire an' Mr. Warner was yellin' at me because I didn't stay with her."

"Where did you go that day?"

The girl looked at him appraisingly. "Tha'll cost you a lot, to know that."

Clementine poked him again.

"Your friend Bill got into a fight the other day," she said.

"That's na strange," Nora said. "Bill likes to fight."

"The fight was about you."

That surprised her. "It was?"

"Yes," Clementine said. "One of Nelson's friends called you a name and Bill didn't like it. And then this other fellow said that your baby would be just as ugly as Hazel's."

"There's no baby," Nora said.

"But there was, wasn't there?"

"It's gone," Nora said. "Gert took it. It near killed me."

"When was this?" Thaddeus already knew the answer, but he wanted to hear it from the girl.

He was met with a stony silence. He reached into his pocket and drew out a wad of notes. Nora eyed it greedily. He shuffled the notes, as though he were counting it, while she watched.

"The day of the parade," she said suddenly. "When they was all marchin' through the streets. There was nobody around, see? They'd all gone to watch. And then, afterwards, I couldna find Hazel, so I went back to the Warners. Might better've stayed in bed. It's what I wanted to do."

He counted out five notes and handed them over.

"Did Nelson go with you?"

Nora nodded. "He wanted to make sure I went through with it. Waited in the next room while Gert did her business. At least he helped me afterwards. I half expected him to bugger off once the deed was done."

"Would you…" he began, but Clementine jumped in before he could ask the question.

"Do you have anybody to look after you now?" she asked instead. "Or are you all on your own?"

"Old Annie's been good to me," she said. "Lettin' me share the cabin an' all. Other than that, there's none. They're long gone. Died of the fever. I'm hopin' to get a little work at the woollen factory. I'm hopin' I don't have to go to one of the houses o'er in East London. I'm about done with men." And then she spat, as if to emphasize her point.

Clementine grabbed Thaddeus's arm and picked off four more notes to give to Nora. And then she took off her hat and pulled out the silver clasp that held her hair in place. Her dark locks tumbled in profusion down over her shoulders. She handed the clasp to Nora.

"I hope you'll wear this, at least for a little while," she said. "But if you have to sell it, don't do it cheaply. It's real silver."

Nora snatched it out of her hand and shoved it into her pocket along with the money. Then without a word she turned to go back into the dilapidated shack. Just before she disappeared, Clementine called out to her. "You should give Bill a chance."

Nora stopped. "Why?" she asked.

"He took a beating for you."

She nodded once and was gone.

They turned and picked their way back along the muddy paths until they reached the road and were able to ride again. Thaddeus climbed into the saddle first, then kicked the stirrup loose for Clementine. She nonchalantly hitched up her skirts, affording Thaddeus a good view of a very shapely leg. He couldn't diplomatically look away. He needed to grasp her arms in order to haul her up to the back of the horse. Once settled, she wrapped her arms around him again.

The wind was at their backs as they rode. Occasionally a gust caught Clementine's loose mane of hair and blew it against Thaddeus's face. It smelled of some rich perfume, an exotic scent from some faraway place.

He made no attempt to brush it away.

Clementine enjoyed having her arms around Thaddeus. He seemed disinclined to talk and she was content to ride in silence. From time to time, she leaned her head into the back of his neck where the hair curled over his collar and breathed in deeply. He smelled of soap, mostly, a clean smell punctuated by a hint of that scent that was his alone. It was pleasant, after the last eighteen months of old-man smell.

She'd met Frederick Bellingham at a resort hotel in Bristol Springs, just outside of Philadelphia, where he'd gone to avail himself of the spa facilities. She'd gone to avail herself of whatever she could find. It had been an extravagance – the hotel was expensive – but as she was traveling as Lady Flora Hargrave and affected an English accent to give credence to her aristocratic claim, it would have seemed odd to stay at a lesser establishment.

The extravagance had paid off. She'd caught Bellingham's eye and stirred his curiosity. He had that peculiar fascination with the English that so many self-made American men had, and it was an easy thing to steer him into a hasty marriage. It was an added bonus that his failing health precluded much in the way of onerous duty on her part. It was companionship the old man was really after. Clementine figured she'd fulfilled her part of the bargain – she'd kept him entertained until his feeble spirit finally sputtered out one night.

But it turned out that he hadn't kept his. There was supposed to have been provision made for her in his will, but when she finally finagled a copy from Bellingham's lawyer, it was clear that he hadn't changed it as promised.

The Bellingham children had been outraged by the marriage in the first place, so she knew that there would be no generous gesture on their part. They laid claim to everything – even down to the presents of jewellery Fred had bought her.

Eighteen months of comfortable living had in no way dulled Clementine's instinct for survival. She knew it was time to cut and run. She packed up the jewellery, the small pieces of silver and as many easily sellable household effects as she could cram into her trunks. And then she turned her attention to the safe that was hidden in the library behind the row of Sir Walter Scott's poetry. She'd discovered it by accident one day when she was looking for something to read to Fred. She had been unable to find the key, but after a few attempts to get it open by herself, she had prevailed upon Joe to pick the lock.

What she found inside took her breath away. There was only a small amount of cash – Fred believed in banks and kept most of his money there, out of her reach. There were bundles of papers that proved to be stocks and bonds of assorted varieties. She left these where they were; they were too easily traceable.

But a wooden box at the back of the safe yielded treasure; a gold watch, five rings with rubies and sapphires and emeralds, and the most stunning of all, a diamond necklace, the centre stone of which was enormous. She would have to take a discount on it, she knew, but when she sold it, it should yield enough to keep her for years. But it made her escape more dangerous.

She didn't know if the Bellingham children or even the Bellingham lawyer knew about the safe, but the jewellery must have been belonged to Fred's first wife and his children would be looking for it. She doubted that they would chase her far to reclaim the other bits and pieces she had taken, but they might be very persistent indeed if they were after the diamond necklace.

Suddenly, London had seemed an ideal hidey-hole. Who would ever look for her in a small town in the wilds of Canada West? And when she collected the Elliott money, it would keep her afloat until she found a buyer for the diamond.

London was as safe a place as anywhere to be right now. Thaddeus's presence was merely a bonus. She had been sincere when she said she'd missed him. True, he was a preacher - often too sanctimonious for her taste and on occasion more than a little pompous - but he was one of the few men she had ever met who was clever enough to keep up with her. He was a challenge that she had looked forward to. She'd been disappointed to find that the stretch of years since they'd last crossed swords had worn down his edges, and that although he remained suspicious of her, he wasn't particularly interested in unmasking her. Only when she needled him did the old sharpness surface, and then it was fun again.

Before long, they reached the centre of London. They returned the horse and then started walking back to the hotel. Clementine took Thaddeus's arm. He made no attempt to pull it away.

"You were awfully generous to that girl," he said.

"At one point in my life, that could have been me, if it hadn't been for Jack."

"Jack who we buried in Wellington? Was he really your husband?"

"Husband, partner, Joe's father. I'd have ended up in gaol if it hadn't been for Jack. And after gaol…" she shrugged. "I've never been quite as successful without him. I still miss him."

"I know what you mean," Thaddeus said, and Clementine knew he was thinking of his dead wife.

She let him have a few moments of reverie before she pounced. "The woman in Cobourg was a fool, you know."

He pulled his arm away. "I'm not talking to you about that."

"After what I just did for you? Now, there's gratitude. Anyway, I figure she should have snapped you up."

"It wasn't that simple."

"Oh, I know, she was married and it went against all your stiff-necked Methodist principles to feel any kind of attraction for her and all that blarney. So it didn't work out. Stop feeling so sorry for yourself. She was a fool and you're better off without her."

"I don't feel sorry for myself."

"Yes you do. You figure if you just pray hard enough you'll get whatever you want, and then you get sore when it doesn't happen."

"What do you know about it? What do you know about anything?"

"I know there's no point in beating myself up about things that don't work out. And I know there's no point in praying for anything. God does what He likes, whether it suits us or not."

"That's nonsense. God can work miracles. We have only to ask him."

She was unimpressed by his vehemence. "Yes. Just not necessarily the ones we want."

"We have no way of knowing God's plan."

"So what's the point of asking in the first place? Just live your life and let God get on with whatever He's doing, since nobody can figure out what it really is anyway. For all I know He could wake up tomorrow morning and decide that I'd make a good Pope."

"Now that would be a miracle."

"Why? I would be a really good Pope. My first decree would be that Thaddeus Lewis should smile a little more often."

"That is utter blasphemy."

"I don't see why you think so. You're not even a Catholic."

He stopped walking and whirled to face her. "Look, if you're interested in a serious discussion about the state of your soul, I will be happy to speak with you anytime. If you're going to persist in being flippant, then stop wasting my time."

"But these are serious inquiries, Thaddeus. These are questions I've been asking for a long time. And nobody seems able to provide adequate answers."

"Pray to God for answers."

"That hasn't done you much good, has it? I would think that if He provided answers for anyone, it would be someone like you."

Thaddeus's face was thunderous. "The devil is a woman who speaks with a crooked tongue."

"No," Clementine said, taking his arm again. "The devil is a woman who sees through all your nonsense."

He brushed her off and strode up the steps of the hotel ahead of her. She could see that he was very angry. It was going to be an entertaining evening.

CHAPTER 14

As soon as they were inside the hotel doors, one of the clerks came bustling up to Thaddeus to deliver a message, but not without first raising an eyebrow at Clementine's disheveled appearance.

"Mr. Ashby is waiting for you in the downstairs sitting room."

"I'll just go and tidy up, then I'll meet you there," Clementine said. She patted Thaddeus's arm as she left.

Ashby was lounging in the most comfortable chair in the room, a drink in his hand.

A waiter hovered near the door. "Would you like anything sir?" he asked.

"A pot of tea would be most welcome," Thaddeus said. "And some cookies if possible?" He was getting far too used to this life of wants met on demand, but just then he was grateful for it.

Ashby held up his glass. "And another of these?" he said. The waiter nodded and departed.

"I hear you've been arguing with your wife again," Ashby said. He seemed to be highly amused by the report. "You certainly have set London on its ear in the short time you've been here. Nobody seems to know who exactly you are, but everybody knows about your extremely stormy marital relationship."

"It doesn't seem to be getting any calmer either," Thaddeus replied. "We just had another set-to on the hotel steps. I'm sure you'll hear about it tomorrow. And by the way, I'd appreciate it if you kept my private affairs private. There was no call to tell Mrs. Elliott about Cobourg."

Ashby seemed surprised. "Oh. Sorry. I didn't think it was a secret.

Everyone in Cobourg knew all about it."

Ashby was right. Cobourg knew. All the Methodist Episcopals knew. Mealy-mouthed Calvin Merritt knew. Was there to be no end to this torment?

"Besides," Ashby went on. "When I arrived it was clear that Mrs. Elliott was fully apprised of the details of our current case. I naturally assumed that she was in your confidence."

Thaddeus had no answer to this. He should never have included her in the investigation. It had been a severe breach of confidentiality. But if he hadn't let her help, would he ever have got this far?

"Speaking of which," he said, desperate to change the subject, "we have some interesting information to pass on."

"I hoped you would. After all, the two of you have been gone all day. I'm pleased to hear it had something to do with the case." Ashby's tone was light, which took the sting out of his words.

"Nora Tobey confirmed that Nelson was with her on July twelfth. He trotted her over to East London to take care of her little problem. She also said that Hazel Warner was seeing someone on the main street, but she didn't know who, and that Hazel had asked her to make herself scarce on the day of the fire. Nora tried to find Hazel later, so they could return to the Warner house together, but, of course, she was dead by then."

"Do you think she would testify?"

"Not willingly. She hates Nelson, but it took quite a lot of money to get her to talk to us at all."

"I suppose I could call her, but I don't like putting a hostile witness on the stand. And her story doesn't exactly speak to Nelson's good character, does it? The jury won't like it."

"I don't like it either. I'm really having second thoughts about all this, Towns. I'm not sure I care whether Nelson Lakefield is found innocent or not."

Ashby nodded. "I understand what you're saying. And you're right, Nelson Lakefield is a dreadful young man. But consider this – just because a man is guilty of some crimes, it doesn't necessarily follow that he's guilty of all the ones he's accused of. And even if he's guilty, he is still entitled to a defence. The rule of law must apply. Otherwise, we descend into chaos, with the mob deciding our fates."

"But sometimes it seems as though it's all just a trick."

"The only trick is getting the court to weigh other possibilities. That's why we have the concept of reasonable doubt. I have no idea if Nelson is guilty or not. I don't want to know, because it makes no difference to me. My job is to provide him with a defence, and I will do that to the best of my ability. It's up to the court to make of it what they will, but I won't let him be hanged because I failed to do my job."

That was fair enough, Thaddeus supposed, and he was impressed that Ashby, as cavalier as he could sometimes be, operated from a set of principles that he was able to articulate so well.

Just then the waiter, Clementine, and Martha converged on the room all at once. Clementine had made short work of restoring her coif, and had changed from her dust-covered traveling clothes into a dress more suitable for the dining room.

"Oh good, I'm starving," she said when she saw the plate of shortbread the waiter set down beside Thaddeus. She reached forward and took one.

"Hey, those are mine," Thaddeus said. "Get your own."

"The waiter can bring more." She held the plate out to Martha. "Would you like one?"

"Yes, actually, I would," Martha said. "And I'd love a cup of tea."

"I'll bring more cups too," the waiter said and departed.

When Joe came in a moment later, he too walked over to the tea tray and selected a biscuit, which he jammed into his mouth whole. Clementine and Martha giggled. Thaddeus sighed and poured himself some tea before anyone else could claim the single cup on the tray.

He took a sip and settled back in his chair. "Just to bring everyone up to date," he said, although it was really for Martha's benefit, "we found the Tobey girl and she confirmed that Nelson was with her on July twelfth, but I'm afraid there's little hope that we could ever get her to confirm it in court."

"There's something I don't understand," Clementine said. "The Warner girl sued Nelson for seduction. Why couldn't Nora Tobey have done the same thing? She would have had a child to weigh her down, but at least she would have got some money, wouldn't she?"

"The suit was actually brought by Hazel's father," Ashby explained. "In this country, that's the only way it can be done."

"And Nora has no father to sue on her behalf," Thaddeus said.

"Remember – she said her whole family died of the fever. And Nelson took care of things in his usual manner – not ideal from Nora's point of view, but taken care of all the same."

"So what are you going to do?" Clementine asked Ashby.

"The circumstantial evidence is pretty weak and I can probably cast enough doubt to get the charge dismissed. But if I can't, I'll have to find some way to introduce Nelson's alibi. Your and Mr. Lewis's testimony would, unfortunately, be struck down as hearsay, I'm afraid." He shrugged. "If I have to haul Nora Tobey into court, I will, but I'd prefer not to. And now, since both you and Mr. Lewis are here and not actively warring at the moment, I have those documents you were looking for."

He pulled some papers from his valise and handed them not to Clementine, but to Thaddeus. "I assume you're willing to attest to Mrs. Elliott's identity?"

Fair was fair. Thaddeus had more or less said that he would expedite matters for Clementine if she helped with the case. And it seemed a simple enough document, outlining the circumstances of the bequest and requiring only a signature to the effect that the money was being given to the woman Thaddeus had known as Clementine Elliott. Since that was the name he knew her by now, he saw no difficulty in signing it.

"I suspect the best thing to do would be to keep this with my files," Ashby said when Thaddeus handed the papers back to him. "That way we know where it is should any question arise. And now, Mrs. Elliott, if you'll sign the receipt, I can give you a bank draft."

She borrowed Ashby's pen and signed. Thaddeus noticed that she misspelled "Elliott", putting only one "t" at the end. It had been a long time, apparently, since she had used the Elliott name. He didn't bother pointing it out. It probably didn't matter. Ashby handed her the draft.

"Thank you." She tucked it away in an inner pocket.

"I suppose this means you'll be leaving now," Thaddeus said.

"Don't sound so hopeful. Having become involved in all your affairs, I have half a mind to stick around to see how everything turns out."

"I'm not going anywhere," Joe announced. "At least not for a couple of days. Martha and I have a picnic planned for tomorrow."

"I have to pick up the report from the phrenologist before we go," Martha said. "He said Wednesday. It's Wednesday tomorrow, isn't it?"

"Oh," Clementine said. "That means my picture will be ready as well. Perhaps I'll give it to Mr. Lewis as a memento."

"I don't need it," Thaddeus said. "Try as I might, you're hard to forget."

And they were off again, trading barbs while Ashby laughed and Joe and Martha did their best to ignore them.

After supper Clementine announced that she was staying in that evening. "I know you're looking for entertainment, but I'm so tired I can hardly keep my eyes open. I'm not used to riding a horse so far."

"You didn't really ride it," Thaddeus pointed out. "You just hung on while I rode it." But he, too was tired. It had been a long day.

"I need to sponge down my dress," Martha said. "It got pretty dusty this afternoon."

"What did you do today, by the way?" Thaddeus asked. He couldn't believe that it hadn't occurred to him until then to ask.

"Joe was teaching me how to throw a 'last resort' with a set of dice. Don't be alarmed, I'm not about to engage in any games of chance. I was just curious about how he manipulated them, that's all."

"And?"

"If you flick them a certain way, one of them will shoot off sideways." She had the grace to look a little shamefaced as she explained. "It's easier to substitute dice that are weighted on one side while everyone's scrambling to find the one that went astray."

"In other words, you were learning how to cheat." Thaddeus glared at Joe, who merely shrugged.

"It's not like I'm ever going to use it," she pointed out. "I just wanted to know how it was done. But I spent a lot of time rooting around in the dust looking for the dice that went flying."

Ashby smoothly deflected the conversation away from Martha's activities. "I'm on my own tonight then?"

Joe gave him a speculative look. "I heard there's a regular card game at the back of Arthur's Saloon. Are you interested?"

"I could be. What kind of stakes?"

"I don't know. But I'm sure we can find a way to raise them, if that's what you have in mind."

Ashby nodded and he and Joe rose from the table. The others lingered for only a few minutes more before they left the dining room and went to their rooms.

Thaddeus read for a while, but he soon grew sleepy and had already climbed into bed when there was a knock on his door. When he answered, he was surprised to see that it was Joe.

"You're looking for Jeb Storms, right? He's at the saloon, holding forth in the tap room."

"Where's Ashby?"

"I don't know. He lost a lot of money and got tired of the card game. Then he went off with somebody."

Thaddeus had no doubt that Ashby had lost the money to Joe and that the somebody was female, but it was none of his business, really.

"Come in. I'll just be a minute."

Joe stood impassively while Thaddeus threw on his clothes and jammed his feet into his boots. Then he went to Martha's door and rapped. She was in her nightgown, and looked alarmed when she saw that Joe was with her grandfather.

"We're just going out for a little while. Joe's found Jeb Storms."

She nodded, and quickly closed the door.

As they walked along the street, Thaddeus tried to formulate how he was going to approach Storms. He'd like to find out how firm the man was in his identification of Nelson Lakefield, but at the same time he didn't want to tip Ashby's hand. Trust Ashby to disappear just when Thaddeus needed some advice.

Arthur's Saloon was on a side street and jammed in between two taller buildings. Its seedy-looking exterior was in no way beautified by the three drunken men who lolled in front of the entrance. Inside was a bar room much like every bar room Thaddeus had ever been in. Scarred wooden tables, sawdust on the floor, the rank smell of beer and smoke and spittoon. He couldn't now imagine why he had ever wanted to linger in such a place. But he had, once, long ago. Before Betsy. Heads turned as he and Joe walked to a table near the door. Thaddeus should have known that he would be unable to slip in unnoticed. Everyone had been speculating on his presence in London. Now, they would have no doubt as to why he had suddenly shown up at Arthur's Saloon on the eve of the trial when Jeb Storms was there too.

Joe nodded toward a table at the opposite end of the room, where a large scruffy-looking man was regaling five others with loud conversation. "Storms is the talker," he said in a low voice.

Thaddeus took careful note of the men who were listening to him. Two of them were quite small. One of them was quite old. But the remaining two were nearly as large as Storms. This could be trouble. Thaddeus had to remember that he no longer had the protection of his clergyman's clothes, which in the past had often served as a deterrent for people wanting to pick a fight.

One of the men leaned over and said something to Storms, then gestured in Thaddeus's direction. Storms turned and stared. Thaddeus stared back.

Joe broke the impasse, for the moment, by getting up to fetch two glasses of beer. He brought them back to the table and set them down. Thaddeus ignored his. After a few more minutes staring, Storms stood up and walked over. There was a sudden hush as everyone watched to see what would happen.

"You the investigator?"

Storms' speech was slurred. He must have been drinking heavily all evening.

"Yes. I've been looking for you."

"I don't know why. Everybody knows Lakefield did it."

"I don't," Thaddeus replied. The room was very quiet. Everyone was listening intently.

"I saw him."

"Are you sure? Nelson Lakefield is such an unremarkable young man I'm surprised his own mother can identify him."

There was laughter at this.

"I don't doubt that you saw a man," Thaddeus went on, "but why are you so sure it was Nelson?"

" 'Cause I'd know that son of a bitch anywhere," Storms hissed.

"I haven't been actively investigating Mrs. Lakefield," Thaddeus said, "so I'm not sure who you're referring to."

There was even more laughter at this, which seemed to rankle Storms.

"Are you bein' smart?" he sneered, leaning over the table.

"Yes," Thaddeus said. "I'm very smart. Which is why I'm

wondering if Albert Warner told you to set the fire, or did he just tell you to blame Nelson for it?"

This obviously wasn't what Storms expected to hear. His face wrinkled up in confusion. "What are you talkin' about? Warner didn't tell me nothin'."

"Oh, I see. So it was your idea? To punish Nelson for what he did to your daughter?"

That was going too far, and Thaddeus knew it as soon as he said it. Storms let out an angry roar and lunged across the table. But before Thaddeus could even stand up and kick his chair out of the way, Joe, in one almost continuous motion, threw his beer in Storms' face and shot a leg out sideways to throw him off balance. Storms fell, bashing his chin against the wooden table.

"Run," Joe said.

Thaddeus shot a quick glance at the men who had been drinking with Storms. The two largest were getting to their feet. Thaddeus ran. He and Joe burst out the door, almost tripping over one of the drunks in the entranceway. In an effort to avoid them, Thaddeus landed badly, and when he regained his balance he just caught a glimpse of Joe disappearing around the corner. Thaddeus ran toward him, trying to put on a burst of speed that just wouldn't materialize.

I'm too old for this. I'm not going to get away.

He could hear voices behind him, as his pursuers stumbled over the same drunk.

Joe grabbed his arm as he rounded the corner and pulled him down an alleyway and into the shadow of a shed at the rear of the building. He held a finger to his lips. Thaddeus was gasping from the run and his knee hurt, but he tried to be as silent as he could while he caught his breath. He heard footsteps go past the alley, then stop and return.

"Did they go down here?" The words were slurred.

"I dunno, maybe." The second voice sounded much closer. "It's awful dark."

"Ah, forget it then. Let's go back to the tavern. Jeb Storms ain't worth this much trouble."

The footsteps retreated. Joe signaled for Thaddeus to wait while he made sure the men had really given up. He disappeared into the darkness, but was back a few moments later.

"Give them a couple minutes more, just to make sure. I didn't know you were going to start a fight."

"There didn't seem to be any point in beating around the bush. You're a good man to have in a tight spot, Joe."

"I've had far too much experience. When we get back out on the street, I think we should go the other way and circle around to the hotel, just in case. There's no point in walking right past the saloon so they can find us again."

"I hope that wasn't one of your favourite drinking spots."

"I'm not going to worry about it," Joe said. "They were so drunk they probably won't remember that I was there. It's a good thing I was, though. Otherwise they might have caught you."

Joe was right, they would have. Thaddeus was far too old for this nonsense.

CHAPTER 15

The next morning, Martha very nearly cancelled Joe's picnic when she heard what had happened to Thaddeus the night before. She blamed Joe for leading him to the saloon in the first place.

"Why didn't you find Ashby and let him take care of it?" she asked.

"I didn't know where he was," Joe said. "All I knew was that everybody was looking for Jeb Storms."

"It's all right, Martha," Thaddeus said. "I'm fine and Joe did the right thing."

"But you're not fine," she protested. "You've hurt your leg again."

"It's feeling better," he said. "I got up early and soaked it in the bath for a half-hour. That did the trick."

"And Joe did do the right thing," Ashby said.

"Did he?" Thaddeus asked. "I was afraid I'd just tipped Storms off."

"No, he must know he's going to be questioned pretty closely in court. After all, a man's life is at stake."

"He seemed genuinely puzzled when I suggested that Warner had a hand in it. I'm beginning to think that we've got hold of the wrong end of the stick."

"But if neither Warner nor Lakefield set the fire, then who did?" Martha said. "And why?"

"It doesn't matter," Ashby said, as he stirred sugar into his third cup of coffee, "as long as I can get a jury to believe that it wasn't Nelson."

Martha thought Ashby looked dreadful. His eyes were red and his hands shook a little, rattling the cup in its saucer. She was pretty sure she knew exactly where he'd been and what he had been doing the night before. But he downed half his coffee in one gulp, and then he seemed to perk up a little.

He looked at Thaddeus for a long moment, and then he said, "Would it be possible for you to come to court with me this morning?"

"Of course."

"I'd like you there for the jury selection. I'm sure news of your confrontation with Storms is all over town, since you seem to be all anybody can talk about at the best of times. I'd like to see the reaction when you turn up in court. With any luck, you've planted a seed of doubt in one or two minds and we can take advantage of it."

"I'm at your service. I've nothing else to do today anyway, since Martha is deserting me."

"Is she?" Joe asked, turning to Martha for the answer.

"I'm provoked with you," she said.

"Does that mean you don't want to go?"

"I didn't say that. I see no reason to spoil the entire day over it. As long as you understand that I'm provoked, and likely to remain that way for the next little while."

"Yes, ma'am," said Joe.

"Oh my," said Ashby.

"Don't look at me," Thaddeus said. "I'm just relieved that she's not provoked with me as well."

Clementine wondered if she was making a mistake by staying in London now that she had Nathan Elliott's money safely in hand. As soon as Ashby handed it over, her first instinct had been to board the next train. So far it appeared that she had covered her tracks effectively. Mrs. Frederick Bellingham had, to all intents and purposes, disappeared. No one in Philadelphia knew her as Clementine Elliott. No one in London knew who she was at all, the most common speculation, fed by the silliness at the Methodist meeting, was that she was Thaddeus's wife. That suited her plans. It was another layer of gauze over her true identity, but she needed to move on soon, before anyone thought to start checking facts.

But Joe had made it clear that if she left before he was ready to go, she would be going by herself. She still needed Joe, for a little while at least. He would have to be her advance man, checking out the reliability of any merchants who might be interested in the diamond necklace she had taken. Once it was sold, she would have plenty of money. She could take her time and look around carefully for the next opportunity.

And then she and Joe would part company. It was the way of the world, she supposed. Sooner or later sons left their mothers, but in spite of the fact that he was often sulky and difficult, his departure would leave a big hole in her life. He had been her anchor ever since his father died.

She was sure he had no idea where he would go yet. For all she knew he would circle back and find Martha again, still looking for something he thought he'd lost.

She'd have another chat with him this evening, and point out that it was dangerous to stay here much longer. In the meantime, she decided, she was finally ready to get out of bed. She'd brush down her dresses and fuss with her hair for a while, go to the bank and walk over to Strong's Hotel to retrieve her picture from the daguerreotypist. After that, she had nothing more to do with her day but look forward to another round of squabbling with Thaddeus.

Martha stood on the steps of the hotel basking in the sunlight while she waited for Joe. He couldn't have chosen a nicer day for a picnic. It was still quite warm for October and the sky was bright blue with no prospect of rain.

He appeared with a wicker basket in hand. "The hotel made up some sandwiches for us," he said. "I thought we could eat them at the lake."

"All right. But I have to go to Dr. Scott's studio first."

"I'll go with you." He seemed determined to salvage their outing.

Martha would let him, eventually, although she still felt mildly annoyed that he had led her grandfather into such peril. Joe was wisely silent as they walked.

Now that she was about to see her analysis, Martha was curious as to what it would say about her. Thaddeus had made it clear that he thought phrenology was nonsense, and she had only agreed to have her head examined in the hope that she might elicit information from Scott, but she hoped it didn't say anything awful. She would retrieve the report, she decided, then she would relax her air of disapproval so she and Joe could spend the rest of the day laughing about it, no matter what it said. It was too nice a day to do anything but have fun.

There was no one in Scott's shop when they entered.

"Hello?" Martha called.

There was no answer. "I guess he's not here," she said. "Maybe we should come back some other time."

But the skulls and the strange diagrams had caught Joe's attention. "What's 'alimentiveness'?" he asked.

"I have no idea. I'm hoping the report will explain it all." He seemed in no hurry to leave, but moved on to peer closely at another row of skulls.

Martha took a few steps toward the desk near the door to the back room. Its surface was piled high with a jumble of items. She was looking idly at this when her own name caught her attention. It appeared to be the bill for her reading. A newspaper lay over the bottom half, obscuring the total. She knew that Ashby would cover the cost of the consultation, but she would have to pay Scott first and reclaim the money on the account that Thaddeus was running. She hoped she'd brought enough to cover it.

She reached out and pushed the paper aside, and gasped when she saw what else was underneath it. The wooden, box-like frame of a daguerreotype had been left lying open to reveal the picture inside. It was of Hazel Warner. Martha reached out and picked it up for a closer look. It was exactly like the one they had been given by Nelson Lakefield.

At that moment, she heard footsteps from beyond the door. She tucked the picture into her pocket and took a hurried step back.

Richard Scott appeared in the doorway. "Sorry. I'm with a client."

"I only came to collect my reading," Martha said. "I didn't mean to disturb you."

"I'll get it for you." To her relief, he went, not to the desk, but back into the examination room. She pulled the daguerreotype from her pocket and was just reaching to put it back on the desk when Scott reappeared. She shoved the picture back into her pocket.

Scott handed her a package. "There you are."

Martha counted out the money she owed, then stood wondering what excuse she could find to linger in the shop.

"Thank you for attending," Scott said. He was evidently anxious to have her leave.

"Ready to go?" Joe asked. He was already holding the door open for her.

She would have to find some way to return the picture later.

She was reluctant to show it to Joe when they got out onto the street. He would tease her about taking it, even though she hadn't meant to. She also wondered if she should take it straight to Thaddeus. But Thaddeus was in court with Ashby all morning, and tracking him down would eat into the day that she had promised to Joe. It could wait until later, she decided. The picture seemed to be a direct connection between Scott and Hazel Warner, but she wasn't sure whether or not it got them any closer to discovering who had set the fire.

She didn't know what Thaddeus would make of her theft of the daguerreotype, even if it did turn out to help the case. She needed to make him understand that she'd meant to put it back, but couldn't figure out how to do it without admitting that she had been snooping. She would tell him that night and if he decided it wasn't important as a clue she would simply take it back to Scott and apologize profusely.

Joe broke the silence. "Do you want to go to the lake now? Or would you rather sit down somewhere and read your report? I'm dying to know what it says about you. 'Excitable'would be my guess."

Martha knew that this comment was a peacemaking gesture on Joe's part and she decided she had been angry long enough. "What do you mean 'excitable'? I'm not excitable!"

"Quick to anger," he added. He began to laugh.

She batted him across the shoulder, but he kept laughing.

"And a tendency to violence. I wonder if there's a bump on your head for that?"

"I don't know. But keep it up and I'll give you a real bump on your head."

That only made him laugh all the harder.

Balance restored, they teased each other all the way to Lake Horn, a tiny man-made body of water beside the military parade grounds.

"Is it even big enough to row on?" Martha asked when she saw it. "It looks like you could jump across it." She was used to lakes that were more like inland seas.

"That's why I suggested it instead of the river. I've never rowed before. This way if we capsize we can probably walk to shore."

They found a grassy bank, where Joe set down the wicker basket that contained their picnic and Martha spread out the blanket she had taken from the hotel. She plunked herself down, stretched out her legs, and reached for the basket.

"Are you hungry?" she asked.

"Yes, but I want to hear what's wrong with your head first."

She opened the package Scott had given her and pulled out a bundle of papers.

"Oh my," she said. "There's rather a lot, isn't there? It's no wonder it took so long for him to write it up."

"Maybe you just have a lot of undesirable characteristics," Joe said.

"Or maybe it's full of praise," she returned, and then she began to read,

"First order – Feelings, First Genus – Propensities."

"Ah, the impulsive part," Joe said. He scooted over beside her so he could read over her shoulder.

Concentrativeness – The area is moderate in size, indicating an over-developed power of riveting attention on one subject, resulting in tediousness.

"Oh my."

"Now there I have to disagree," Joe said. "You are many things, but you are not tedious."

Philoprogenitiveness. She stumbled over the unfamiliar word.

"An inability to read?" Joe suggested.

She ignored him. *Moderate. Showing an indifference to children and pets.*

As Martha read on through the endless list of categories separated into order and genus, she discovered that she was weak and irresolute, quarrelsome, crafty, deceitful and given to intrigue, while at the same time proud, arrogant, over-bearing and desirous of applause.

"Really?" she said, dismay in her voice.

"No, not really," Joe said. "You're none of those things."

Amativeness, she went on. *Moderate. Fastidious in selecting a lover with a tendency to be cold and reserved.*

"I certainly hope you're fastidious," Joe said, "but I'd guess you're anything but cold and reserved." And as if to prove his point, he leaned over and kissed her lightly on the cheek. She was flustered by this, but not at all displeased. To cover her confusion, she read on quickly, then began to laugh.

"All right, now I know for sure that this is nonsense.

Tune: Medium. Only an average talent for music.

"Why is that nonsense?" Joe asked.

"You've never heard me sing, have you? I'm not even average. I'm tone deaf. It's so bad that when I was eleven years old my grandfather took me aside and suggested that I just pretend to sing the hymns in church. I kept throwing everybody else off."

"So you're not perfect then?"

She was laughing so hard she didn't notice the wistfulness in his voice. "Far from it. Especially when it comes to music."

Joe covered his remark quickly. "I wonder why Scott gave you such an unfavourable analysis? Do you think he was trying to warn you off? All that stuff about crafty and deceitful and - what was it? – given to intrigue. Maybe you asked too many questions and he hoped that you would be so annoyed that you would never darken his door again."

"Do you think he might be Hazel's lover?"

Joe shrugged. "He could have been, I suppose. But even if he was, that doesn't mean he set the fire."

"No, it doesn't, does it?" Her discovery of the picture didn't really advance the investigation very far at all. It might provide a motive for someone other than Nelson Lakefield, but that was about it. She took the top sheet of the report and began folding it.

"What are doing?"

"Making a boat. I think we should make a whole bunch of paper boats and float them on the lake. It's not as if this nonsense is good for anything else."

Clementine thought she looked quite lovely as she regarded her reflection in the mirror. She'd spent most of the morning playing with her hair and had finally arrived at a style she was happy with. She put it in a knot at the nape of her neck as usual, but she braided the sides, looping them under her ears and tucking them into the bun. The braids were visible under her hat. It was really quite fetching.

She wondered if she should take a ring or two with her when she went out, but then she decided that she had disposed of enough items for the time being. After all, she had the Elliott money, and she'd already sold the gold watch and a strand of pearls. Better to wait until she was in another town to deal anything more.

Heads turned when she stepped into the London branch of the Bank of Montreal. Several distinguished-looking gentlemen tipped their hats as she made her way to the counter. It was the reaction she had been hoping for, and she graciously nodded in return.

The clerk studied the bank draft for a long moment, then jotted down some numbers on a piece of paper.

Clementine tensed. Had Ashby added some lawyer-trick to keep her from getting the money after all?

"Is there a problem?" she asked.

The clerk looked up at her and smiled. "No, not at all. I'm required to check very carefully because of the amount, that's all. But the draft is made out to "bearer" and it's from an escrow account, so I don't see any difficulty. Are you sure you want to take it all in cash?"

"Quite sure, thank you." So Ashby hadn't double-crossed her after all.

She deposited the money in a string-purse that she'd brought for the purpose, then as soon as she was out on the street again, she ducked down a side alley, unbuttoned her jacket and slid the bag inside her bodice.

She would go to the daguerrotypist's first and then maybe she'd visit a milliner's or a dry goods store. If she could find something pretty, she'd get some new ribbons for her hair. She could thread them through the braids.

Charles Pearsall was nowhere in sight when Clementine entered the lobby of Strong's Hotel, but the clerk reported that he was "just out the back" and would be with her in a moment. He emerged a few minutes later, carrying a case which proved to be full of carved wooden boxes.

He smiled at Clementine. "Choose the one you like, and then I'll pop the picture in. It won't take long."

She pointed to a filigreed frame made of some dark wood that she thought was a little prettier than the others.

"Excellent choice," Pearsall said and disappeared again. Only seconds later, he returned.

"I forgot to ask you if wanted copies or just the one," he said. "A copy can be made at any time, but it's a little easier to do before it goes into the frame."

"You can make copies?"

"Yes. Basically I take a picture of the picture, so there's a slight loss of definition, but not much."

"Do many people get more than one?"

He grinned. "Not enough of them. It would be more lucrative for me if they ordered copies for everyone in the family. But most seem to think one will do."

Since Clementine had a vested interest in making sure that not too many people knew what she looked like, she decided it was most prudent to decline.

"I'm sorry," she said. "I really have use for only one."

"That's all right," Pearsall said. "I just thought I'd ask." And then he disappeared again.

He was gone a lot longer this time. Clementine stood waiting in the hall, while she thought about what he had said to her. She hadn't known that it was possible to make copies of a daguerreotype. She wondered if Hazel Warner had had a copy made. It would explain why both her father and Nelson Lakefield had been in possession of her picture.

Pearsall finally returned and laid the frame on the hotel desk, flipping it open so she could see her likeness. She looked quite pretty, she decided. Her head was tilted slightly and she looked directly into the camera with a small, mischievous smile on her lips. Clementine was quite delighted with it, and so, apparently was Pearsall.

"Most subjects look stiff, because they sit still so long, but you managed to maintain an animated expression without moving. I'd love to make a copy of this just so I can show customers that it's possible."

"I'm not entirely sure I can agree to that," Clementine said, and Pearsall's face fell.

"Oh," he said. "I hoped you'd be flattered."

"And I am. But surely you have other photographs that would do as well?"

"Not as nice as this."

A foolish thought floated through Clementine's mind and she gave voice to it before she really thought it through. "I'll trade you," she said.

"What do you mean?"

"You may make a copy of my picture in exchange for some information. I know you're reluctant to discuss the Warner girl, and I'm not sure why that is…"

Pearsall looked wary. "I have no real reason except that I don't know anything and I don't want to get involved."

"Then I'm sure you'll have no objection to answering my question. How many copies of her picture did you make?"

"She asked for two. She took the original away when it was ready, then she came back a few weeks later and got two copies. She said they were for other members of her family."

"Thank you."

"That's it? That's all you want to know?"

"Unless you can think of something else that might be useful."

"Not really. As I said before, I have no interest in the case other than not wanting to be drawn into it. So… I can make a copy of you?"

"Yes."

"I'll need to keep the original for a day or so then."

"That's fine. I can come back. I'll be at the Western for the next few days."

She exited the hotel wondering what on earth possessed her. A copy of her daguerreotype would place her in London on a specific date should anyone come looking and might well lead them to wherever she went from here. But knowing that there was one more copy of Hazel Warner's picture could help solve the Lakefield case. It was a foolish risk. She didn't know why she'd done it. Except that, she suddenly realized with a pang, she knew that it would help Thaddeus.

CHAPTER 16

After their day in court Ashby and Thaddeus returned to the hotel and headed for the sitting room. One of the waiters saw them and asked if he could bring them something in the way of refreshment. Ashby ordered a drink. Thaddeus again asked for tea, but this time suggested that multiple cups and a very large plate of biscuits might be in order.

The court proceedings had been long and tedious, mostly taken up by preliminary formalities and the selection of jurors, but Thaddeus had to admit that the young barrister's instincts were good. As soon as the many spectators spotted him with Ashby, they had begun to lean over to their neighbours and whisper.

Thaddeus knew that they were probably passing on an account of his previous night's confrontation with Jeb Storms. He had no way of knowing how much of the story would reach the jurors.

And there had been a bonus.

The sheriff drew a card from a box and called out a name. The man who stepped forward was the older gentleman who had been drinking at the same table as Storms. Thaddeus nudged Ashby and shook his head.

"Objection!" Ashby called out.

He was allowed to reject up to twenty jurors without cause, so with no further ceremony, the man was directed to stand down.

Earl Jenkins turned and glared at Thaddeus's intervention.

After that, the selection continued without further comment from anyone.

Testimony from the coroner and two constables occupied the rest of the afternoon. There were no surprises. Dr. Bratten's account was much the same as he had reported to Thaddeus and the constables repeated the information that had been in their statements.

Thaddeus hoped that Ashby wouldn't ask him to attend the next day.

Just as the waiter was arriving with their order, Clementine flounced into the room. She had dressed her hair differently, Thaddeus noticed and seemed very pleased with herself.

"Guess what I found out today?" she said, reaching for a teacup. "Hazel Warner had two copies of her picture made. The daguerreotypist told me."

"Three altogether?" Thaddeus said. "So Nelson had one, Albert Warner had one. What happened to the third?"

"I'll warrant if you can find that out, you'll know who Hazel's lover was," she said.

"I expect we would," Thaddeus said. "But how do we do that? Go around and knock on doors and demand to see what pictures people have on their mantelpieces?"

"I found out what," Clementine said with an air of high dudgeon. "The how is up to you."

"I'm not sure we need to find out," Ashby said. "All I need is a little doubt planted in the minds of the jury. Since the prosecution's case rests almost entirely on the notion that Nelson was the baby's father, the existence of a third picture can be used to insinuate that he wasn't. There's not much motive left if that's the case."

"See?" Clementine said. Thaddeus ignored her.

Just then Joe came in.

"How was your picnic?" Clementine asked.

"It was great. The hotel made some sandwiches for us, but we ate them all up a long time ago. I'm hungry as the dickens again." He dove for the biscuits.

"Why didn't you get sandwiches for us yesterday?" Clementine said to Thaddeus. "You could have arranged it just as easily as Joe did. Honestly, you could be a little more thoughtful."

"We weren't exactly on a picnic," he pointed out. "Where is Martha now, Joe?"

"She said she wanted to get cleaned up before dinner, and that she'd meet us here. She'll be along in a minute. Can we order some more cookies?

Martha looked forward to finding out what had happened in court that day, and to sharing her own discovery, but first she needed to change her clothes. After they had eaten their picnic, Joe found a man who was willing to rent them his skiff for a couple of hours. Joe proved to be terrible at rowing. At first he didn't seem to realize that he needed to pull the oars evenly, and they spent several minutes going around in circles while Martha giggled. He frequently caught crabs and one time nearly upset the boat. Then he concentrated on creating huge splashes of water with the oars, until Martha reached down for a bailing can, filled it and threatened to dump it over his head.

All in all, it was a most satisfactory outing, but now her dress was quite wet and muddy along the hem. She'd drape it over the back of the chair to let it dry for now, and sponge it off later.

She slipped into her best dress, which looked quite lovely with the new trim attached to it, but she was annoyed to discover that the edges of one of the frogs was already starting to pull loose. Clementine was not much of a seamstress, and she had sewn them on in a hurry. Martha would have to redo them at some point, but just then she was in a hurry to join the others.

She slipped the picture of Hazel Warner into her pocket, tidied her hair, slid into her leather slippers and skipped down the stairs.

When she reached the bottom, a porter stopped her to say that he had a message for her.

"The gentleman you travel with...", he evidently was taking no guesses at the exact relationship between she and Thaddeus, "...Mr. Lewis? He wants you to meet him outside."

"Did he say why?" Martha asked. When it was clear that Thaddeus wasn't in his room, she had assumed that he would be waiting in the sitting room.

"I didn't speak with him directly," the porter said. "Another gentleman relayed the message."

It must have been Joe or Ashby, she decided. She hesitated for a moment. She hadn't realized that she would be going outside again. She had no cloak. And although the day had been warm, it was

October and the evenings cooled off quickly. She wondered if she should run back upstairs and grab her cloak or a wrap, then decided that she should go and see what her grandfather wanted first. If he needed help, he would expect her to come straight away.

She stepped out into the night. The porter hadn't given her any indication of where she should go. The street was quite empty, with only a pedestrian or two off in the distance. It was suppertime. Most people were at their dining tables. She walked south toward Dundas Street. If she didn't see her grandfather by the time she reached the first intersection, she would turn around and go the other way.

She was only half-way to the corner when she heard a voice call from an alleyway that led from the street. She hesitated, unwilling to step into such a dark place without knowing what lay in wait for her. "Grandpa?" she called.

"Come quick, he's been hurt," a voice called back. And without thinking about it a moment more, she rushed into the darkness.

She could just make out the shape of a horse, and behind it a wagon. When she stepped into the alleyway, she had expected to see Thaddeus lying on the ground, some good Samaritan bent over him, or doubled over in agony, clutching his chest and gasping for breath. She could see no one. Something wasn't right.

She turned to go back to the street. She would go for help. Better to lose a little time than venture any further into the darkness on her own.

She had taken only a step when someone wrenched her arm and clapped a hand over her mouth, then dragged her over to the wagon. She was flung over the side so hard that the breath was knocked out of her and she couldn't scream in the split second before someone stuffed a wad of cloth into her mouth. Her arms were pulled roughly behind her back and rope wound tightly around her wrists. She tried to kick at her assailant, but he grabbed her legs and tied those too. She was helpless as he bound her gag in place and unceremoniously threw a blanket over her.

Her heart was pounding and she found it difficult to catch her breath through the cloth that had been jammed into her mouth. She twisted her hands frantically, trying to pull them free but they had been too firmly tied. She was helpless.

Calm down. Breathe.

She forced herself to take air in through her nose in measured breaths and she was rewarded when her heart stopped thudding quite so wildly. The wagon started to move. She tossed her head free of the blanket that covered it and then twisted her hands again, but she couldn't bend them far enough to discern where the knot might be.

Think. There must be something you can do.

She wondered if she could get herself upright, so that someone might see her and intervene. The wagon stopped after rolling forward only a few feet. The driver must be waiting to make sure that no one would see him when he pulled out into the street. Even if she were able to sit up, she knew that there would be no one to see her. It was suppertime. Everyone was inside. A fresh panic hit her.

Calm down. Think.

She needed to get free of the ropes that bound her. She tried to pull her hands apart, but there was little give in the knot. And then one finger brushed against the loose edge of the decorative frog braid that held her left pocket closed. Her dress had been rucked up and pulled sideways when she was thrown so roughly into the bed of the wagon. She strained her arms, shifted her body to one side, and found that she could reach the frog just well enough to stick her little finger through a loop. She pulled. Nothing. On the second try, she yanked as much as she was able, and was rewarded when it ripped partially away. One more hard tug and she had it.

She needed to find a way to leave the frog in the open, out on the street, so her grandfather would know she had been there when he came looking, for there was no doubt in her mind that Thaddeus would look for her when she failed to appear in the sitting room.

She kicked at the blanket and pulled it away far enough so that her hands were exposed. She would have only one chance. She would need to flick it over the side of the wagon. Hard. Just like Joe had shown her how to do with the wooden dice. She squirmed around until she was facing away from the back of the wagon, and then when it lumbered onto the street, she let the piece of braid fly.

She had no way of knowing if it had cleared the side of the wagon, or where it landed. But at least she had done something, and that was better than lying there helpless.

She braced her feet against the side and rolled herself over. Now her dress was bunched up under her and she had to wiggle herself forward in order to straighten it out enough to reach her other pocket. The fastener on this side was a little more firmly attached, but after several hard tugs, it too came free. Again, she flicked it as hard as she could. This time she could see that it cleared the side and landed in the road.

She didn't have a hope of leaving any more – the rest of the frogs were clustered on the bodice of her dress and it wouldn't matter how hard she craned, she could never get her hands around that far in front.

Think.

She didn't know how far she would be taken, or how long she would be in the wagon, but surely there was something else she could find, some identifier, that would serve as a signal to Thaddeus. He would read the signs and come to her rescue. She was sure of it.

The wagon hit a bump and a hank of hair slid down into her face. The snood that held it at the back of her head must have come loose when she was grabbed. Was it still hanging there or was it lying on the wagon bed? Or worse yet, had it fallen on the ground in the alleyway where no one would ever see it?

She arched her back and rotated her shoulders as far forward as they would go, then stretched her hands upward. It was still there. She could just feel the edge of it. She tried again, this time craning her head backward as far as it would go. She hooked a finger into the netting and pulled, stifling a yelp as her hairpins pulled out with it.

She debated what to do next. The frogs had been made of hard, twisted piping and had been small enough to lend themselves to popping over the side. The snood was a bag-like piece of netting that hung limply unless it was filled with hair. It would never reach the street. Better to wait until she was taken out of the wagon. Then she could simply drop it. She scrunched it up into a ball and hoped her closed fist would hide it.

She didn't have long to wait. The wagon slowed, then rumbled around a sharp corner and came to a stop. The wagon jounced as someone climbed down. Then she heard a door open.

A minute later her abductor returned and lifted her roughly out of the wagon, threw her over his shoulder and carried her to the door. Just as he crossed the threshold, she dropped the snood against the side of the building.

There was a lamp burning and she could see where she had been taken, although it looked very different from the last time she had been there.

It was Richard Scott's back room, the room where he examined heads and measured skulls. The shelves that had held his books were stripped bare. There were no diagrams or charts on the wall, and the table no longer held the large book that he had recorded his measurements in. There were only boxes stacked on the floor and a trunk near the door.

Scott slammed the door shut behind him, then carried her through a curtained doorway and down a very steep set of stairs. He was panting and stumbled once or twice under her weight. She didn't dare struggle. She was afraid he would drop her, or worse, throw her down the steps if she tried to resist.

He dumped her against the far wall, then roughly patted her, and quickly found the daguerreotype of Hazel Warner that she had put in her pocket. He looked at it sadly for a moment, then abruptly turned and went back up the stairs. He had not said a word the whole time.

Martha managed to inch her way into a sitting position by using the wall as leverage. She had to do it slowly; she was having a lot of difficulty getting her breath. Once upright she rested until her heart stopped pounding and her breathing slowed again.

Above her she could hear Scott's footsteps, and once or twice the sound of something heavy being dragged across the floor. The trunk, she assumed. He must be moving it out to the waiting wagon.

She tried to get some notion of her surroundings. It was very dank in the cellar; it had the fusty smell of a place that never quite dried out. The floor was dirt. The walls were rough stone. Beyond that she could discover nothing. Little light spilled down the stairwell from the lamp above and she was unable to tell if there were any doors or high windows. She pulled her hands against the ropes, but the knots still held fast. But she realized that the strip of cloth that held her gag in place was loose.

She rubbed her jaw against her shoulder and it loosened a little more, but not enough that it would fall completely away. She steeled herself against the pain and rubbed her cheek against the rough stone at her back.

She was lucky. The cloth caught on a rough edge and by pulling her head up in one smooth motion, she was able to slip it past her mouth. She spat the gag out and breathed deeply. Now she could think.

In one respect she was fortunate, she realized. If she'd been kidnapped by some stranger with sinister intent, no one would know where to look for her. But surely her grandfather would figure out that her disappearance had something to do with the Lakefield case. If that was so, the list of suspects was narrow. Joe and his mother would look for her as well. Maybe even Ashby. If they split up, surely it wouldn't be long before they arrived at Scott's studio.

All she had to do was stay alive until then.

Ashby had finished his drink and all the biscuits were gone by the time Thaddeus decided that Martha had had plenty enough time for primping. He, too, was starving. He stood up.

"Are you sure she said she'd meet us here?" he asked Joe. "Maybe I'll just check the dining room in case she misunderstood." But when he went to look there was no sign of her amongst the diners.

He went up to his room and knocked on the connecting door. "Martha?"

When there was no answer he opened it slowly. Martha was normally very tidy, but it was clear that she had changed in a hurry. One of her dresses was thrown over the back of the chair and her hairbrush was on the bed. He checked the cupboard. Her best dress and the leather slippers that she wore indoors were gone. She had changed her clothes for dinner and never quite made it to the sitting room.

Just to make sure that she wasn't still upstairs, he went down the hall to the water closets, but they were all unoccupied.

He returned to the sitting room.

"I can't find her," he said. "She's not upstairs and I didn't see her in the dining room."

"Let's go check again," Ashby said, rising. "You may have just missed her."

But again there was no sign of her, and the waiter who stood at the door to take meal tickets claimed he hadn't seen her that evening. One of the porters who passed by at that moment overheard their conversation.

"I believe the young lady went out," he said. "There was a message that you wanted to meet her outside."

"A message? When was this?" Ashby asked.

"Perhaps a half-hour ago."

"Who gave you the message?"

"I don't know who it was. He seemed like a respectable gentleman. He said that Mr. Lewis wanted her to meet him outside."

"What did this man look like?"

But the porter recalled few of the details. "Not old, not young. He was just…a gentleman. Not a labourer, that's for certain, but other than that I really can't say. I see too many people in a day. I'm sorry."

Thaddeus felt a rising alarm. *Calm down*, he thought. *There's probably a perfectly reasonable explanation.* But he could see that Ashby was concerned as well.

"I'll take a look outside," he said. "Go get the others."

Thaddeus stepped outside. There was no one on the street. No one to ask if they'd seen a pretty, dark-haired girl. He slowly started walking south, but there was little to see. There was an alleyway in the middle of the block, a passage to allow carts and drays access to the rear of the buildings. It was very dark, flanked as it was by the three story buildings on either side of it. He hesitated before he stepped into the shadows. Surely she wouldn't have ventured into such a dark place on her own.

"Martha?" he called. But there was no answer. He turned to make his way back out onto the street. At that moment a gust of wind blew a cloud of dust down the alleyway and into his face, stinging his eyes. He reached the street blinking, his eyes watering. He turned his back to the wind and pulled out his handkerchief to dab at them, hoping to dislodge the grit. He stood with his head down to guard against a further blast of dust, and when his vision finally cleared he saw something that well and truly alarmed him. It was a green frog fastener exactly like the ones that Martha had recently added to her best dress. He stooped to pick it up. There were threads dangling from the edges. It had been torn from the fabric it had been attached to.

He was standing there with it in his hand, trying to decipher what it meant when the others joined him.

Clementine gasped when she saw what was in his hand. "That's Martha's."

"I know. And it's been torn from her dress. How could this have happened?"

"It's decorative, so I didn't attach it very securely. I tacked it on, that's all. Could it have caught against something and been ripped away?"

"Maybe." And then Thaddeus gave voice to his fear. "Or torn off if someone handled her roughly."

Clementine understood his concern immediately. "Was there any sign of her in the alleyway? It's dark and there's no one around if someone…

"I did. But before I found this. Let's check again."

Joe was down the alley before anyone else could even move. "There's been a horse and cart down here, and fairly recently by the look of it." He gestured toward a mound of dung. "That's fresh. And a wagon wheel ran over it not long ago."

Joe was right. The wheel had dragged part of the muck with it. Thaddeus followed the track which began as a smear against the ground but soon petered out into flecks that were nearly impossible to see. But they were there.

"What do you think?" Thaddeus asked. "Did the cart turn south?"

"Hard to say." Joe stood looking at the nearly non-existent trail. "But at least it's someplace to start."

"Wait a minute," Ashby said.

"I'm not waiting," Thaddeus said. "If someone's got Martha, I'm going after him."

"I know how you feel, but let's think this through. Is this some stranger who grabbed her off the street, or does it have something to do with the case?"

It was a good point.

"Someone gave her a message," Ashby went on. "That someone knew your name and he knew that Martha would come if she thought the message was from you."

"But everybody knows me," Thaddeus said. "I'm apparently the talk of the town." He glared at Clementine.

"No, everybody knows that you're a gentleman who has some connection to the Lakefield trial. They don't necessarily know who you are, just that you're here. The porter very definitely said 'Mr. Lewis'. The same is true of Martha. Whoever did this would have to know her name so that the porter would know who to give the message to."

"He's right," Clementine said. "I don't think this was a stranger. It was someone who knew her."

"But who does she know?" Thaddeus said. "We've only been in town a few days." But even as he said it, his mind was racing with the possibilities. "Lawrence Lakefield, for one, I suppose."

"Really?" Ashby asked.

"She came with me to take notes the first day I interviewed him." Thaddeus thought back over where he had been, who he had talked to. "I was by myself when I talked with Albert Warner."

"Jeb Storms?" Joe said. "Or one of his drinking friends?"

"No. I don't think he would know about Martha. She wasn't at the tavern and she wasn't with me when I went to his house."

"Bastard Bill?" Clementine offered. "Martha is the one responsible for his new nickname. Maybe he's still sore about it."

Ashby considered this for a moment, then shook his head. "The porter said the gentleman was neither young nor old. And not a labourer."

"True, Bill is just a boy, and looks it," Clementine agreed. "And he doesn't know our names."

"There's the hotel staff," Ashby said. "They know us all."

"The local Methodists know Martha too," Thaddeus pointed out. "The minister, Calvin Merritt, knows me by name and he probably knows Martha's as well. But that doesn't make any sense. Why would any of them kidnap her?"

"Maybe they're trying to lure you back into the church," Clementine said. "They'll hold her hostage until you promise to preach a sermon."

Thaddeus ignored this remark.

"I'm going to the police," Ashby said. "In the meantime I don't know what else to do but look wherever you can. Mrs. Elliott, perhaps you should stay at the hotel in case Martha returns."

"No," Clementine said. "We can just as easily leave word at the desk that we're looking for her. I'm going with Joe and Mr. Lewis. It's another pair of eyes," she said in response to Thaddeus's look of exasperation. "Don't worry, I'll be back in five seconds." And she went flying down the street in the direction of the hotel.

"You don't think that whoever took her will hurt her, do you?" Thaddeus asked Ashby, the anxiety evident in his voice.

"Quite frankly, I don't know what to think," Ashby replied. "But I'll be just as happy to have the police in tow." He too set off.

"Which way?" Thaddeus said to Joe. "Or should we split up?"

"I say let's keep heading south. Whoever took her waited in the alley until she came by. If he intended to go north, wouldn't he have waited somewhere on the other side of the hotel?"

"Unless he went east or west when he reached the corner. But we have to start somewhere. Let's go. Your mother can catch up as best she can."

"Look carefully," Joe said, walking at a far slower pace than Thaddeus would have liked. "There may be other signs."

Thaddeus had to admit that Joe could be right, and forced himself not to run, but the sun was starting to set, casting long shadows across the street and making it difficult to see anything.

"Let's split up and cover both sides of the road," he said.

Joe crossed, his eyes glued to the ground.

By the time they reached the intersection with Carling Street, Clementine had caught up with them, even though she had obviously taken time enough to retrieve a coat and, unaccountably to Thaddeus, her umbrella.

Rather than joining Joe, she walked beside Thaddeus. "You're in such a state, you're apt to miss something."

The street was largely deserted. Only three or four vehicles passed, none of the occupants seeming to express any interest in what they were doing.

They had nearly reached Dundas when suddenly Clementine said, "That's Bill crossing the road down there. We can ask if he's seen anything. For once, he's not with a gang."

As Thaddeus looked up, a figure ahead of them stopped in the middle of the street, bent over and picked something up.

Clementine broke into a run. "Bill!" she called.

Bill looked around wildly to see who was hailing him. When he saw who it was, he turned and scurried to the other side of the road, without noticing that Joe was coming up fast behind him. Joe clapped a hand on his shoulder, effectively cutting off his retreat.

Thaddeus was only seconds behind Clementine, hampered as she was by her long skirts.

Bill eyed them warily.

"What did you find Bill?" Clementine asked.

"Nothin'. It was lying in the street. It isn't anything."

"Show me."

He held out his hand. Lying in his palm was a decorative frog fastener, just like the one that had been left outside the alleyway.

"Did you see who dropped this?" Clementine asked.

"No. It was just there."

"You know the girl who was with me the other day? The dark-haired one who called you fatherless? Have you seen her?"

"No."

"Have you seen anybody else tonight? Or anything unusual?"

Bill shrugged. "No. It's real quiet." He thought for a moment. "The Mayor went by in his buggy. There's a drunk Irishman down on the corner, but that's not unusual. The quack that reads heads is moving out, but that's about it."

"The phrenologist? He's leaving?" Joe looked at Thaddeus. "We were there this morning. Martha picked up her reading."

"Which way?" Thaddeus demanded.

"Follow me."

Joe was off like a shot, Thaddeus on his heels.

"Thank you Bill," Clementine said. "Find me later at the Western and I'll have something for you."

"Thanks," he said, but she didn't hear. She was running to catch up with the other two.

CHAPTER 17

Martha strained to hear what was going on over her head. There was no longer any sound of heavy things being dragged across the floor, just a tattoo of footsteps back and forth. Scott must be loading the boxes, she decided. And then she saw a light at the top of the stairs and he descended into the cellar.

She shrank back against the wall as he reached the bottom step, but he paid no attention to her. He set his lamp on the ground a few feet in front of her, then disappeared underneath the stairs.

He emerged with a glass carboy and set it down next to the lamp. Martha stifled a gasp when she realized that the jar held the body of an infant, floating lifeless in liquid. Even with the light from the lamp the cellar was shadowy, but she had no difficulty discerning the raised purple stain that covered fully half of the baby's face. Hazel Warner's child, withered not in a fiery death, but in a watery one. There was something else, too, she realized. Something was wrong with one arm. It floated in an odd way, and looked as though it was somehow not attached to the shoulder anymore.

"Have you ever seen such a monster?"

Martha shook her head. Scott didn't appear to notice that she had managed to remove her gag.

"She should have been perfect. Hazel was perfect, or so I thought. Hers was the most incredible analysis I have ever seen. Every trait was favourable, every genus in balance, the orders the most auspicious I have ever seen. I thought she was a superior human being in all respects. We should have produced a paragon, an exemplar, the personification of all that is admirable and exceptional in mankind. Instead – this." Scott pointed at the child in disgust. "This loathsome thing of bestial intellect. I went over and over the measurements, analyzed them again and again. I could find only one tiny error, but its impact was enormous. A small mathematical mistake that nevertheless threw all else into disorder. I failed to predict her propensity to amativeness. I knew then, that the child was not mine – it couldn't be. She had bestowed her favours on others. She was a whore just like my wife, a harlot, and this monstrosity was the product of her promiscuity."

A wife? No wonder Hazel had kept her lover's identity secret. "Why didn't you just walk away?" Martha said in a low voice. "No one would ever have known. Hazel didn't tell anyone."

Her words seemed to agitate him more and Martha wondered if she might have been wiser to say nothing. Except that she needed to keep him talking until Thaddeus arrived. For surely he was on his way.

Please be on your way.

"I tried. But the harlot wouldn't let me." Scott spat the words. "She plagued me, and lied about what she had done. But nature will tell. Every time, nature will tell. And then it occurred to me that I could have the proof of it."

Martha struggled to make sense of Scott's words. Proof of what?

Hurry Grandpa. Come soon.

"But Hazel wouldn't give it to me. I don't know why. Who would want to mother such a thing? An example of everything that is odious in mankind. It didn't deserve to live. And yet I couldn't make her understand what a lesson it could be. I could display it beside the murderer who was hanged twice and then the whole world would see what comes of miscegenation, of consorting with the lower orders of man."

"You arranged to meet Hazel, didn't you? That day at the warehouse."

"She thought she could change my mind. As if she could persuade me ever to touch her again. That somehow I could forgive her harlotry. All I wanted was the child."

"Did you kill it?"

Soon, please, Grandpa. I don't know what he's going to do.

"I wanted to. I wanted to kill it before her eyes, so she could see what her betrayal had come to. But she wouldn't give it up." Scott stopped speaking and gazed at the small floating body for a moment. "I damaged it a bit, when she wouldn't let go. I pulled too hard, and its arm came loose. And then they both began to shriek."

He turned his gaze on Martha. "She made me hit her. It was the only way to stop her before someone heard. And then the child was so small that it was but the work of a moment to smother it."

Martha was shaking.

Keep him talking. Keep him talking until Thaddeus comes.

"Did you set the fire?" she asked. She struggled to keep her voice even as she asked.

"Yes, I burned her. It was a lovely fire. All that chaff and sawdust and wood. Much the best thing. No one would ever know. No one, that is, except you." Martha shrank against the wall as he took a step toward her. "I knew with the first measurement what you are. Quarrelsome and deceitful. Stubborn and self-willed. Your lack of prudence has brought you to where you are and now you'll reap the whirlwind. Just like Hazel did."

There was a faint creak from a floorboard above her head. Scott heard it too. He cocked his head on one side and listened, and there it was again.

Thaddeus.

"Who did you tell?" Scott hissed. "Who else knows?"

"My grandfather knows," she said defiantly. "And now he's here.

When Thaddeus reached the building that housed Scott's studio he found that it was dark and the door locked. He cupped his hands around his eyes as he peered in through the front window.

"Do you see a light in the back?" he asked as Joe and Clementine caught up with him. "Or am I imagining it?"

"Maybe," Joe said. "I can't really tell if it's a light or a reflection of some sort. Is there a laneway at the back of these buildings?"

"Yes, but you have to go down aways to get to it." It was Bill, who had followed them, curious, no doubt, to see what they were up to. "Follow me."

He led them down the street and showed them the alley that gave access to the rear of the buildings.

Joe raced ahead, but Thaddeus stepped gingerly into the darkness. Behind him, Clementine stumbled over some unseen obstacle. He took her by the hand so she wouldn't fall. Bill brought up the rear. When they reached the lane that was parallel to the street they turned to make their way back in the direction of Scott's studio. Somewhere ahead of them a horse nickered, and as they got closer Thaddeus realized that it was hitched to a cart piled high with trunks and boxes. Bill had it right. Scott was moving out.

Joe was peering in through the back window. "The light's gone, if it was ever there at all," he said when Thaddeus and Clementine reached him. "But look, I found this."

He held out his hand to show the snood that Clementine had loaned to Martha.

Thaddeus felt a constriction in his chest that he thought might choke him. Martha was here. *Please God*, he began, and then he stopped himself. No bargains. No deals. No special pleadings. He had to trust that God was looking out for Martha. But he wasn't prepared to take any chances with the details. God might keep her safe, but Thaddeus would find her himself.

The door was firmly locked.

"Should we smash it open?" Thaddeus asked.

"No," Clementine said. "That will make too much noise. Here." She reached up and removed a pin from the knot of hair at the back of her head. She handed it to Joe. He inserted it into the lock and began wiggling it back and forth.

Joe was evidently well-acquainted with the art of picking locks, but it still seemed to take an eternity before Thaddeus heard the faint clunk of the bolt sliding open.

"Gee, can you show me how to do that?" Bill asked.

"No," Joe replied. "But I'll give you a nickel if you run and find a constable."

"What am I supposed to tell him if I find him?"

"Tell him there's been a kidnapping." Thaddeus said. "And tell him to hurry."

Joe cautiously opened the door and slid inside. A moment later he waved at Thaddeus and Clementine to follow him. The door opened to the back room of Scott's studio. There was nothing there but a table, two chairs and an empty bookcase.

Thaddeus stepped through the doorway to the public room at the front of the building. Clementine tiptoed behind him. Light from the street made it easier to see, but there wasn't much to look at – just an old desk and a few empty shelves.

"Somebody's doing a runner," Clementine said softly.

"Psst." It was Joe, waving at them to show what he had found in the back room. They joined him as quietly as they could. He had pulled aside a black curtain that hid another doorway. There was a set of steps leading down to the cellar. A faint light glowed at the bottom.

Thaddeus was about to go down the stairs when Joe put out an arm to stop him.

"That's a real bottleneck," he whispered. "It'll be dangerous if he's waiting for us."

"Do you think he knows we're here?"

"We're making so much noise I don't see how he couldn't. And I haven't heard anything from the cellar since we arrived. He knows, all right." He leaned over to his mother. "Give me your umbrella." She handed it to him.

"You plan to beat him over the head with that or something?" Thaddeus asked.

Joe held his finger to his lips, as an indication that they should stay as quiet as possible. Then he pushed on some hidden button on the handle of the umbrella and a long, narrow stiletto popped out.

"Remind me to keep on your mother's good side," Thaddeus muttered.

"That was always the best idea anyway," Joe whispered back.

Thaddeus and Joe jockeyed at the top of the stairs over who would go down first. Joe had one foot on the top step when Thaddeus reached out to pull him back. He shook his head and pointed to himself.

Joe scowled, but Thaddeus pushed him out of the way. And then, wary and apprehensive, he began to descend the steep steps that were more like a ladder than a stair. Halfway down he saw Martha - his Martha, his last girl - huddled against the wall opposite the steps. Her eyes were wide, her face illuminated in a ghostly light from the lantern in front of her. She gestured toward her left with her head, then her eyes slid sideways. Thaddeus nodded to show he understood.

Even though he had been alerted, Thaddeus was still knocked to the cellar floor when Scott slammed into him. He turned as quickly as he could to avoid being pinned by a knee in his back, at the same time jabbing both arms up in an outward sweeping motion. One fist connected with Scott's jaw, but it wasn't enough to slow him for long. Thaddeus felt hands at his throat. He jerked a knee up sharply and Scott's grip wavered long enough for Thaddeus to get a good grip on his hands and pull them away. Then he twisted them and Scott fell back. But before Thaddeus could get to his feet again, Joe rushed forward and plunged the stiletto into Scott's chest.

The attack seemed to slow Scott for only a moment. He scrambled sideways toward Martha, grabbed her head and wrenched it back, then pulled the blade from his own chest and held it at Martha's throat.

One tiny part of Thaddeus's brain registered the fact that the scene in front of him was ludicrous – the lacey folded fabric at one end of the umbrella made a strange contrast to the bloodstained shank of steel at the other. The rest of his brain registered his horror at the threat to Martha.

"Stand back, or the whore will get it," Scott snarled.

"It's all over you know," Thaddeus said. "The police are coming. You can't hope to get away."

"Then maybe I'll take her with me." He pulled her hair again and gestured with the knife. She cried out and Thaddeus thought his heart would leap into his throat and strangle him, it was pounding so furiously.

He could see that the wound in Scott's chest was bleeding quite freely and he wondered if they could simply wait it out, but he had no way to judge if the blood loss was enough to weaken Scott to the point where he collapsed on his own.

Joe took a small step to his right. He was hoping, Thaddeus realized, to get close enough to make a rush forward. Divide and conquer. It would take only a momentary distraction, and between the two of them, he and Joe should be able to get to Scott before he had time to harm Martha.

It was Martha herself who provided the opportunity. She suddenly pulled her knees toward her, then kicked out at the glass carboy at her feet. It teetered for a moment, then fell over and cracked against a stone, the liquid from it spilling across the floor.

"Nooo," Scott screamed and leapt to right it, but Joe stopped his forward motion with a tackle and a grab at the hand that wielded the odd, umbrella-ended weapon. Thaddeus lunged at the same time, but he ignored Scott. He grabbed Martha by the arms and dragged her out of harm's way.

Scott struggled with Joe for control of the unwieldy knife, each of them attempting to wrench it out of the other's hand. Just as Thaddeus was about to jump into the fray, he realized that Scott was no longer trying to turn the weapon on Joe. He was trying to turn it toward himself. Joe must have realized this at the same moment, for he suddenly let go of the stiletto and jumped back.

Scott glared at Martha for a moment, then knelt and placed the end of the stiletto at the corner of his right eye, grasped the base of the umbrella with both hands and without a word, fell forward. The weight of his body drove the blade deep into his brain.

There was nothing Thaddeus could do but watch as Scott fell over sideways onto the floor. He tried to turn Martha's head, so she wouldn't have to see, but she pushed his arm away. Joe stood over the writhing body with a strange, impassive look on his face as Scott convulsed in shuddering spasms.

Thaddeus heard a gasp from behind him. He had forgotten that Clementine was there. She came down the steps and grabbed Joe by the arm.

"We have to go," she hissed. "We can't be part of this."

At the sound of his mother's voice, Joe turned to her. She pulled him toward the stair. With one foot already on the bottom step, she said to Thaddeus, "Are you all right? Ashby should be here at any moment with the police." And then, "We have no idea where the umbrella came from, right?"

Thaddeus nodded, and then she and Joe disappeared.

He turned his attention to Martha. "Are you hurt?"

"Not really, but my arms and legs have gone numb from the ropes."

Thaddeus began to work on the knots that held her hands, but it took him a long time to loosen them. It would be easier if he could just cut them, he thought, but he could see nothing sharp in the cellar except the stiletto that was currently stuck in Scott's head. He was reluctant to touch it.

"I'm so sorry this happened to you," he said, as he teased the knots apart. "It's my fault. I shouldn't have got you involved in this."

"No, it's my fault," Martha said. "I should never have gone down that alley. But it's all right. I knew you'd come for me."

He was just freeing her legs when Bill led Ashby and one of the local constables down the stairs. Ashby rushed over to Martha and helped Thaddeus get her to her feet.

"My word in heaven," the constable said as his gaze swept the scene in the cellar. "What happened here?"

"This man kidnapped my granddaughter," Thaddeus replied, pointing at Scott. "I came after her. When I told him that police were on their way, he took his own life."

"Kidnapped her? But why?"

"Because of…" Martha said, but that was as far as she got. Ashby interrupted her in mid-sentence.

"Later," he said. "You can tell it all later."

"Someone needs to fetch the coroner," the constable said.

It would have been most sensible to send Ashby, but when he made no move to go, the constable's eye fell on Bill.

"Billy, stop gawking and go fetch Dr. Bratten," the constable said. And when Bill had disappeared back up the stairs, "I just hope he remembers what I told him to do."

"He will," Thaddeus said. "He's been useful tonight."

"First time in his life," the constable muttered.

"Can we leave?" Martha asked.

"I'll need a statement from you first, Miss," the constable said.

Ashby intervened again. "She's been lying here in this cellar tied up for some time. She's cold and possibly in shock. I think it makes far more sense for you to get a statement later, after the coroner has made his examination. We'll wait for you in the sitting room at the Western Hotel."

"I don't know if I should…"

At that point, Martha tried to take a step forward, but stumbled and gave a little gasp. Thaddeus and Ashby each grabbed an arm to keep her from falling.

"My legs are all pins and needles," she said.

"She needs medical attention," Ashby pointed out.

The constable gave in. "All right. The Western, you said. I'll be along in due time."

Thaddeus wanted more than anything to sweep Martha up in his arms and carry her out of the cellar, but the steepness of the stairs was daunting, and his knee was hurting again. He couldn't see how he could manage it. More likely he would need help himself.

It was Ashby who picked her up and climbed the stairs with her cradled in his arms. Thaddeus limped up behind them.

When they reached the street, Ashby flagged down a passing buggy whose driver agreed to take them to the Western. By the time they reached it, Martha insisted that she could walk on her own, but they made a sorry sight as they entered the hotel lobby. Thaddeus was limping badly. Martha's face was smeared with grime and her hair had tumbled down her back. Her dress was filthy. They drew even more stares as Ashby shouted orders for hot tea and brandy.

"Do you think I could get something to eat?" Martha asked.

Ashby looked at her in surprise.

She shrugged a little. "I didn't get any supper. I'm starving."

CHAPTER 18

Joe and Clementine must have been watching for their arrival, for they appeared in the sitting room almost immediately. Thaddeus sat on one side of Martha. Joe claimed the other side, while Ashby sat in a chair across from them. Clementine took one look at the graze on Martha's cheek and the nasty welts on her wrists and disappeared again.

The waiter arrived with a tea tray and a bottle of brandy. He must have realized that the situation was fraught in some way, and required sustenance, for he had added a plate of gingersnaps.

"I know it's late," Ashby said to him, "but do you think the kitchen could rustle up some sandwiches, or at the very least some bread and butter? We none of us have eaten tonight. And if you can, please keep the other guests away?"

The waiter nodded and left. Ashby reached forward and poured a cup of tea, then opened the bottle of brandy and poured a generous tot into the cup. Joe leapt up and took it from Ashby, then handed it to Martha. She looked at her grandfather.

"It's all right. In these circumstances, it's medicinal."

Clementine returned with a small jar in her hand.

"It's salve," she said. "It will help prevent scarring." She rubbed it on Martha's cheek, and on her wrists. "What about your ankles?" she asked.

"They're not as bad. My stockings kept the ropes from rubbing too much."

Clementine set the jar on the table beside the tea tray. "Take it with you and use it twice a day." Then, apparently satisfied with her ministrations, she took a seat at one of the writing desks.

"Are you all right?" she said to Thaddeus.

"Only fair to middling," he replied. "My nerves are shattered and my knee hurts again."

"I have some liniment if you need it," she said. "It'll take the ache away."

"I'll see how it goes. But thank you."

"Well," Ashby began. "If you're up to it Martha, I think it would be a good idea if you told me what happened. Then I'll tell you what you should say to the police."

"The porter said grandpa needed me outside." Martha spoke slowly, careful to reconstruct the sequence of events as they had happened. "I heard somebody yell for help as I passed the alleyway." She turned to Thaddeus. "I thought you were in trouble."

"I'm sorry," he said. "I am so, so sorry."

"It's not your fault," Martha replied. "Obviously Scott was trying to fool me. Unfortunately, it worked. Anyway, he grabbed me and shoved a piece of cloth into my mouth, so I couldn't scream. He tied me up and threw me into the back of the wagon, but I managed to reach one of the frogs on my dress. I ripped it off and threw it over the side. Did you find it?"

"Yes, we found it. You left us a grand trail."

She beamed. "I'm quite proud of myself for thinking of it. But I wouldn't have been able to do it if Joe hadn't shown me how to throw dice."

The resilience of the young. Right now I wish I could borrow a little of it. Thaddeus felt battered and exhausted and quite, quite old.

Martha took a sip of her brandy-laced tea. She made a face at the taste of it, then resumed her story.

"Scott left me in the cellar for quite a while. I think he was loading his things into the wagon. Then he came down the stairs."

She stopped for a moment. Thaddeus reached out and gripped her hand. "It was dark down there so I couldn't see much until he came down with the lamp. Then he showed me the baby in the jar. Poor thing."

"But what did he want from you?" Ashby asked. "Why did he do this?"

"I'd figured out that he was Hazel Warner's lover."

With a sidelong glance at Thaddeus, she recounted how she'd taken the daguerreotype from Scott's desk that morning.

Clementine gave a little gasp. "I told you," she pointed out. "The daguerreotypist told me that Hazel had made copies," she said in response to Martha's puzzled look. "I was going to tell you earlier but you weren't here."

"Well, he wanted it back. And he wanted to know who I'd told about it. I said that my grandfather knew, but before that he was … I don't know… *raving*." She took another sip of tea and grimaced a little less with the second tasting. "He said something about his wife, and that Hazel was just like her. He tried to take the baby and when she fought him, he hit her. Then he set fire to the warehouse. And he killed the baby. He said it was an abomination and better off dead, but he wanted to display it as a warning." She turned to her grandfather. "He blamed Hazel. He said she was unfaithful. And that's why the baby was so disfigured."

"You need to be very clear about this Martha," Ashby said. "As distressful as it is, you should try to fix his exact words in your mind, so you can repeat them to the police."

"Don't worry. I don't think I'll ever forget them," Martha replied.

"There's no question in my mind that it's a valid confession. But don't offer that conclusion on your own. As far as possible, just repeat what you said to us."

She nodded.

"So now tell me exactly what happened in the cellar after you got there," Ashby said to Thaddeus.

"I went there looking for Martha. Scott attacked me. Then he took his own life."

"With a knife hidden in the handle of an umbrella."

"Yes."

"And where do you suppose this strange – and I might add, most probably illegal – weapon came from?"

"It was just there in the cellar, I guess," Thaddeus said.

Martha shot a glance at him. He nudged her to keep quiet.

"I see," Ashby said. "And Mrs. Elliott? Where were you and your son while all this was going on?"

"We were looking for Martha. In a different direction," Clementine answered.

Ashby was silent for a few moments. Then he nodded. "All right. That will do. That's our story, so let's everybody stick to it."

Clementine sent Joe out to the lobby to watch for the constable, and as soon as he indicated that he and the coroner had arrived, she excused herself and beckoned Joe to follow her. A short time later Dr. Bratten was shown into the reading room, along with the constable, whose name they were told was Thomas.

Much to Thaddeus's approval, Martha repeated her story almost word for word.

Constable Thomas questioned her for several minutes about Scott's confession. And as many times as he rephrased and reworded his inquiries, she answered in a way that confirmed her original account. Finally, the constable seemed satisfied.

"So young Lakefield will be off the hook, I guess," he said to Ashby.

"It would appear so," Ashby replied. "But that will, of course, have to wait until Dr. Bratten has conducted his inquest."

"Will that be necessary?" Thaddeus asked. "My granddaughter has had a very trying time and is quite distraught. Will she be required to testify?"

This statement was belied by the fact that the waiter had brought a plate of sandwiches and Martha had eaten three of them while she told her story.

"Yes, I'm afraid she'll have to put in an appearance," Dr. Bratten said. "It's clear to me that Scott died by his own hand, but I haven't heard anything about the wound in his chest. Can you shed any light on that?"

"We did have quite a struggle at first," Thaddeus pointed out. "It may have happened then."

This seemed a satisfactory answer, and the coroner announced that he had no further questions. He stood, and bowed slightly to Martha.

"Is there anything you need me to attend to, my dear?" he asked.

"I don't think so. My wrists hurt, but I have some salve for them."

"Then I hope you have a restful night. It would do you good to have a tot of brandy before you go to bed."

But Martha was already stifling a yawn.

"I think that will do it for me tonight as well," Constable Thomas said. "The newspapers will be onto this by morning. Could you please not talk to them until after the inquest?"

Thaddeus nodded, glad to have the interview over.

Ashby stood as soon as the doctor and the constable made their exit.

"We should all get some rest," he said. "It will be a long day tomorrow. I'll brief you on what to expect at the inquest, but I think it should be reasonably straightforward. Is there anything else you need. Martha?"

"I'm fine, thank you," she said. "I just want to go to bed."

Thaddeus limped out of the room. He should have asked Dr. Bratten for something for his knee, but he hadn't wanted to prolong the interview. His nerves were stretched to the breaking point.

"Call me when you're ready for bed," he said to Martha when they reached their rooms. "I want to come in and say good night."

He removed his cravat, shrugged out of his jacket and waistcoat, then sank into the chair and pulled off his boots, but after that he didn't have energy enough to do anything more but sit and think about what might have happened if he hadn't got to Martha as fast as he did. Would Scott have killed her too? Probably.

He was sitting with his head in his hands when she opened the connecting door and came in.

"I thought it would be easier on your knee if I did the walking," she said. "You're limping again."

"You must have been terrified," he said without looking up.

She took a seat on the bed across from him.

"I was really scared at first. I didn't know who had grabbed me. But then I thought of leaving the frogs and having something to do helped. Then when I saw it was Scott, I knew you'd figure it out and that it was just a matter of time until you found me."

"But what if I hadn't seen them? What if I hadn't found you?"

"But you did."

Thaddeus was astounded at her faith in him. Astounded, humbled – and alarmed.

"You should trust in God, Martha, not in me."

"It's more or less the same thing, isn't it? After all, if God isn't on your side, whose would He be on?"

In the past, Thaddeus would have had a ready answer for this. He would have pointed out the fault in her logic and admonished her to read her Bible more carefully. Now he wasn't sure what to say. He himself had been unwilling to leave it all up to God.

"I just had to…not panic until you got there," she went on. "He was mad, wasn't he?"

"Scott? Yes, he was.

Follow the money, Josiah Blackburn had advised. *Sometimes sex can gum up the picture, but follow the money and you won't go far wrong.* The newspaperman had forgotten to add madness to the mix.

"Poor Hazel."

She stood up and came over to hug him. "I love you grandpa."

He held her tightly for a moment. "And I love you. Will you be able to go to sleep?"

"I can barely keep my eyes open. It must be the brandy. What about you?"

"I'll be fine."

But he wasn't.

After Martha left, he hobbled over to his bed and stretched out on top of the covers. As tired as he was, his mind was buzzing and he knew that sleep would be a long time coming that night.

He didn't quite know what to make of Martha. At the moment she seemed none the worse for her experiences, but that could change when she'd had time to think about what had almost happened to her. He wondered if he should send her back to her father. He didn't want to, but this was the second time she had been involved in a series of events that put her in danger. No, not the second, Thaddeus reminded himself. The third. She had been threatened by the man who killed her mother. And back in Wellington, when they'd met Joe and Clementine for the first time, Martha had been unwittingly instrumental in helping Thaddeus find a murderer. "Adventure" as she put it, seemed to find her as often as it did him. If only she didn't have such a certainty that it would always turn out all right in the end. That was the essence of faith, he supposed, but it didn't help him in deciding what to do.

He would talk with Martha later, when things had settled, and see if he could persuade her to go home. She would be safer there.

Tomorrow, after the inquest, when they had both told their stories and could begin to put her kidnapping behind them.

He needed to consolidate his own version of what had happened so that he could answer any questions succinctly and without confusing the jury. He didn't know why he had gone along with Clementine's wish to be excluded from the narrative, except that she had been extraordinarily helpful, and he was in her debt. He knew there would be lurid accounts of the affair in the papers. No doubt she wanted to avoid being mentioned, even though it was unlikely that anyone else knew her as Clementine Elliott. He doubted it mattered where the umbrella had come from; the fact remained that Richard Scott had taken his own life, and if he hadn't done it with so handy a weapon he would have found some other way. He could easily keep Clementine out of it, without jeopardizing the truth of his testimony.

Joe was a little trickier. The jury would find it difficult to believe that Thaddeus had wrestled Richard Scott to the ground single-handedly. He would have to emphasize the fact that the police had been on their way, and that he had managed to persuade Scott that it was hopeless to resist. Constable Thomas would confirm that Ashby had called on him for help, and that Bill had led him to the cellar. Everything would make sense if Thaddeus told it correctly.

He found Joe's actions in the cellar oddly disturbing. The boy had deliberately released his grip so that Richard Scott could gain control of the knife, but it wasn't the act of letting go that bothered Thaddeus so much. It was the impassive look on Joe's face while he stood and watched Scott convulse his life away. It had been such a cold-blooded blankness.

Even though he was lying down, Thaddeus's leg was aching badly.

Old bones. Falling apart, in more ways than one.

He had some willow tea that his son had given him, but brewing it up would require boiling water and it was far too late to cause such a fuss with the hotel staff. He should have asked Dr. Bratten after all.

After another half an hour of trying to ignore the pain, he got up. He opened the door to Martha's room and peeked in. She was sound asleep already, one fist balled up against her cheek, the same way she had slept as a child.

He hesitated for only a moment, then left his room, closing the door behind him as quietly as he could. He limped down the hall and tapped softly on Clementine's door.

A minute or so passed. Thaddeus was about to leave when the door opened.

"I wonder if I can get some of that liniment?" he said. "I'm not going to get any sleep otherwise."

"Of course, come in."

He remained standing in the doorway. Clementine was in her bare feet, her hair down and plaited into a braid and she was wearing a loose wrapper that rustled when she moved. Her room was in an uproar, clothes in piles on the chair, trunks open, hats in a row on the dressing table.

"Going somewhere?" he asked.

"I think it's best if we leave tomorrow," she said. "There will be far too much attention paid to this little town in the next few days. I'd hate any of the light to shine too brightly on us."

It was as Thaddeus suspected. She wasn't taking any chance that someone might find her.

"Thank you for all your help," he said. "We'd have been a long time figuring things out without you."

"Is Martha all right? She was bearing up awfully well while she was talking to the police, but sometimes people can have a delayed reaction once the immediate crisis is over."

"She seems to be fine. She's sound asleep already." Then, as if to prove Clementine's point, the horror of the evening's events suddenly washed over him again. He slumped against the door frame, his hands shaking. "I couldn't have borne it if I'd lost her. Not after everything else." He could feel the tears forming behind his eyes and fought to control them.

"Come in," Clementine said in as gentle a tone as he had ever heard from her. "Sit down and I'll find the liniment."

He hesitated. There was nowhere to sit but on the edge of the bed.

"I should go," he said.

"Don't be silly. You look done in. Sit down." And then when he didn't move she took him by the hand and led him into the room. "Sit. I'll just be a moment."

He sat, grateful to take the weight off his leg.

She went to one of the trunks and began rummaging through it.

"I'm sorry," he said. "I didn't mean to burden you with this."

"Don't be sorry. You've had a trying time. It's not surprising that you're rattled."

"She said she knew I'd come for her."

"And you did."

"I'm going to have to send her back to her father. I can't keep her safe."

"No you can't. But who's to say she'd be any safer there? You'll break her heart if you send her away. Besides, you're not giving her enough credit. She gave you an awful lot of help."

Thaddeus realized that this was true. He'd never have found Martha if she hadn't had the presence of mind to leave him a trail.

"You have to let them grow up, Thaddeus. And you're one of the lucky ones. Most of them grow up and want to leave. Martha wants to stay."

Clementine's tone was wistful. Joe must be setting off on his own soon.

"Ah, here it is." She held up a brown bottle, then grabbed a small towel from the washstand. "I'll rub it on for you." She knelt down in front of him.

He was startled. "You don't have to do that. I can manage," he said.

"It's better if you knead it into the muscle," she said. "And that's easier for someone else to do. It won't take long."

"I really shouldn't be here at all."

"Why? Because someone might see you? It hardly matters. Half the town thinks I'm your wife anyway."

She pulled up his pant leg.

"It's the other one," he pointed out.

She giggled a little and switched her attention to the other leg, but gave a small gasp when she saw the white, knotted mass of scar tissue that wound across his knee and down his calf.

"What is this?"

"I told you. I got shot in the war. It's bothered me on and off ever since. It's been better since I stopped riding so much, but I aggravated it again yesterday."

"I don't know if liniment will do much for this. It may help a little, but you really need something stronger."

"I'll get something tomorrow. I'm old bones, that's the problem. I don't cope as well as I used to." And he felt old. Old and defeated.

"Nonsense. You're in your prime." She looked up at him. "And don't you dare argue with me, because then I might have to admit that I'm not in mine."

She began to massage the lotion into the scars, rubbing her thumbs along the lines of gnarled tissue and loosening the knots in the muscle. She seemed unaware that the loose wrapper she wore gaped open when she bent over. Thaddeus could see the lacy edge of her chemise, and above it, the round tops of her breasts. He tried not to look.

As the heat from the liniment crept in, he began to feel a lessening of the ache, and, he realized with surprise, a lightening of his mood. Maybe Clementine was right. Maybe he should keep Martha with him as long as she wanted to stay because all too soon she might want to leave. Just like Joe.

"Where are you headed to now?" he asked.

"I'm not sure yet. I'll go west, I think. Chicago, maybe. The trains will connect from here. If I don't like Chicago, maybe I'll go south. They say New Orleans is an interesting town. To tell the truth I'm sorry to have to leave so soon. I've been enjoying myself." She grinned up at him. "It was fun being your wife. I don't think I've ever had such a combative husband."

"Especially in public. People are feeling sorry for me, you know, because you're so obviously bad-tempered."

She dug her thumb into his flesh with quite unnecessary force.

"Ouch."

"Watch your tongue, then." She continued to work in silence for a few minutes. Then she asked, "So what are your plans? Where do you go from here?"

"I don't know. Ashby threw me a lifeline once. I can't expect him to keep doing it."

"Can you go back to preaching?"

"I'm not sure they'll have me again."

"Maybe we should team up and run our own show. It could be a lot of fun, couldn't it? You and me? You could preach and I could fleece the congregation."

It was such an outrageous statement that it made him laugh.

"I don't think there would be a lot of money in it. I doubt it would keep you in hats."

"Really? What a shame. There. That's all I can do for now. It's too bad I'm leaving. It would be best if that leg was massaged a couple of times a day, but at least I can leave you the bottle of liniment."

"I'm grateful. It feels much better already." She began cleaning her hands on the towel, but made no move to get up from her kneeling position.

"I'm going to miss you Thaddeus," she suddenly said in a low voice. "I like you. I always did. Even when you were working against me."

He was instantly wary at her change in tone. She was angling for something. He was sure of it. "What are you after, Clementine?"

Her head was bowed as she finished wiping her hands. Then she looked up into his eyes very directly, and he could almost fool himself into believing that what she said next was sincere.

"That depends on what you're really asking me. If you want to know what I need, the answer is 'a safe place to hide'. But if you're asking me what I desire, I think maybe, just now, it's this." She stretched up to kiss him lightly on the lips, her hands resting on his thighs.

He didn't respond. "You tried that once before and it didn't work," he pointed out.

"I wasn't serious that time. And you weren't available."

"What makes you think I'm available now?"

"A girl can ask, can't she?" She leaned forward and kissed him again.

He grabbed her by the arms, to hold her off from going any further, but she didn't persist. She simply waited.

Put an end to this right now, the voice in his head told him. *She's after something.*

But suddenly he was swamped by a sense of his own loneliness. He felt like he could drown in it.

Get up. Walk out.

She moved slightly and again he caught a whiff of the scent she used.

Don't do this. Go. Now.

She really looked quite lovely in the low light with her braid hanging over her shoulder.

You're a fool.

Instead of pushing her away, he pulled her closer and the voice in his head fell silent.

CHAPTER 19

Thaddeus was used to waking up in strange places. In all his years of riding circuits he had slept in plenty of barns and haylofts, on kitchen beds and floor pallets, upright in chairs, and even once or twice on horseback when he dozed off while his horse plodded on. He had learned to orient himself by taking time before he opened his eyes to backtrack, to think of where he had been and what he had been doing before he fell asleep.

When he first woke, he realized that he was very comfortable. Just for a moment he was almost able to convince himself that he was curled up with Betsy in the corner bed at their first farmstead, the quilts pulled up against the cold, his firstborn already stirring in her cradle. But he knew this wasn't so; that had been many years ago when he was young, and both Betsy and the baby had long since left him.

And then the present came flooding back to him. He came fully awake with a start that jostled Clementine, who had fallen asleep with her head on his shoulder. She groaned, blinked and rolled over, then burrowed deeper under the covers.

"I need to check on Martha," he said to the top of her head.

There was no response. She appeared to have gone back to sleep.

Thaddeus slid out of the bed and gathered his clothes, which were in a tangled mess on the floor. He couldn't find his boots. Then he remembered that he hadn't been wearing them when he'd arrived at Clementine's room. Once dressed, he opened the door a crack and peered out. He had no idea what time it was. There was no one in the hallway, but there was always the danger that the hotel's staff would soon begin their day. He stepped out cautiously, and quietly closed the door behind him, panic rising as he neared his own room. He had left Martha alone. What if she had called out and he hadn't been there? What if she'd had nightmares after her nightmarish experiences and he hadn't been there to soothe her back to sleep?

But everything was as he had left it, the connecting door slightly ajar, and when he tiptoed into Martha's room she appeared to be deeply asleep. She had turned over, and at some point kicked the bedclothes loose, but that was the only sign of disturbance that he could see.

He left the door open and stretched out on his own bed only to face a fresh panic. What had he done? And with, of all people, Clementine Elliott? What had possessed him to go to her room? True, his knee had been aching, but he could have asked the doctor for some laudanum to take the pain away. Yes, he had been upset, but he could have taken his troubles to God, as he so often counseled others to do. What had he been thinking?

For a moment, he wanted to blame her. She was a Jezebel. She had seduced him with her exotic scent and loose clothing. She had mesmerized him, just like the night she'd made him kiss her cheek. But even as he thought it, he knew it wasn't true. It had been he who had gone to her. He'd sat on her bed willingly. He'd let her massage his aching leg. And when she made her intentions clear, he had not stood up and walked out. He stayed because he wanted to and now there was no blame to be assigned to anyone but himself.

He had blotted his record in Cobourg. Now, in London, he had virtually torn the page out of the book. And his indiscretion put him in the power of a proven fraud, liar and swindler.

The question was: what did she want? His experience of her was that she seldom did anything without it being part of some opportunistic scheme. What did he have that she could possibly use? He had no money, and she must know that. He had no prospects. Even his integrity as a minister was under siege.

I like you, Thaddeus. I always did.

Her words had fallen pleasantly on his ear. He had always been enormously grateful that his wife had loved him, and while she was alive he'd been indifferent to the opinions of other women. But after Betsy died he'd grown used to thinking of himself as old, convinced that the best part of his life was over. And then he had gone to Cobourg, where the first spark of interest he'd felt in anyone else had been extinguished before it even had a chance to ignite. But maybe he wasn't so ancient and used up after all. Was it possible that Clementine had, for once, been honest?

He instantly rejected the notion. Her words had been honeyed, meant to deceive. To believe anything else was foolishness.

If you want to know what I need, the answer is 'a safe place to hide'.

That sounded more like the truth. But how far was she prepared to go to cover her tracks? She'd certainly seized fast enough on the excuse of the Elliott money to come to London. Had her schemes included him, right from the start? If so, he had been skillfully played. He would have to give her whatever she wanted now.

The Bible was clear on the matter.

And if a man entice a maid that is not betrothed, and lie with her, he shall surely endow her to be his wife.

She was scarcely a maid, and he wasn't the one doing the enticing, but was that what she was after? A seamless change of name so that whoever was looking for her would be thrown off the track? A marriage of convenience that would be convenient only to one of them?

And then a startling thought intruded.

Would it be such a terrible thing?

He found their verbal battles entertaining, much as he hated to admit it. She sharpened his wits. She was a match for him, no matter where the conversation turned. Then last night, when he had been so overwrought, she had unexpectedly provided a sympathetic ear and words of comfort. And what had followed…

He wrenched his thoughts away from the details, and turned them back to the difficulties Clementine presented. He couldn't afford her, for one. He could barely support himself. Nor could he trust her.

You could preach and I could fleece the congregation.

Far too close to the truth to be amusing anymore.

But was there any guarantee that, having got what she wanted, she would stick to it? Far more likely that she had planned to waltz into town with one name and waltz right back out again with another. That might be a relief, under the circumstances, but where would it leave him?

It made no difference, he decided. He needed to behave like a decent man. An honourable man, guided by his conscience and the dictates of his church. He would answer for his actions. What happened after that was up to her. But in one thing he had to admit that she was correct – he had been feeling very sorry for himself, and had lost his way because of it. No more. From now on he would take responsibility for everything he had done and face up to whatever consequences there were.

But really - lust and fornication? Two sins he thought would never tempt him. God must have a wicked sense of humour.

Thaddeus must have fallen into a doze at some point because the next thing he knew Martha was tapping at the door and asking if he was ready to go down for breakfast. He rolled off the bed, and was pleased to discover that there was only a slight twinge of pain when he put weight on his left leg. Clementine's liniment had done the trick. Or maybe it had been the massage. And then he remembered all the rest of it and his pleasant mood evaporated.

"I'll be a few minutes yet," he said to Martha. "Go on down if you're ready and I'll meet you there."

She seemed none the worse for wear after her experiences of the previous evening. Unlike himself, he decided, when he looked in the mirror. He was rumpled and red-eyed. There was a tear in the sleeve of his shirt and bite marks on his neck. He hoped that his cravat would wind high enough to hide them.

Heads turned when he finally walked into the dining room, and there was a rustle of whisper as he made his way to the table where the others were gathered. He was taken aback by it, until he realized that reports of Scott's gruesome death would already be in circulation. It was not Thaddeus, personally, they were whispering about; just his connection with such a lurid case.

Martha was not sitting, as had become usual, at one end of the table with Joe, but was next to Ashby. They were deep in conversation, their heads close together, Ashby failing to remember to eat as he explained something to her. Joe was watching them closely.

Thaddeus slouched into the only unoccupied chair across the table from Clementine.

She beamed at him. "Good morning."

To his surprise, she seemed her usual self.

"Good morning," he muttered.

"I've just filled Martha in on what to expect at the inquest," Ashby said. "It should be straight-forward enough. Tell the jury what you told me last night and there should be no difficulties."

"Will you be there?" Thaddeus asked.

"No, don't forget I still have a court case to argue, although it shouldn't take me long. I'll ask for a recess in light of the new information, and as soon as I have the ruling from the inquest, I should be able to get the charges against Nelson Lakefield dropped."

"Another triumph for Towns Ashby." Thaddeus hadn't meant it to sound ungracious, but that was the way it seemed to come out.

"Well, yes." Ashby said. "Thanks to you, yes."

"Somebody's grumpy this morning," Clementine observed.

"Yes, somebody is." Thaddeus wished the waiter would bring his tea soon. He felt fragile and beset with troubles.

"You should cheer up, Mr. Lewis. It's a beautiful day, after all. The mystery is solved, Martha is safe, Mr. Ashby will win his case. What more could you ask for?"

He stared at her bleakly for a moment and then said, "I'd like a few minutes of your time later, if you'll give it. There's something I need to talk to you about."

She looked perplexed. "Of course. I need some time to finish packing, but my train doesn't leave until this evening."

"You're still going?"

"Yes. Why wouldn't I?"

"Oh. I thought… maybe… in light of…" He was confused. She seemed so unconcerned, almost as though she didn't understand what he was referring to.

Ashby's eyes darted back and forth between the two of them, then, ever so slightly, his lips twitched into the faintest hint of a smile.

"I expect it will be sometime after eleven before the jury is ready to hear from you," he said. "The sheriff will come and fetch you when you're needed. You should have plenty of time before then to talk about… whatever it is you need to talk about."

The waiter finally arrived with Thaddeus's tea. He spent the rest of the meal glumly sipping it while the others chattered around him.

Ashby, who had finally settled down to polish off his breakfast, rose from the table first. "Good luck at the inquest," he said. "Remember, keep it simple."

Martha and Joe were finished as well.

"Let's go for a walk," Joe said.

"Don't go far," Thaddeus cautioned. "The sheriff needs to be able to find Martha."

"We'll be back soon," he promised.

"Are you nervous about the inquest?" Joe asked Martha as he walked along idly kicking bits of rubbish off the plank walk in front of the hotel.

"A little," she admitted. "It's not easy to stand up in front of a lot of people and talk, but I've watched my grandfather do it so many times, I'll just try to copy him and I should be fine. I'll speak clearly and tell them exactly what happened."

"All of it?"

"Well, the important bits anyway." But she knew what he was referring to. Thaddeus had tried to prevent her from watching Joe's struggle with Scott, but she had seen the whole thing. She knew that Joe had deliberately let go. It bothered her, a little, that he hadn't tried to stop Scott from killing himself.

"You should cry," Joe said. "Especially if they ask you something tricky and you don't know how to answer."

"I'm not doing that."

"But if they think you're a poor, weak helpless little girl, they'll feel sorry for you and they won't be so persistent."

"If I don't know something, I'll just say I don't know. I don't need to do anything else."

"Is that what Ashby told you?"

"Yes. I'm assuming he would know. He's a barrister after all."

"I'm just teasing."

But she could tell that he wasn't. Not really. He had been annoyed when she'd sat beside Ashby, that was the problem.

"What, exactly, do you think we were talking about, if it wasn't the inquest?"

Joe shrugged. "I don't know."

"Are you jealous of Ashby?"

"No."

"Yes you are! Ashby, of all people."

Joe scowled. "Why wouldn't I be? He's rich. He's good-looking. He likes you."

"I don't really think that's true," Martha said. "He puts up with me because my grandfather is working for him, that's all. We don't really get along at all."

Joe brightened up a little then. "I wish we weren't going. I'll miss you."

"I'll miss you too. Have you decided what you're doing yet?"

"No, not really. I'll go as far as Chicago with my mother, but after that, I don't know. Further west, maybe. Or maybe I'll come back to Canada. Where are you going when you're done here?"

"Wherever my grandfather goes, I guess."

"Not back to Wellington?"

"No. I don't think that's the plan."

"How can I find you if I don't know where you'll be?"

"Oh. I see what you're asking. Send a letter to the Temperance Hotel in Wellington. My father will know where we are." She wanted to stay in touch with Joe, of course she did, but she was uncertain as to how closely. "I'd love to hear a description of your adventures," she finished lamely.

"If I get settled somewhere maybe you can come and visit. Your grandfather too, of course."

"Maybe. It depends on how far it is. Or I suppose you could come back and visit us again."

"Or maybe you could just come on your own." He cast her a sidelong glance.

"Oh no," she said. "Wherever I go, my grandfather is coming too."

"So," Clementine said, after Joe and Martha had gone. "Where do you want to go for this conversation? The sitting room?"

But Thaddeus didn't want to take the chance of being interrupted or overheard.

"Let's go outside." He needed air for what he was about to do.

"You're not going all preachery on me, are you?" Clementine said when they reached the street.

"I don't know what you mean by "preachery". I'm not a preacher any more. But I do still have morals. I want to apologize for last night."

"Trust me, Thaddeus," she said with a smile that could only be described as smug, "there's no need to apologize for anything."

"Yes, there is. I took advantage of you and that was wrong."

"Hard to say who took advantage of who, if you ask me."

He knew she was laughing at him, but he was determined to soldier on anyway. "I want you to know that I'm prepared to make it right. I want to do the honourable thing."

"All you've offered up so far is a half-hearted apology. What is it, exactly, that you're trying to say to me?"

He took a deep breath. "I'm trying to say that I'm willing to make you an honest woman."

"No you aren't. You just think you should, that's all."

"It makes no difference. It's the right thing to do."

"Oh, I see. My goodness, that's not very romantic. How on earth did you ever get your wife to marry you, if that's your notion of a proposal?"

"I have no idea why she married me. Will you just give me an answer?"

"No."

"No what? No, you won't answer, or no you won't marry me?"

"Oh, don't be ridiculous, Thaddeus. We joked about this last night. It would be no time at all before I was caught with my hand in the collection plate, and then where would you be?"

He halted abruptly.

"So what is it you want then? I haven't any money."

Their raised voices caught the attention of a man walking on the other side of the street. No doubt the town would be buzzing yet again with another breathless account of a public argument. Thaddeus glared at the man, who hurriedly walked on.

Clementine turned to face him. "There were no strings attached, Thaddeus. I thought I made that clear."

"I know, but…"

"She married you because you're a lovely man and you have no idea why. And if I had any interest in being an honest woman, I'd marry you too." She giggled. "But I don't. So maybe we should just leave things the way they are, all right?"

She sauntered off down the street. "Stop trying to bargain for everything, Thaddeus," she called over her shoulder as she walked away. "It never turns out the way you think it will."

And he was left in her wake feeling exasperated, flattered and far less relieved than he knew he ought to be.

CHAPTER 20

As Ashby predicted, Martha and Thaddeus were not called for until nearly eleven-thirty.

"Are you ready for this?" Thaddeus asked as they followed the sheriff to the town hall.

"Yes. It helps that I saw some of the trial in Cobourg. I sort of know what to expect."

"This won't be nearly so intense. They just want to hear what happened. No one will be trying to make out that it didn't."

The room was full of people, news of the phrenologist's death having spread like wildfire through the town. An added inducement for the curious was the involvement of the man they had all been talking about anyway. Perhaps they would now hear who, exactly, Thaddeus Lewis was, what he had been doing here and how, exactly, he was related to the various members of the entourage he had brought with him.

The results of the autopsy were reported first, then Constable Thomas gave his account of being called to investigate a kidnapping, and his recollection of the scene in the cellar beneath Scott's studio. To Thaddeus's surprise, Bastard Bill, whose real name turned out to be William Hendricks, testified that he had aided the desperate search and had discovered the pocket fastener that had been thrown into the street. He looked directly at Martha and grinned while he spoke.

"Looks like you've got a friend," Thaddeus whispered.

"Just what I need," Martha replied.

Thaddeus gave her hand a reassuring squeeze when she was called. She held herself very straight as she walked to the front of the room. Then she sat in the chair set aside for the witnesses and modestly lowered her head until she was addressed directly.

"Would you tell us, please, in your own words, what happened last night?" the coroner asked.

She briefly recounted the events of the night before. There were a few gasps from the crowd when she described her abduction. After all, young girls weren't supposed to be snatched off the streets in a respectable place like London. There was even more reaction when she repeated Richard Scott's confession that he had seduced Hazel Warner, killed her and stolen their child before setting the fire that destroyed the Warner warehouse. At that point, Martha happened to look across the crowd of spectators and spotted a man who had his arm around the woman beside him. The woman had tears running down her face, and she made no attempt to hide them. Martha wondered if they were Hazel's parents. When Martha reported that Scott had pickled the murdered infant in a glass jar, the woman began to sob openly and the man led her out of the room.

The coroner had only a few questions after that, but they were the ones Martha found most difficult to answer.

"Why do you think Dr. Scott kidnapped you?"

"My grandfather, Mr. Thaddeus Lewis, is currently in the employ of the barrister retained by Nelson Lakefield. My grandfather was investigating the case on the barrister's behalf." There was a murmur through the crowd as Thaddeus's role was confirmed.

"I took an interest in the case," Martha went on, "and when I was in Dr. Scott's office, I accidentally picked up a daguerreotype picture of Hazel Warner. As it directly connected Dr. Scott to Miss Warner, I expect he was anxious to get it back."

"And could you describe, please, the events that took place after your grandfather arrived to retrieve you?"

"There was a struggle. Dr. Scott grabbed me. I kicked over the glass jar and he lunged for it. The next thing I knew, he was dead. I'm sorry, I'm not too clear on the details. My grandfather tried to keep me from seeing."

The crowd murmured its approval that Thaddeus had shielded such a young girl from the horrific scene. And then Martha was excused.

"Well done," Thaddeus whispered when she returned to her seat.

And then it was his turn.

The first part of his testimony was straight-forward enough. Martha's absence, his growing concern, the hunt for her, guided by the clues she had left, the desperate struggle in the cellar, Scott's use of Martha as a hostage.

"I informed Dr. Scott that Mr. Ashby was contacting the police and that there was no hope of him escaping," Thaddeus said. "When my granddaughter kicked the glass bottle over as a distraction, I was able to pull her out of harm's way. At that point, Scott must have realized that there was no way out. He plunged the knife blade through his eye. There was nothing I could have done to save him. Mr. Ashby and Constable Thomas arrived a few minutes later, but Scott was already dead."

"It was an odd weapon that he used, was it not Mr. Lewis?"

He nodded. "Very odd indeed. A knife blade attached to an umbrella."

"Do you have any idea where this weapon could have come from?" Thaddeus relaxed a little. The phrasing of the question allowed him to answer truthfully. He had no idea where such a thing might be obtained.

"None at all." His answer would have been quite different had the coroner asked if he knew whose it was.

The coroner seemed satisfied enough, even though Thaddeus thought there were still a few glaring holes in the story. But he seemed unconcerned about Martha's purloining of the picture, or how Thaddeus had managed to overpower a far younger man.

And that was the end of the testimony. After a very short deliberation, the jury ruled that Dr. Richard Scott died by his own hand, in order to avoid arrest for arson, murder and kidnapping.

"That was kind of a let-down," Martha said as they walked back to the hotel.

"I told you it wasn't like a trial."

"I know. But it wasn't very exciting."

"I should think you've had enough excitement for your young lifetime."

"I said I wanted adventure."

Thaddeus decided the time was opportune for the second difficult conversation of the day. "Listen, Martha, I know I said you could live with me, but I didn't realize what I was getting you into when I said it. I've been wondering if you should go back home."

"No. I don't want to."

Thaddeus had expected an argument. He hadn't expected outright refusal, and it took him aback.

"You will if I say you will," he pointed out.

"No I won't. I turn seventeen in a few weeks. Old enough to be on my own." Her face was stubborn.

"And just what, exactly, do you think you would do instead?" He had never before encountered outright defiance from Martha. He wasn't entirely sure how he should respond to it and wondered if he should have heeded Clementine's advice and just let things be.

"I don't know," Martha said. "Stay here, maybe. You said the man at the newspaper office wants to hire women typesetters. Maybe he'd give me a job. I know how to spell. Surely I could learn how to set type."

"I don't think he was serious."

"Well then, maybe I could go to Normal School and learn how to be a teacher. I'm sure Uncle Luke would let me stay with him in Toronto. Or maybe Mr. Ashby knows someone who would put me up."

"But…"

"I suppose I could be a cook. After all, I cook almost as well as Sophie. Maybe the hotel needs someone in the kitchen."

She reeled off a couple of other things that she thought she might be able to do, but the one option she didn't mention was the one Thaddeus had been afraid he might hear. She made no mention of Joe or Joe's plans.

"Is that what you want to do? Go off and work your fingers to the bone trying to make a living?" he asked.

"Women work their fingers to the bone no matter what they do. It might be refreshing to be paid for it, for once. But no, those other things are only second choices. I want to stay with you. But I won't go back to Wellington. Not yet."

Martha was far more like her mother than Thaddeus had realized. Downright obstinate once she decided to dig her heels in. His objections to his daughter's plans had gone unheeded. Evidently they would go unheeded with his granddaughter's as well. He was powerless in the face of determined women.

"Oh all right, but if you get murdered don't blame me," he grumbled.

"I won't," Martha said, and she slipped her arm through his. "You won't let that happen anyway."

The scene in the dining room that night was both a victory supper and a farewell celebration.

"I sent our luggage to the station with a carter," Clementine said to Thaddeus. "But the train doesn't leave until this evening, so at least we can have a last meal together."

It would be her last meal with Ashby as well.

"All charges against young Lakefield were dropped late this afternoon," Ashby reported. "Jeb Storms is lucky the case didn't go to trial or he'd be facing a perjury charge right now. He must have figured it was a golden opportunity to get Nelson back for what he did to the daughter."

"So Nelson is completely off the hook?" Thaddeus asked. He didn't know if he should be happy or not.

"Yes, but now his father thinks he shouldn't have to pay my bill. He's sadly mistaken."

"I know Lakefield is strapped for money. I hope you can collect."

"He can pay me or he can hand over his business. His choice." Ashby appeared unconcerned.

Thaddeus was relieved. He had totted up his list of expenses that afternoon, and it seemed to him that they had reached an exorbitant sum. "More bad news," he said, handing it over.

Ashby merely glanced at it. "I'll get you a bank draft tomorrow morning and I'll include what I still owe you in salary, if that's convenient." He tucked the paper into his pocket.

It was more than convenient. Ashby's generosity meant that Thaddeus would not have to worry about money any time in the immediate future.

"Where are you off to now?" he asked the young barrister. "Back to Toronto?"

"No, I head west tomorrow. The assizes move to Kent County and I have a couple of cases there." He turned to Clementine. "It's a shame I still have a few odds and ends to clear up here, otherwise I'd travel with you."

"That would have been charming, Mr. Ashby. I must admit that it's very tempting to stay in London another night, especially with the promise of dashing companionship. However, since I've sent my luggage on already, I expect it's best if I catch my train tonight." She smiled at Thaddeus. "Don't you agree, Mr. Lewis?"

"As delightful as another evening in your company would be, yes, I think that's best." He smiled back, just as ingenuously.

"And you, Mr. Lewis, where do you go?"

"I was thinking, if it meets with Martha's approval, that we might go visit two of my sons. I've seen them only three times since they decided to take up farming north of here. Since we're this close, it seems a shame not to take advantage of it."

"Two more sons?" Ashby said. "Are they as charming as Luke?"

"Not at all. They're rough and ready farmers, not city boys. But it would be nice to see them again. What do you think Martha?"

She smiled, rather saucily, Thaddeus thought. "I go where you go, boss."

"So if I need you again, where should I look?" Ashby asked.

"The Temperance Hotel, Wellington. Francis will know where to find us."

"No guarantees, but I doubt this is the last case I'll need help with."

Thaddeus had been hoping for just such an offer. He could make what he had last a long time, but it was nice to know that the prospect of more work might in the offing. He would just have to figure some way to keep Martha out of whatever it was.

"I'm becoming a very busy barrister," Ashby said to Clementine. "And Thaddeus really is a most useful fellow."

"I agree entirely," Clementine replied.

"And now, a toast." Ashby poured out five glasses of wine from the bottle he had ordered, and handed them around. "To another successful collaboration," he said, holding up his glass and bowing toward Thaddeus, "to unexpected assistance", this with nods toward Clementine and Joe, "and most of all to Miss Renwell, who is the most intrepid young lady I believe I have ever met. I know it's not customary for people to drink to themselves, but bottoms up, folks."

Thaddeus and Clementine laughed, Martha blushed, and Joe scowled. Thaddeus took only a small sip to be sociable, but Ashby's toast lent a festive air to the occasion and Thaddeus was glad that he had proposed it.

"Walk us to the station?" Clementine asked when their meal was finished.

"Only if you promise not to start an argument on the way," Thaddeus said.

"I suppose the good people of London have enough to talk about today," she said. "So, yes, I promise."

They didn't, in fact, talk much at all. Clementine took his arm when he offered it and they walked along in silence while Thaddeus tried to sort out what, exactly, he felt about this woman. There were so many ifs and buts and maybes about her. He was not sorry she had turned him down; neither was he glad. She was devious and exasperating and had an uncanny ability to worm her way into his soul and poke at the sore spots, but then she had turned around and unexpectedly applied a balm to soothe them. She claimed that he was the only one who ever saw through her, but the opposite was true as well – she had seen through him, with a clarity that had yanked him out of the slough of self-pity he had fallen into. He was grateful. He liked her. He would miss her.

Just as they neared the train station, she broke the silence. "If I ever find myself in a jam, an absolute pickle that I can't get myself out of, could I call on you for help?" She sounded wistful, and a little melancholy.

Thaddeus was surprised. Was this what she had been after all along? Somebody she could turn to when all else failed? A friend? She was so artful it was difficult to remember that she was a woman who was alone in the world. And who would now be even more dependent on her own wits with Joe's departure.

"Are you trying to strike some sort of bargain with me?" he said. "A deal? You know it never turns out the way you think it will."

She laughed. "All right, I guess I deserved that."

"Yes."

"Yes, I deserved it, or yes you'd help me?"

"Yes, I'll help you. No strings attached." He fixed her with a mock glare. "But it had better be a really big pickle."

When the train finally pulled into the station well behind schedule, Joe took charge of making sure their luggage was aboard, and when he was satisfied that it had been safely stowed, he and Martha took one last walk along the platform. After a few minutes, the train signalled it's impending departure with a blast of the whistle. Thaddeus took a quick look around him. Everyone's attention was on the train. He grabbed Clementine's hand and pulled her around the corner of the station, into the shadows where no one could see them. Then he cradled her face in his hands and planted a long, lingering kiss on her lips. It made him feel eighteen again, stealing kisses from a girl while no one was watching.

She was breathless from it. "If you're going to be like that," she said when she recovered her voice, "maybe I should stick around for another couple of days."

He shook his head. "Your bags are already packed." He waved her toward the train. "You'd better go." And then, when she had taken only a step away from him, "Wait. I don't even know your name."

She turned to him with a smile that lit her entire face, and for the first time, Thaddeus thought that she was really quite beautiful.

"Just remember me as Clementine."

Then she walked to the waiting train without taking a single look back.

He leaned against the corner of the building to watch as the last of the passengers boarded, then the engine gained a head of steam and slowly chugged away.

CHAPTER 21

Clementine stared out the window as the blackness rolled by, wondering how she could have miscalculated so badly. She had gone to London with the simple intention of lying low until she judged it safe to move on. Teasing Thaddeus was no more than an amusing diversion. Even after she realized how attractive she found him, she really hadn't been after anything more than a dalliance. A romantic interlude with an interesting man. She hadn't anticipated the fireworks. Even so, in the cold light of the next morning she saw no reason to change her plan to catch the next train.

And then he had been so contrite, so *decent* in such an endearingly awkward way, her heart had melted. But her resolve held firm. She remained determined to leave.

It was the last kiss at the train station that had nearly undone her. It had taken every ounce of will power she possessed to walk away from that kiss. How strange to fall in love so late in the game. What a shame he was a preacher. What a shame he wasn't rich.

She was startled out of her reverie by a sudden jolting of the train as it slowed to a stop. Then, to her annoyance, the train began to move backwards. She looked out the window, but in the black of the night she could see no indication of what the problem was.

"At this rate, it will take forever to reach Detroit," she remarked to Joe. "We'll have to go the long way – around the world."

He made no reply. He was sulky, unhappy to be on the move again.

Well, my love, you just have to get me as far as Chicago and then you can go wherever you want.

But she wasn't looking forward to being alone.

Eventually, the train began moving in the right direction again. Clementine hoped they wouldn't miss their connection. Then she decided that there was nothing to be done about it anyway, so she folded her cloak to make a pillow and settled down to doze the journey away.

She woke at intervals, when she became aware that the train was speeding up or slowing down, or had jounced over a particularly rough stretch of track. Sometimes she would see Joe sitting across from her. At other times, his seat would be empty.

Got up to stretch his legs, she would think, and then she would doze off again. At some point she fell into a deep sleep.

She came to abruptly, startled awake by a massive jolt and the sound of shattering glass and splitting metal, and the screams and shrieks of her fellow passengers. Then the car tilted at an alarming angle and slid sideways until it came to a final shuddering stop.

Clementine was surprised to find that she seemed to be unhurt, but she could discern no pain. Tentatively, she attempted to move. Everything seemed to be in working order except for her right foot, which wouldn't budge when she tried to get up. It was pinned by something, but in the darkness she couldn't see what had trapped her.

If only people would stop screaming so I can think.

She became aware of an earthy, fetid smell coming from somewhere in front of her, and as her eyes adjusted to the lack of light, she realized that a hole had opened up in the side of the train car. If she could just get her foot free, she might be able to wiggle through it. But she was lying in an awkward position, and she couldn't get enough leverage for a good, sharp tug.

And then she heard Joe calling her name.

"Here," she said. "I'm in here."

He couldn't hear her over the noise the other passengers were making. She took a deep breath and yelled "Joe" as loud as she could, and then he was there, just outside the car.

"I'm stuck."

"Take my hand."

It was just a little too far away. She tried to pull herself loose again, and was rewarded when she felt her foot slide out of her shoe a little. She pulled as hard as she could. Her foot slid a little further. She stretched her arm out as far as it would go.

If only she could reach Joe's hand he could pull her free.

The next morning's breakfast seemed a tame affair with only three of them at the table, although Ashby did his best to animate the conversation by teasing Martha.

"You're nearly as good as your grandfather at solving crimes. Maybe next time I should just hire you," he said.

"I would be happy to solve all your cases for you," she replied, "but I'd want to do it for a percentage of your fee instead of as a straight hire. I expect it would be far more lucrative."

"And far less likely to happen." But Thaddeus could see that he was impressed that such a notion had even occurred to Martha.

"Should I just hand your money straight over to Martha?" Ashby said. "She seems to have a flair for the financial aspects of the business."

"I have always found it wise to leave the management of money to women," Thaddeus said. "They seem able to do magical things with minimal amounts."

Ashby laughed. "Wise man. I have a bit of business to conclude at the courthouse this morning, then I'll visit the bank. I should be back here well before your stage leaves. I hope you don't think this is presumptuous, but I intend to include a little extra for Miss Martha, as compensation for her rather harrowing adventures."

Thaddeus was about to protest that it wasn't necessary, but Martha jumped in first. "Thank you Mr. Ashby. I must admit my best dress is looking a little woeful and I'd like to repair it." She turned to Thaddeus. "I'm going to slip out this morning and get the things I need, if that's all right with you. I'm already mostly packed."

"Try not to get kidnapped," he said.

She grinned. "Yes, boss."

Thaddeus had little to do that morning but pack up his belongings, the work of only a few minutes. Their stage didn't leave until that afternoon, and with several hours to kill, he had time to browse through the newspapers that were stacked up in the hotel lobby. *The Canadian Free Press* wouldn't come out until the next week, but the daily papers from the bigger centres might have coverage of the kidnapping and subsequent exoneration of Nelson Lakefield. Thaddeus was curious to see what they said. He hoped that Martha's name would not be too prominently displayed, but he wasn't sure how they would be able to tell the story without mentioning her. Or himself, he supposed. Another thrilling episode in the Thaddeus Lewis chronicle, to be repeated ad nauseum at Methodist meetings.

He found a copy of *The Detroit Free Press*, but it was several days old. Ah well, he thought, recent enough that he could catch up with the events of the world. Except that it was full of nothing but discussions of recent American events, most notably the dissolution of the Whigs and the formation of the Republican Party and all of the new railway lines that had been chartered. He returned the paper to the table where he had found it and selected a several weeks old edition of The Globe. He settled into a chair and had just opened it when the desk clerk approached him.

"I'm sorry to bother you, sir, but there's a gentleman here with a package and I'm not sure who it should go to," he explained. "Perhaps you could advise?"

Thaddeus hoped that the 'gentleman' didn't turn out to be a reporter hoping to interview him. He liked reading the news, but was less enthusiastic about being it. Besides, Ashby had told him not to talk to any of them.

Thaddeus was led to a pleasant-looking young gentleman who held out his hand. "I'm Charles Pearsall," he said. "I have a daguerreotype for Mrs. Elliott. She said she would be here until today, but apparently she's left already."

"Yes, I'm afraid she was called away on rather urgent business," Thaddeus said. "I'm not entirely sure where you could reach her."

Pearsall looked perplexed. "I'm not sure what to do. This is paid for already. I could hang on to it until I hear from her, but I'm leaving London shortly and she might have difficulty finding me."

"I'll take it, then" Thaddeus said. "Perhaps I can send it on when I'm apprised of her address."

If he ever was.

Pearsall handed him a small, carved wooden box. "Have a look. I'm really quite proud of it."

Thaddeus opened it, and was quite astonished at what he saw. In spite of the stillness of Clementine's posture, the picture had captured her perfectly. She wore a half-smile and a mischievous look. He almost expected the picture to come to life and say something calculated to annoy him.

"This is lovely," he said. "It's just like her."

"She's a wonderful model. I made a copy of this, to show to other customers. She drove a hard bargain over it, though."

Thaddeus was puzzled. "What did she ask for?"

"Information. About the Warner girl's picture." Pearsall hesitated for a moment and then he said, "I take it you were investigating the case, so I assume I'm not speaking out of turn. Miss Warner's daguerreotype led you to Scott, didn't it? At least that's what they're saying on the street."

"Yes, it did. And I didn't give Mrs. Elliott enough credit for it." She'd come into the sitting room that day, excited by what she had discovered and Thaddeus had dismissed it as irrelevant.

"If I'd known how important it was, I'd have spoken up sooner." Pearsall's face was anxious and apologetic. "I hope you understand that."

"We all have things we wish we'd said when we had the chance," Thaddeus replied. "I wouldn't worry about it. It turned out all right in the end. Good luck. And I'll keep the picture safe until it can be delivered."

Thaddeus tucked the picture into his pocket and returned to his newspaper, but he had read only a couple of articles when Ashby came in the front door. He came straight to where Thaddeus was sitting. His face was grim.

"There's been an accident," he said. "There was a crash on the Great Western line early this morning. The mail express collided with a gravel train."

"That was Clementine's train," Thaddeus said.

"Yes. They say it happened a few miles the other side of Chatham. A telegram came through to the courthouse because the judge is supposed to travel on to the Kent County Assizes, but the trains are delayed."

Thaddeus felt a sickening in his stomach, and he realized his hands were shaking.

"Have you heard any other details?"

Ashby knew what he was asking. "Not yet. And we probably won't know for some time."

"What should we do? Where will the news come in?"

"I've already sent a runner to the train station. He'll let us know as soon as he hears anything. In the meantime, all we can do is wait."

They weren't the only ones with an anxious wait. As the morning wore on, news of the crash spread and other guests began to congregate in the lobby to make inquiries and clamour for news.

Thaddeus kept his attention fixed on the front door, hoping to intercept Martha so he could tell her the dreadful news himself. The boy who had been sent to the station appeared first, breathless, scanning the lobby for Ashby. Martha came in just behind him.

Thaddeus pulled her aside.

"I've already heard," she said. "Do you think they're all right?"

"We don't know yet."

Ashby finished speaking with the boy, who disappeared again, back to the train station, Thaddeus guessed.

Ashby joined them, his face tense. "It happened at a place called Baptiste Creek, a few miles the other side of Chatham," he said. "The loss of life has been terrible. They're still looking for bodies."

"How could this have happened?" Thaddeus asked. "What was the gravel train doing on the track?"

"A dreadful miscommunication of some sort. The Express was late leaving London. The driver of the gravel train may have thought it had already gone through. There was a heavy fog, which made it difficult to see. Apparently the second-class cars took the brunt of it."

That was good. Joe and Clementine had been traveling first-class. And then Thaddeus took himself to task for the thought. If the second-class cars had taken the brunt of the crash, then so had the second-class passengers.

"It may take some time before we hear anything more," Ashby said. "I don't expect anyone is hungry, but perhaps we should wait in the dining room."

"We're supposed to leave this afternoon," Martha said.

"Don't worry, we're not going anywhere until we know what's happened," Thaddeus told her. "We can stay here another night if necessary."

Bit by bit the details trickled in. At least twenty-five dead, said one report, although there were many bodies still in the wreck. The gravel train had been heavily loaded said another, and presented an immovable barrier across the track. The second class cars had been full of immigrants on their way to the American west. One of the first class cars had been badly smashed. And all through the hours, the report of the death-toll kept rising.

Then, finally, late in the afternoon, a porter walked up to Thaddeus. He had a telegram in his hand.

"Mr. Lewis?" The porter's face was full of concern. "This came for you. I sincerely hope it's not bad news, sir."

Ashby tried to give the man a coin for his trouble, but the porter waved it away. "Not today, sir," he said. "It's not a special service today."

Thaddeus's hands were shaking so badly he had difficulty holding the piece of paper still enough to read it. It was the news he had been dreading.

Regret to inform C. Elliott did not survive crash. Joe.

He let the paper flutter down to the table. Ashby grabbed it, then looked up quickly at Martha. "Joe's fine," he said.

"And Clementine?"

Ashby shook his head.

She let out a little shriek and began to cry.

"I don't know what to say, Thaddeus." Ashby's face was a mask of concern.

"We have to go to Joe," Thaddeus said. "He doesn't have anyone else."

"I'd advise against it."

"We can't leave him alone at a time like this."

"It will be a madhouse and the authorities will be overwhelmed. Let me go. I'll have better luck dealing with any arrangements that need to be made. And I have to go to Chatham anyway."

Ashby was right. As a barrister, he would be better able to chivvy and command. But would he be able to comfort? There had been uneasiness between he and Joe, a jealousy-tinged tension that simmered just below the surface.

"You and Martha stay here. With any luck the trains will be moving in a few hours. I'll go and telegraph you as soon as I find out what we can do to help."

"Tell Joe we can take her to Wellington. That's where her husband is. We can put her beside him." He couldn't bring himself to say the word "bury".

"That sounds fine, Thaddeus. I'm sure he'll be grateful for the offer."

"All Joe wanted was to go back to Wellington," Martha said. "I'm sure he didn't think it would be this way."

"I know," Thaddeus said. Clementine had been right. There was no knowing what God intended.

There was little point in them staying in the dining room any longer. The only news they would hear would be of the mounting number of deaths.

"I need to go to the bank yet," Ashby said as they reached the lobby. "Then I'll go on to the station and hope that there's a train for me to catch. I'll leave your bank draft at the hotel desk." And then he shook Thaddeus's hand. "Thank you again. And I'm so sorry it ended this way." He held his hand out to Martha.

She ignored it. Instead she stepped forward and gave him a quick hug. "Thank you for everything," she said, scarcely able to stem her tears, and then she turned toward the stairs.

As he climbed the steps behind her, Thaddeus happened to glance back at the lobby. Ashby was standing where they had left him, his gaze fixed on Martha.

In spite of the fact that he was exhausted, Thaddeus knew that sleep would be elusive that night. He was tormented by the notion that he should have been more persuasive with Clementine. If she had agreed to marry him she would never have been aboard the train. But she had dismissed his proposal and she had been right to do so - it had been grudging and craven, more concerned with salvaging his own honour than with anything else.

Would she have taken him seriously if he had managed to sound more sincere? He didn't know. After all, the fundamental difficulties between them would still have been there, but he wished now that he hadn't been so weaselly.

His mind told him that it would have made no difference. His heart clamoured for a second chance.

When he finally fell asleep he did not dream, as he feared he might, of shattered bodies and severed limbs, but of soft flesh and hard passion. He awoke and wished that she was beside him again.

CHAPTER 22

Thaddeus and Martha both slept in the next morning, worn out by grief and waiting. A murmur went through the dining room when they finally appeared for breakfast. None of the other diners were entirely sure what the relationship with Clementine had been, but they knew that she had been lost in the accident and many concerned glances were cast in their direction. He and Martha dawdled over their meal, and drank extra cups of tea to pass the time while they waited for a message from Ashby. Finally, they could sit at their table no longer. They rose, but neither of them seemed to know what to do next.

"I don't want to leave the hotel," Thaddeus said. "I'd rather wait here for the telegram."

"I don't want to go back to my room," Martha said. "It's too easy to think there."

Eventually, they wandered out to the lobby and simply sat without speaking, watching the ebb and flow of guests and the bustle of the porters, checking the time again and again, only to realize that no more than a few minutes had passed since the last time they checked.

There was still no word by noon, so they stood and made their way back to their table in the dining room and picked at their food while the time dragged on.

Finally, just after one o'clock, a waiter handed Thaddeus what they had been waiting for. Thaddeus read it quickly, but the message made no sense. He sat, his brow furrowed while he read the words again, trying to figure out what they meant.

"What is it?" Martha asked.

"I'm not sure."

He studied it once more, and when he finally realized what it signified, a great wave of anger swept over him. How could she have put him through this? He had thought it was his fault, somehow - retribution for what they had done, or for what he had failed to do, or for any number of sins he knew he was guilty of and had yet to ask forgiveness for. And then, when he fully understood the sheer audacity of what she had managed to pull off, he began to laugh.

Martha snatched the message out of his hand and read it out loud.

> *All fine. Joe identified body, claimed baggage, disappeared. I viewed body. Definitely not her. Towns*

"What does he mean it's not Clementine?" she asked. "Who else would it be?"

"My guess is some poor immigrant woman," Thaddeus said. "Someone who won't have anyone looking for her."

"But…"

"Clementine must have got out of the crash unscathed. Towns said it would be a madhouse and that everyone would be overwhelmed. No one would question Joe's identification, they would just be relieved that he'd accounted for one more body."

"So he took their luggage…?"

"…met his mother and got out of town."

Martha was beginning to understand. "So now everyone will think Clementine Elliott is dead?"

"That's right. And whoever might be looking for her will never find her now. Even if someone discovered that she was going by the name of Elliott and traced her to London, the trail would end at the crash. She has completely and utterly covered her tracks."

"I thought the first telegraph message was a little strange," Martha said.

"What do you mean?"

"It said that C. Elliott didn't survive the crash. Why would Joe refer to her as 'C. Elliott' and not 'mother'. That would be like me calling you 'T. Lewis' instead of 'grandpa."

Martha was right, and Thaddeus hadn't been quick enough to catch it.

"It was a code, I guess. Joe was trying to let us know that she wasn't really dead. It was the name that died, not the person. And that's why Ashby's message is so cryptic. He didn't want to give the game away."

An alarmed look crossed Martha's face. "You don't think she caused the accident do you?"

Thaddeus chuckled. "She is a remarkable woman in many respects, but no, I don't think even Clementine would be capable of making a train crash. She took advantage of the circumstances that's all."

"So if whoever she was hiding from won't be able to trace her, I suppose that means we won't be able to either, will we?"

"No, but that was the case regardless."

"Do you think we'll ever see them again?"

"Only if Clementine gets herself into serious trouble. In other words, yes, I think it's quite likely we'll see her again. And when she turns up, you may have to persuade me not to wring her neck."

They still had time to catch the stage that would carry them north, if they hurried. They rushed upstairs and packed last-minute articles, then called for a porter to take their luggage to the lobby, and from there to the coach. When Thaddeus tried to pay for their extra night's lodging, the clerk informed him that Mr. Ashby had taken care of it, and that he had also left a bank draft for Mr. Lewis. The clerk's face then settled into an expression of concerned sympathy. "On behalf of myself and the rest of the hotel staff, I'd like to say how sorry we are, sir."

Thaddeus had to remind himself that he was supposed to be in mourning for his lost wife, or mistress or ladyfriend or whoever they all thought Clementine might be. He thanked the clerk and left a substantial tip.

He and Martha were about to walk out the front door when they came face to face with Calvin Merritt.

"Mr. Lewis! Thaddeus! I came as soon as I heard. I am so, so sorry."

"Thank you, Mr. Merritt."

"How dreadful to lose your wife so soon after your marriage,"

Merritt went on. "And in such a terrible accident."

Thaddeus knew that Martha was watching him to see what he would do. By all rights, he should confess the deception to Merritt, explain that Clementine was not his wife, but merely an acquaintance with a peculiar sense of humour. But he wasn't sure if an admission would undo the subterfuge that Clementine had been at such pains to construct. All right then, one more prevarication. He owed her that at least.

He countered Merritt's comment with a quote from Psalms.

"My flesh and my heart may fail, but God is the strength of my heart and my portion forever."

Martha was open-mouthed, but Merritt nodded in agreement. "We must turn to God in times of trouble. Would you like me to pray with you Thaddeus? Ask God for His mercy on her soul?"

"Thank you, Calvin, but no. I'm afraid that in this case, prayers will do absolutely no good whatsoever."

And with that, he and Martha walked out the door, leaving Calvin Merritt, once again, at a loss for words.

The lurching stage coach was not nearly as easy to fall asleep in as the train had been, but Martha found she could doze a little if she jammed her cloak between the seat and the window so she could rest her head against it. She could drop off easily enough, but would come to blinking and disoriented whenever the coach's wheels hit a particularly deep rut in the road. Somewhere past Lucan, she was jolted awake for what seemed like the twentieth time and saw that Thaddeus had taken out the little carved box frame that held Clementine's daguerreotype. He was sitting with it balanced on his knee, one hand holding it steady against the sway of the coach. He stared at it, lost in thought, the faintest hint of a smile on his lips.

Martha was careful not to disturb him. She would never tell him that she knew. She'd been half-awake when he'd come tiptoeing into her room to check on her. She had smelled Clementine's perfume on him.

She closed her eyes again and tried to drift back into sleep. No, she would never tell him. She would never tell anyone.

ACKNOWLEDGEMENTS

For readers who would like to learn more about the historical background of this story, I am indebted to a number of sources, in particular *Petticoats and Prejudice: Women and Law in Nineteenth Century Canada* by Constance Backhouse, (published for The Osgoode Society by Women's Press 1991). Ms. Backhouse succinctly outlines the many legal disadvantages that governed women's lives during the period in question; *The Conventional Man: The Diaries of Ontario Chief Justice Robert A. Harrison, 1856-1878*, (published for The Osgoode Society for Canadian Legal History by University of Toronto Press 2003) provided insight into 19th century Upper Canadian society; and *Nothing "Improper" Happened: Sex. Marriage and Colonial Identity in Upper Canada, 1783-1850*, a doctoral thesis by Robin Christine Grazely, (Queen's University, June 2010) provided a wonderful account of Upper Canadian courting practices.

Both the *Doty Docs* website (dotydocs.theatreinlondon.ca) and the delightfully snarky *This Was London: The First Two Centuries* by Orlo Miller, (Butternut Press Inc. 1988) outlined the early history and social structure of London, Ontario; and *The Meaning of Misadventure: The Baptiste Creek Railway Disaster of 1854 and its Aftermath* by Paul Craven, published in *Patterns of the Past: Interpreting Ontario's History* (Dundurn Press 1988) provided details of what was, at the time, Canada's worst railway disaster.

I consulted *Self Instructor in Phrenology and Physiology* by O.S. and L.N. Fowler, (Fowlers and Wells, Publishers 1853), but the many websites devoted to the phrenology movement of the 19th century were far clearer.

I would like to thank my husband Rob, my agent Robert Lecker, and most of all, my faithful readers who, like me, have fallen in love with Thaddeus.

Praise for the Thaddeus Lewis Books:

"Love the Murdoch Mysteries? Then you need to discover Janet Kellough's terrific series featuring preacher-detective Thaddeus Lewis. Who says Canadian history is boring?

Margaret Cannon, The Globe and Mail

"Kellough does a fine job of bringing life to the times and to her ministerial hero on horseback."

The National Post

"...it is hard to think of any crime fiction set in Canada's rich historical past. *On the Head of a Pin* by Janet Kellough is doubly welcome, since it is firmly historical and also extremely well done."

www.whodunitcanada.com

[*The Burying Ground*] "is an engaging historical mystery. Fans of Chesterton's Father Brown or Anne Perry...will find this Canadian variation much to their liking."

Booklist

[*Wishful Seeing*] "is an appealing look at life in mid-1800's Canada, full of historical detail, engaging characters, and a murder investigation that takes many surprising twists and turns before it can be solved."

Kirkus Reviews

[*Wishful Seeing*] "Kellough smartly brings her trails of intrigue and misunderstanding to a fine finish...suspenseful, complex, satisfying – and entertainingly instructive, as well."

Joan Barfoot, The London Free Press

Janet Kellough's novel *Wishful Seeing* was short-listed for the 2017 Crime Writers of Canada Arthur Ellis Best Novel Award.

CPSIA information can be obtained
at www.ICGtesting.com
Printed in the USA
LVOW10s1230301017
554281LV00004B/521/P

9 780993 720062